I0772318

NICK ROBERTS

For Cora

PROLOGUE

Ann squinted at her numberless watch as rain pelted her clear umbrella. On a sunny day, she could barely read the time; forget about a rainy night. But her grandmother had given it to her mom who'd passed it down to her when Ann received her admission letter from The Claymont Residency for Writers last year after she graduated college. So, she wore it, just not for practical purposes. None of that mattered at the moment, though. She knew it was almost ten, and she needed to get to town. To the airport.

Lightning reflected off the slick stone street that was barely a street —more of a path surrounded by a mile of trees on one side and a tall iron fence on the other. But it was the only way to or from the front gate of Claymont. Ann looked around to see if anyone was coming for her, but as far as she could tell, she was alone in the storm, in the nightmare.

Everything had gone so terribly wrong. It seemed like only yesterday when the horse-drawn carriage had dropped her off at the property's entrance as a day-one writer—a tradition carried over since the medieval castle had been renovated and named Claymont. She remembered how excited she'd been, and for the briefest moment, she foolishly felt the wonderment of when she'd first laid eyes on the building. She saw through the façade now and prayed it wasn't too late.

Thunder exploded across the heavens. She jumped and looked at the trees looming above her like they were silently judging her decision to leave. There was no going back, though. Not after what she'd seen. And she knew it would keep happening until she succumbed to it or left like the other girls. But she wondered now if anyone had actually left, and her heart skipped a beat. She made sure she was hidden by the stone pillar that was part of the arch above the front gate and snuck one last glimpse of the castle.

The torrential downpour obscured her view, but she could still make out the fifty yards of stone pathway that led to the front of the castle that everyone called 'The Keep.' It stood five stories tall with one arched window on each floor, though she only saw dark, blurry caves from her vantage point. Even if someone stood at one and looked straight in her direction, she knew she was concealed by the storm. For once, she was grateful for the darkness that descended on Claymont, a darkness that made the blackest night back in Chicago feel like a sunny day.

Ann looked at her watch again and saw that the minute hand was pointing straight up. It was precisely ten p.m., and she was officially breaking curfew. Residents were not permitted to roam the castle grounds after ten. She'd always found this rule ironic since the structure housed writers, most of them nocturnal by nature. Her face soured when she thought about the others. Some were her friends—the closest she'd had since college—but there were a select few who'd stab her in the back if it meant a positive note from The Reader. She looked at the fifth-story window in The Keep where the mysterious recluse dwelled. No one met The Reader. At least, that's what everyone was made to believe. She shuddered at what was really up there.

She also now knew the real reason why cell phones weren't permitted on the grounds. Ann had to sneak into the main hall to call a cab. It was the only landline at Claymont. Well, the only one that she knew of, at least. The longer she stayed there, the more she understood that uncovering one mystery only led to another. There were secrets upon secrets upon secrets. The castle might have been built out of stone, but it stood on a foundation of deception. She regretted that it took her so long to figure it out, and she would've warned the other girls if she thought they'd actually believe her. Her justification for fleeing unannounced was that she'd phone the authorities when she got to town and tell them what was really going on at Claymont, what its real purpose was. They'd think she was insane, but hopefully they would at least go investigate and maybe even find the note she hid.

After she'd phoned the taxi, she ran back to her room and packed what she could. She made sure she had her passport and wallet, grabbed her umbrella, and snuck out through a passage in the kitchen. If anyone had been actively monitoring the cameras, she knew they would've come for her. They would surely begin the search once they discovered her empty room, which should be right at that moment.

"Come on," she said, leaning against the stone archway that adorned the front gate.

The rain started coming down even harder, to the point where it peppered any exposed parts of her body like little bee stings. She grunted and looked down the road to her left, trying to will a set of headlights into existence. It didn't work. She considered making the trek to town on foot and just getting a ride to the Perugia Airport. But the thought of what could be out there with her squashed any attempt to go roaming through the night. It was after ten p.m., after all.

A twig snapped in the tree line in front her. She looked straight ahead and stared into the forest, going from tree to tree and peering into the abyss between them. A thin layer of mist hovered above the forest floor like it was threatening to come out. It undulated like something just walked through it.

No. Please, no.

Another snap came from her right. There was no road in that direction, only the edge of the woods that ran parallel with the fence, separated by about ten feet of perfectly manicured grass. A few miles in that direction would eventually lead her to a steep descent down the hill on which the castle stood. Trying to navigate that terrain at night during a thunderstorm was a death march.

Something darted across the road to her left. Ann gasped and watched the area, praying that it wouldn't reveal itself. She held her breath as her heart thumped against her chest. She gulped, feeling the burn of a parched throat. The rain continued to beat the earth, but nothing was moving in that direction except the mist. She looked through the gaps in the fence. It had to be out there with her. Was it just toying with her?

Ann placed her suitcase on the ground and peered around the stone pillar. She mentally prepared herself for anything. As she surveyed the courtyard in front of the castle, she felt her gaze being drawn to the window on the fifth floor of The Keep. An outline of a tall figure stood motionless in the darkness. She recognized his build, and he most certainly was not The Reader. She squinted like that would give her a better view through the rain but turned away as soon as she saw the taxi's headlights appear down the road.

"Oh, thank God," she said and picked up her suitcase and stepped onto the road.

The taxi crept along the narrow path while its windshield wipers struggled to provide a view for the driver. She looked back at the window, but there was no one there. The yellow vehicle was fifty yards away and moving slowly. Just as she made up her mind to meet the cab halfway, the gate squeaked behind her, and she thought she heard something run back into the forest.

Ann spun around to see the front gate hanging ajar. A strong gust of wind blew it the rest of the way open, banging it against the stone pillar. She jumped at the loud sound just as another gust turned her umbrella inside out before completely ripping it from her hand.

"Shit!" she said, struggling to even stand upright.

The rain stung her eyes. She shielded her face with her jacket and turned toward the cab that was almost there. Her saving grace that would ferry her away from this dreadful place was approaching. She went to grab her suitcase, but it was gone. She looked all around and saw nothing. There was no way the wind had taken that heavy thing. At best, it would've just knocked it down.

"Looking for something?" a man said from the other side of the fence.

Ann recognized the voice immediately. It belonged to the man she'd just seen at the window. Her blood ran cold. She'd been caught. The only option now was to run for the approaching taxi. There was no way she would go back in that building on her own accord. Just as she was about to sprint, a hand grabbed her arm through the fence. She looked at the tall, hooded figure but couldn't see his face, not that she needed to.

"You know we can't let you leave now," he said, almost apologetically while gripping her bicep.

"Help!" she screamed toward the vehicle that was struggling to stay on the road in the torrential downpour.

With one swift motion, the hooded figure yanked her arm, slamming her head against the iron fence. Fireworks exploded in her field of vision as the world swirled around her. Her adrenaline pumped away the pain before it could settle in.

"Let me go," she mumbled.

Though dazed and dizzy, she could still see the headlights, which meant she still hand a chance.

"Just know that you were so close. It could've been you. And all this would've been over."

Ann's stomach went sour at the thought. He was crazy, and she was a fool for taking so long to realize it. Her survival instincts kicked in as the headlights grew brighter. All she had to do was grab his wrist and use her body weight to lean forward and let the iron fence do the rest. She reached for him with her right arm, but he jerked even harder than before, and she heard her shoulder pop out of socket as the left side of her head crashed into the metal.

"You chose to go. Not me," the man said as Ann struggled to maintain consciousness. "So, go."

The hand released her, and she stumbled and fell on the wet stone road. That's when she saw her for the second time that night. Even in her dazed state, she knew it was her standing between the trees, watching. The incoming taxi's headlights shone on the girl's feet that were standing in the mist and gradually crept up her body, exposing more of her form. Ann couldn't move. She knew what was about to happen, but she just wanted to see her face before it did.

The taxi didn't slow down because the driver couldn't see her lying there in the middle of the road. As soon as the light reached the girl's neck, she receded into the forest. Ann released a scream of terror that was cut short by the tire that twisted her neck and split her skull.

ONE

Lyla Robbins stared at the blinking cursor on her MacBook. Each flash was the device flipping her the bird, taunting her for pretending to be a writer but having nothing to say. She minimized the word processor and opened her web browser, briefly catching a reflection of her dark-haired silhouette. If she couldn't get the creative juices pumping, the least she could do was brainstorm ideas to get her out of her parents' house.

It still felt weird, calling it that. She'd spent the first eighteen years of her life there. The place used to be her home; now it was her *childhood* home. In the four years she'd been gone, they'd turned her bedroom into an office since her dad worked remotely most of the time now.

She no longer felt like a resident, more like a roommate who never contributed to the bills. But after graduating from West Virginia University with a BA in English, the world wasn't exactly banging on her door with job opportunities. Her dad had told her to at least take courses in teaching so she would have some job security, but the thought of facilitating a room full of middle-schoolers on how to write a thesis statement was anathema to her at the time.

Now, twenty-two years old and sitting on the foldout couch in the basement while Mom and Dad were getting ready for work upstairs, she felt the pressure to do something with her life. And the worst part was that Lyla knew her parents would never say anything to her about it. They'd let her live with them until she inherited the house if she wanted, but that just made her feel worse.

She'd only been back for a month after graduation. The plan had been for her to crash with them while she looked for a job and found her own place, which she assured them wouldn't take very long. Her mom had proposed applying to more grad schools to get her Creative Writing MFA if she truly wanted to be an author, but after being shot down by her top choices, she'd convinced herself that she didn't have what it took even though she really knew her lack of persistence was holding her back.

Lyla had watched her friends get accepted into their dream programs—Katie went to Columbia University School of the Arts, Olivia got in the University of Michigan's Helen Zell Writer's Program, Melanie went to New York University, Kurt somehow was admitted to The Michener Center for Writers at the University of Texas at Austin, and Brandy went to Brown University—but she got rejection letter after letter.

Even though it hurt, she knew why. It was her genre, her unapologetic love for the genre. She wrote horror and had done so ever since she went to her first Scholastic Book Fair in elementary school. While her cohort was focused on writing the next great American novel or trying to change the world with important social commentary embedded in distinguished prose, Lyla just wanted to scare people. Even in creative writing courses as an undergrad, she had to "elevate" her genre fiction if she expected a good grade. She did, of course, because she just had that ability, but it took the fun out of it.

When her advisor suggested different writing samples to send to her desired programs, it punctured a hole in her ego after years of unanimously being told by her classmates that she was the most naturally gifted writer among them. If she couldn't get in because she wouldn't be taken seriously as a writer for not mimicking Sylvia Plath or Cormac McCarthy, then that route simply wasn't for her. But once graduation rolled around and she had to empty her apartment and say goodbye to her friends just to drive back home, her defiant confidence waned.

On the first day after she'd moved back in, she looked up writer residency programs, amusing herself at the thought of getting a free ride to do nothing but focus on writing. The irony that she was living with her parents and basically had that same luxury was not lost on her. Using the same writing sample she'd sent to all the grad schools that turned her down, she filled out applications to various places throughout the country and sent email after email. She'd always been told that writers need life experience, and as she was about to go to sleep on that first night, an idea to do just that flashed through her mind: travel abroad.

Lyla stayed up all night jumping from country to country, researching writing residencies. If she got into one of those and got to see the world, maybe she wouldn't look like a loser to her friends. She would be the one who took the road less traveled. The thought renewed her sense of purpose, exciting her in a way that her previous searches did not. Out of all the places she found and applied to, the one that stood out the most was in the heart of Italy. She'd never left the east coast, let alone visited Europe.

The Claymont Residency for Writers was a relatively new program and fully funded if she were to be accepted. The biggest drawback was that the program had an extensive waiting list, and its rate of admission made the other residencies look as accessible as the public library. Once she clicked on the pictures of the actual location, she understood why.

Claymont was located in Umbria in the Perugia province of Italy. The building itself was a medieval castle that had been modernized with over 9,000 square feet of living space containing thirteen bedrooms and seventeen bathrooms on a one-hundred thirty-six-acre plot. The castle stood on a hill surrounded by green trees and looked like something out of a fairy tale. And that's not even taking into account the luxury amenities: an infinity pool, tennis courts, outdoor terraces with fire pits and lounges, flower gardens, and olive groves. There was also a fitness center, recreation room, a quiet room, and a guest house.

It looked so nice that it made her wonder how anyone would actually get any writing done. She'd be too distracted by learning about the history of the place that was built over one thousand years ago and had undergone several additions and renovations. The current owners were philanthropists whose only desire was to provide a "haven for new writers to find their voices." One stipulation that struck Lyla as being too good to be true was that once you were admitted, you could stay until you completed your work. Just as she was fantasizing about sitting by the pool with her MacBook, she read that only ten writers were permitted to stay there at a time. Even if a vacancy did become available, the odds of getting in were astronomically low.

Still, Lyla clicked on the admissions guidelines which requested a summary about her life, why she desired a residency, and a writing sample. There were no formal stipulations on the writing sample, no minimum word or page count. The only instructions were to "submit a piece that best showcases your narrative voice and skillset," and to mail print copies of the requested documents.

And that's what she did the very next day. After three weeks of either being rejected or ignored by the other residencies, she got an automated email from Claymont informing her that there were no vacancies at that time, but she would be added to the waiting list. There was no doubt in Lyla's mind that she could retire from teaching long before the powers that be at Claymont would ever get to her submission.

The worst part about her current predicament was that she wasn't taking advantage of her free time to write. She had talked herself out of being a writer, and now she sat on the bed in the basement looking at the West Virginia State Department of Education for requirements to become a certified teacher. She spent the day compiling a to-do list and didn't stop until she had a detailed plan of action. She ate lunch, went to the gym and ran on the treadmill for an hour, and drove home.

As she pulled onto her street, Steve the mailman—the same friendly face who'd ran the same route since she was a child—passed by with a wave. She smiled and nodded back, slowing when she reached her parents' mailbox. She rolled down her window, withdrew the contents, and parked on the side of the driveway so her mom had space to park in the garage.

In the kitchen, she made herself a protein drink and sat at the table with her MacBook, determined to give it one last shot for the day, hoping those endorphins she'd released from the gym would jar an idea loose.

"Just start with one good sentence," she mumbled to herself.

The corner of a purple envelope poking out from under a magazine caught her eye. She hadn't noticed it when she first emptied the mailbox. She cocked her head and lifted the magazine. Her eyes widened when she read the name on the return address and saw the customs clearance stamps on it.

"Dad!" she yelled, temporarily forgetting that he could be on a conference call.

The office door opened down the hallway.

"Yeah?" he hollered back.

"I need you, please."

She waited and listened to his footsteps, never taking her eyes off the letter for fear that it would disappear if she did.

"What's up?" he asked.

"Can you open this?"

She handed him the purple envelope and watched his face as he examined it.

"Is this from one of the programs you applied to?"

"Yes, please open it. I can't do it."

"You opened all the other ones just fine. Or did you have your mother do it?"

"I opened them. This one is different."

"Okay," he said and tore away.

She watched him pull out the letter from the corner of her eye. The passing seconds felt like hours, and his silence as he read was too much for her to tolerate any longer.

"Well, what's it say?" she asked and finally took a breath.

"It appears as though you're going to need a passport because The Claymont Residency for Writers has cordially invited you to join their—"

"Oh my God!" She jumped up. "Oh my God. I mean, holy shit!"

She yanked the paper out of his hand and read it for herself.

"I'm really going. I can't believe it," she said, fighting back tears as she looked at him. "They liked my story, and I'm really going to Italy."

"We never doubted you for a second, Lyla bug."

He hadn't called her that in years. She wrapped her arms around him and squealed.

"I'm going to Italy!"

TWO

Lyla checked the status of her passport online every day since she filed the paperwork at the post office. In the nearly two months that had passed since she received her acceptance letter, she'd made all the formal arrangements with Claymont, and they set her start date as September fifteenth. The person she had been in contact with was Julia, the residency's admissions liaison. Beyond logistical questions regarding travel, Julia didn't disclose much about the program itself. She assured Lyla that it was all-inclusive and once she arrived, she need not worry about anything but writing.

She was still in a group chat with her cohort from WVU, and when she told them about her new path, they were ecstatic. And they all wanted the link, of course. They expressed their disbelief that Lyla would actually be living in a medieval castle in Italy for, according to the website's guidelines, as long as she wanted to if that's how long it took her to finish her book, though she knew there must be some stipulation. Katie brought up the fact that a residency wouldn't yield her an MFA, and Lyla, at her most optimistic, said, "Well, I might just write something great there. Tons of writers didn't go to grad school."

Lyla fully planned on doubling down on turning her passion for writing into a profession, and she was willing to do whatever it took. Unlike at WVU where she would second guess professors or dismiss critiques of her work outright, she knew now that she must remain teachable. She was not the naïve freshman or the cocky senior. To keep herself grounded, she'd created a folder on her computer's home screen and labeled it *REJECTION LETTERS*. True to its name, she filled it with every denial from the school and other residencies to which she'd applied. Every time she opened her laptop, she would see it and use it as both a source of gratitude and motivation.

Her passport arrived on September first, two weeks before her flight. She packed everything she thought she'd need, and her parents assured her that they'd mail anything she might have forgotten. Claymont provided no list of supplies or suggested items because, as her liaison said on each call or email exchange, "It's all-inclusive."

One of her biggest concerns was the language barrier, though her parents and her friends who'd traveled abroad assured her it wouldn't be that big of an issue. The other residents were American. Everyone who worked at Claymont spoke English, and they even had translators upon request if they wanted to travel down the mountain to Umbertide. That had eased her anxiety somewhat.

In addition to not knowing anything about the program or being able to locate any notable alumni, she couldn't find any pictures of what the interior of the castle looked like. There were plenty of gorgeous exterior shots on their website and Google Images, but nothing that revealed what type of sleeping quarters she'd have or what the bathroom situation would be. When she brought this up to Julia, she simply said, "You will be more than pleased with the accommodations and daily routines. Relax, and think of nothing else but ideas for what you want to write."

Lyla sat in the backseat of her dad's Nissan Pathfinder, watching her hometown disappear street-by-street as they headed for the highway; she had the same bittersweet feelings that she did when they drove her to Morgantown and helped her move into her dorm. Soon they were on the interstate and headed for the airport. Her mom kept asking what she was excited about the most, but Lyla was more focused on her flight itinerary.

Flying out of Yeager Airport in Charleston made the trip a little over twenty hours long with two stops, one in Chicago and one in London. With her two checked bags, the one-way flight cost over five thousand dollars. This was all covered by the Claymont Trust, however. It wasn't until then that she realized she basically won the lottery by getting accepted. Still, she didn't like to fly. And the idea of being in the air that long, having to catch different flights, and then getting acclimated with her new environment while inevitably having to deal with jetlag, quickened her pulse.

"Honey are you going to talk to us before you move across the world or just stare at your phone until we get to the airport?" her mom asked.

The question stung. Lyla didn't realize how self-centered she was being. She remembered how much her mom had cried just from dropping her off at a university a few hours from their house. She couldn't imagine how her parents were feeling in this moment.

"Sorry," she said and slid her phone in her purse.

Her dad made eye contact with her in the rearview mirror.

"You still nervous about the flight?"

Lyla let out a long sigh like she'd been holding her breath.

"Yes. I'm starting to freak out," she said, feeling better having voiced her fears.

"It's going to be just fine," he said. "Think about sitting by that sweet infinity pool with no distractions and being able to do nothing but write. Focus on the good stuff."

She smiled at him as he looked back and forth between her and the road. He was right, though. If her choices were between this minor inconvenience and living in her parents' basement while taking courses to become a teacher, then it wasn't really much of a choice at all. As they neared the steep hill that would eventually take them to the airport, she accepted that she only had about twenty more minutes with her mom and dad.

"Thank you," she said.

Her mom looked over her seat.

"For what, sweetie?"

"For everything. For believing in me. For letting me write what I like to write and for reading it even though you don't like horror. For encouraging me to follow my dreams. I wouldn't be here without you guys."

That made her mom tear up.

"Thank you for being a sweet little girl who grew up to be an amazing young lady, Lyla," she said.

Now Lyla felt the moisture in her eyes, especially when she looked at her dad again and noticed that he was fighting back tears, too.

"You make parenting easy, honey," he said. "We really lucked out with you. And so did this Claymont place. I know you feel like you won the lottery, but they don't know who's about to show up at the front door. You'll be queen of that castle before you know it."

Lyla laughed and looked through the windshield at the first sign for the airport.

"Almost there," he said.

She took a deep breath.

Her mom, still facing her, said, "Everything's going to be all right. I promise."

"I think so, too," she said.

A few minutes later, they were pulling into the short-term parking lot. Her dad unloaded the large suitcases, and she wheeled her carry-on. It was a short walk to the terminal. They stepped through the automatic doors and made it through the line in no time. After she checked her big bags and got her boarding pass, she felt like her heart was going to explode.

"Come here," her dad said and gave her a hug and kissed the top of her head. "Let us know when you land."

"Each time," her mom clarified. "Chicago, London, and Perugia. I don't care how late it is in any time zone."

"I will," she said and hugged her next.

The three of them stood there until her dad put his arm around her mom.

"Any idea what you're going to write about?" he asked.

"Not sure yet," she said and smiled. "I just know it's going to be scary."

THREE

Lyla boarded her first flight on time and took her window seat, looking at the dark runway lit up by air traffic control lights. She watched the workers in their reflective vests wheel a train of luggage below her line of sight. After sitting for ten minutes while everyone else boarded, the air started to get muggy. She looked above her at the little light angled directly at her. Not being the most experienced world traveler, it took her a few tries to figure out the air conditioning situation.

Her fingers twisted the knob, and room temperature air eventually hit her face with the strength of a child blowing out birthday candles. She sighed and prayed no one would sit in the two empty seats beside her. If it was going to be this humid, she at least wanted some personal space. But, judging by the backed-up line of people still stuffing carry-on luggage in overhead compartments and finding their seats, the odds didn't seem to be in her favor.

A man and woman who looked around her parents' age seemed confused as they made their way down the aisle.

"Oh, here we go," the woman said, pointing to the number above Lyla's row.

"Shit," she muttered under her breath.

"Is that 17 C and D?" the man asked.

"Yes, Don."

She looked down at Lyla and smiled. Lyla forced one back, but she was oddly comforted by the woman's friendly demeanor.

"Watch out, Delores. I'll get the bags," Don said.

He lifted his small suitcase and wedged it in the storage bin above them. Dolores handed hers to him, and he heaved it up but couldn't squeeze it in. Lyla felt a moment a panic when she realized that everyone else on the plane was putting their overhead luggage in longways; she had just turned hers sideways and tossed it up there. She was about to say that she might need to move her bag, but the couple were already bickering out a solution.

"Just shove it in there, Don," Dolores said and sat in the middle seat beside Lyla.

"I can't. Someone just shoved a damn Dracula suitcase up here."

Lyla's face reddened, and she slowly turned back to the window and watched the men drive away the empty luggage train.

"Well, turn it sideways. You're causing a traffic jam."

Lyla heard him grunt and then felt the *THUMP* of his suitcase landing directly above her head. He sighed like he'd just finished one hundred jumping jacks and shut the bin door. Her seat shook when Don collapsed into his. She just focused on the fact that this leg of the flight would take less than two hours which helped her work up the nerve to turn around and properly greet them.

"Hi," she said to Dolores.

"Hello, dear. What's your name?"

"Lyla Robbins."

"Lyla. That's such a pretty name. I don't know that I've ever met a Lyla. Have you, Don?"

Don looked at his wife and then to Lyla and back to his wife; he obviously hadn't been listening to a damn word she'd said. Even though they appeared the same age as her parents, they seemed to be about twenty years behind the times.

"What'd you say, hon?"

Dolores turned to Lyla and rolled her eyes.

"Don, this nice young lady is Lyla. We're trying to get acquainted."

"Oh, sorry. Hello, Lyla." He extended his arm across his wife's chest, and they shook hands while Lyla did her best not to accidentally brush against Dolores' boobs. "I was a bit flustered with the overhead storage situation—or lack thereof, I should say."

Lyla winced.

"Yeah, that's my fault. I put my suitcase in sideways. I don't fly much."

"Oh, it's no big deal, Lyla. No need to apologize," Dolores said.

Her husband's eyes widened like he just remembered that he'd made fun of her suitcase. For a second, she thought he was going to apologize, but he just smiled and said, "Yeah, no worries."

He'd called it Dracula's suitcase, and she couldn't blame him. She'd picked out a shiny black one on wheels and went a little crazy decorating it with horror decals. To be fair, her mom had told her to mark all of her bags in some way so that they'd stand out when coming through baggage claim, but she'd ordered so many stickers from Etsy that she used the leftovers to cover her carry-on as well.

"Well, I'm Dolores, and this is my husband, Don."

"It's nice to meet you," Lyla said, nodding and looking at the headrest in front of her, hoping the moment would pass. No, if she was going to grow, she needed to step out of her comfort zone. That goal had germinated when she first decided to study abroad, and she chose to apply the philosophy to more aspects of her life.

"So, what awaits you all in Chicago?" she asked like she was a hostage being forced to read a script.

"We're headed back home," Don said.

"Oh, okay," Lyla said, not sure why she automatically assumed they were native West Virginians.

The more she thought about it, the more obvious their midwestern accents were, as she was sure her Appalachian drawl was just as easily detectible to them. It had been to her non-native friends at WVU. That was her first experience being exposed to a melting pot of people from all over the country—the world, rather, and it gave her anxiety at the time. Now, she was going overseas, and campus life seemed like a walk in the park compared to that.

"What brought you to West Virginia?" Lyla asked.

"Gauley Season," Dolores said with raised eyebrows.

Lyla looked them both over and could tell they were awaiting her reaction. The Gauley River was known for its whitewater rafting, specifically for a few weeks in September and October. She'd gone several times—twice with her family when she was younger and three more times with her classmates at WVU. West Virginia brought tourists from all over for its scenic beauty and outdoor excursions such as Bridge Day (where bungee jumpers and skydiving enthusiasts leapt off the New River Gorge Bridge), hiking through the mountains, and, of course, whitewater rafting.

"Gauley Season?" Lyla repeated, trying to gauge to which version they were referring.

During Gauley Season, one can either raft on the Lower Gauley River or the Upper Gauley River, with the latter being for thrill-seekers or veteran rafters prepared for a fourteen-foot waterfall drop and category five rapids. Lyla suspected they meant the Lower because it was known for its tranquil, scenic float.

"Oh, yes," Don said.

She could tell just by the sheer gusto in his tone that they were fucking extreme.

"You all did the Upper Gauley?" she asked.

"Third year in a row," Dolores said. "Don and I have been rafting for over twenty years now. We actually had our wedding party on a kayak float festival in West Virginia, believe it or not."

"No shit," Lyla said, genuinely impressed and interested.

They both nodded with knowing smiles.

Maybe this wouldn't be such a bad flight after all.

"Attention ladies and gentlemen, this is your captain speaking..." the voice over the intercom began.

Lyla listened as she watched the flight attendants demonstrate what to do in the event of an emergency situation. They moved so fast with how to inflate a life jacket and depart the plane that she struggled to keep up and just wished for the best. At least if they went down, she had the extreme tourism couple beside her to lead the charge.

She smiled and got comfortable as the AC finally kicked on. Too much excitement coursed through her veins to even think about taking a nap, not that she was much of a napper anyway.

After the captain's spiel and the plane lined up for takeoff, Lyla felt her hands get clammy. She peered out the window at the flashing red lights on the wing of the plane, waiting for it to propel forward. Her heart beat to the point that she had to take deep breaths to suppress it.

"Lyla, we never asked you why you are traveling to Chicago," Dolores said.

"I'm just connecting to another flight," she replied, gripping the armrests like she'd float away without them.

"And what's your final destination?"

Did she seriously just say "final destination" on an airplane? she thought. *They might be thrill-seekers, but they're damn sure not horror movie fans.*

"London."

"London, eh?" Don began, "I adore London. What—"

"Sorry, that's not my actual final dest…uh, not my last stop."

"So, what is?" Dolores asked.

Before Lyla could respond, she felt her center of gravity move from her butt to her back as the plane angled up. She didn't even realize it had been going that fast. Dolores patted her on the back of her taut hand.

"It'll be okay. Planes are the safest way to travel," she said, smiling like she'd just distracted a kid while the doctor administered a shot.

The older woman did have a calming reassurance to her that reminded her of her mom. She looked out the window at Charleston and the city lights and the blinking cars on the highway and watched them get smaller and smaller the higher she went. Her sense of direction was completely thrown, especially in the dark, but she imagined that she could see her parents' house down there. She comforted herself by imagining them pulling into the driveway and walking into the living room for a quiet evening alone. Her pulse slowed, and she turned back to Dolores.

"That noticeable, huh?" she said, loosening her grip on the armrest.

"No, no. When you fly as much as we do, you just pick up on the subtleties of people who have flight anxiety."

Don nodded.

Lyla smiled, appreciating the gesture but recognizing the bullshit.

"I'm actually going to Italy," she said.

"Italy! *Eccellente!*" Don said. "Which part? Venice? Milan?"

"Oh no," Dolores interjected. "She's a Rome girl through and through. Am I right?"

Lyla laughed.

"No. I'm actually going to Umbria," she said, eagerly awaiting their reactions but only receiving blank stares. "It's in the province of Perugia, like two and a half hours southwest of Tuscany, apparently."

She felt weird talking about a place like she was some kind of authority on it when she'd never been. The extent of her knowledge of Italian geography rested with Google Earth and pictures from Claymont's website.

"Interesting," Don said. What's taking you there, if you don't mind my asking?"

Lyla felt the same butterflies in her stomach that appeared when she saw the purple acceptance letter. She was getting to talk to someone outside of her small circle about her new venture in life, and for the first time in a long time, she felt proud.

"I'm going to a writer's residency program."

"You're a writer," Dolores said with impressed eyebrows. "How interesting."

"I love to read," Don said, leaning over his wife, clearly fascinated by the direction in which the conversation was headed.

Lyla braced herself for the inevitable question that he did not fail to deliver.

"What do you write about?"

"I mostly stay within the horror genre."

"Oh."

Dolores stepped in.

"That's interesting. I'm not a horror reader myself—I typically stick with nonfiction and the occasional legal thriller—but I do admire anyone who can manage to produce anything, especially in this day and age."

"Yes," Don said, seemingly trying to redeem himself, "Kudos to you, young lady. So, you're going to a residency, you say?"

"I am. It's called The Claymont Residency for Writers. The residents actually stay inside a modernized castle in Umbria."

"Well, that's simply fascinating," he said.

"And a castle, no less. The perfect place to write a horror novel, I would imagine."

Lyla took a deep breath, suddenly feeling the weight of producing a story now that she'd been given a chance.

"I guess we'll see."

FOUR

As promised, Lyla called her parents as soon as she landed in Chicago. She was now an hour behind them in her new time zone and knew that stretch was only going to elongate in the opposite direction once she crossed the Atlantic, or "hopped the pond" as she'd heard one of her British classmates from college say.

Other than the initial anxieties of takeoff, the flight had actually been quite peaceful. The couple beside her had once again distracted her during the descent by asking what she planned on writing. She was so stuck in her head, trying to brainstorm some sort of an elevator pitch that would get her creative juices flowing, but she ultimately settled on, "You know what? I don't think I'll know until I get there. I want to be inspired by the place and let it tell me its story."

Lyla could tell her Mom was tired when she called, so she kept it brief and said she had an uneventful flight and even described Dolores and Don and how she hoped she and Dad would be active and outgoing once she returned and moved out. That segued into another reminder from Dad that there was no rush for her to leave, even when she got back. Lyla knew there was no going back. She was going to stake her claim at Claymont and have something lined up before she left. The only reason she would go to her parents' place once she got back to the states—other than to see them, of course—would be to get her belongings and move out.

If they had any objections, they didn't voice them, and Lyla definitely didn't want to keep them, so she said she was going to grab something from Starbucks and go read a book until they called for her flight. After a reminder to phone when she got to London and some quick "I love you's," they ended the call, and Lyla found the closest caffeinated beverage near her terminal. As she stared through the open window at Chicago O'Hare International Airport, she couldn't help but feel equally intimidated and excited. Just the difference in the size of the airports gave her enough foreshadowing of the big changes yet to come. As an English major, she naturally thought in literary devices.

Lyla unzipped her backpack and took out her Kindle. She tried to pick up where she'd left off in SHUTTER ISLAND by Dennis Lehane, but the caffeine was quick to kick in and fan the flames of excitement. She couldn't focus on the tablet, looking around instead at her fellow passengers who would be heading to London. Having made it through international customs had been a milestone of relief itself. It was the first time she used her new passport, and as she sat in her chair and watched the massive British Airways plane pull up to the tarmac, those belly butterflies returned.

Boarding for her flight began about forty minutes later, and she listened for them to call for first class. Claymont had covered travel arrangements, and she'd heard that flying first class was a completely different experience than coach, but she was not prepared for *how* different. The flight attendant packed her carry-on for her, and Lyla put her backpack down by her legs where she had all the leg room she needed and more. The muggy, stale atmosphere had been left in the previous plane and replaced by cool, crisp air. Or maybe it was all just in her head. Either way, she was enjoying it.

Lyla took out her cell phone and checked her app's itinerary. The flight from Chicago to Heathrow Airport in London still said it was on time and would take a little under eight hours, but now, she would be flying into the future. She smiled and shook her head as the rest of first class found their seats. Shortly after, business class and coach filled the rest of the plane that was by far the largest aircraft she'd ever been on.

The doors closed, and she was once again given the rundown on flight safety, but this briefing had a more detailed rundown of a water landing. Being fascinated by the power of word choice and linguistics, she found it morbidly humorous that they referred to it as a "water landing" when she pictured something more akin to a hellish descent into the maelstrom like in LOST, her favorite TV show of all time and one that she would debate with her roommates until she ran out of breath.

Shit, she thought. *First FINAL DESTINATION and now LOST. Are there any other movies or shows revolving around airplane crashes that you want to bring up?*

But this time was different. When the plane readied for takeoff, she wasn't scared. She still watched from the window and saw a much more populated terrain below her. The big city lights made Charleston pale in comparison. Just as before, she kept her eyes on the ground until it was no longer visible.

Once they reached cruising altitude, the reality of flying across the Atlantic Ocean set it. Luckily, the service she received kept her mind distracted. She gladly took the free food and drinks; well, free to her, at least. Yes, she would love a neck pillow and a warm face cloth. She didn't know if she'd ever experience a luxury trip again, so she took full advantage of all the amenities.

Lyla took out her Kindle and tried to give Lehane another go, but the combination of the caffeine crash and the comfortable seating made her eyelids heavy. She pushed on, but once she dropped her tablet and jarred herself awake, she conceded that it was time to take a nap. Minutes after tucking the device into her backpack, she was resting against the pillow and lulled by the hum of the engines into a dreamless sleep.

———

A man's voice woke her up, and she looked around, completely disoriented. It was the pilot talking telling them that they were beginning their initial descent into London. She'd slept the entire flight. She wiped her eyes and yawned, trying to blink herself awake. When she looked out the window, she stared at the sunny city below. Her watch displayed 9:13 a.m., but that was West Virginia time, EST. If she was in London, then that meant her watch was five hours behind the time zone in this part of the world. Even though she knew she would have to adjust her watch again once she got to Italy, she wanted it to show the current time, so she didn't get too discombobulated. She moved the hour to 2:13 p.m.

Once the plane landed and the flight attendants ushered off first class, Lyla went through Heathrow Airport, marveling at her surroundings, looking for signs that she was, in fact, in a foreign land. The first vendor sign she saw was Starbucks.

What did you expect? To step off the plane and into a pub? Hear locals ordering pints with fish and chips?

She hit up Starbucks and refueled. Between the power nap on the plane and the Americano, she was properly prepared to find her connecting flight which was in two hours. She walked around for a little bit until she discovered a restaurant she hadn't heard of and sat for a quick meal. The anxiety of not being in her terminal forced her to scarf down her food, which was too good to be eaten that fast. She put on her backpack that had been sitting beside her in the booth, wheeled her carry-on from under the table, double-checked her app to make sure she knew where she was going, and headed to her destination.

It took her longer than expected to find her terminal, and walking around with a full belly and two pieces of luggage didn't help the situation. By the time she got to where she was supposed to be, she practically collapsed into the barely cushioned seat. She checked the time and still had an hour until boarding, so she figured she'd give SHUTTER ISLAND another go. The pages and the minutes flew by as her mind toured the mysterious island with its psychiatric hospital and mysterious happenings through the lens of a vulnerable U.S. Marshal who seemed to be losing his grip on reality. She knew his situation wasn't going to end well by how the author used budding atmospheric dread and paranoia to create a truly unsettling mood.

When the ladies working her terminal announced that boarding would begin soon, she didn't want to stop reading. She tucked the Kindle back in her bag and got prepared, her anxiety about not being ready winning the battle over her narrative curiosity. One task she did not forget to do this time was to set her watch to the local time in Umbria, which was one hour ahead. Her watch moved from 4:10 p.m. to 5:10 p.m.

There was no first-class section on this flight. She looked at her app and saw she was seated in business class and got mad at herself for being disappointed, already noticing herself getting spoiled. She got in line and noticed the couple in front of her conversing in Italian. Using her basic knowledge of Latin root words, she impressed herself with what she was able to comprehend, or so she thought. Most people were still speaking English. She smiled at the flight attendant who checked her boarding pass and welcomed her to the next leg of her journey.

Already feeling like a seasoned pro, she placed her suitcase in the appropriate spot and took her seat, looking out the window once again at the trolley car of luggage. According to her itinerary, this British Airways flight would take just under two and a half hours. She let out a deep sigh and regretted not having gone to the restroom while she was waiting to board. That damn book had just been so engrossing. It didn't matter; the plane's lavatory was only a few rows in front of her seat.

Lyla figured she still had thirty minutes until the plane was in the air, so she grabbed her Kindle and resumed reading as passengers filled the seats behind her. Two pages in and she remembered to call her parents. She put it down, took her phone out, and realized she'd never taken it off airplane mode after her London flight.

"Shit," she whispered as she switched it back to normal operations and a flurry of social media notifications and text messages populated the screen, turning the device into a nonstop vibrator for about forty seconds.

Lyla responded to her mom's text which was just asking if she'd made it to London yet. She apologized for forgetting to call and told her she had just boarded the flight to Italy and she would land at 8:30 p.m. her time, which would be 2:30 p.m. back home. Mom messaged back immediately and said she loved her and to call her when she landed. A second text came through that said, "We miss you already!"

"Aww," Lyla said involuntarily, a word she rarely used unless kittens were involved.

She switched the phone to airplane mode and tucked it in her pocket.

"And back to SHUTTER ISLAND we go."

By the time she finished the book and was shocked by the ending, the plane's wheels touched down in Perugia San Francesco.

FIVE

As soon as Lyla departed the plane and entered the airport, she found a spot against the wall near the restroom to stay out of everyone's way. Her phone was still in airplane mode, so she switched it back and waited for all of her notifications to settle, which there were significantly less since the last time she checked. She knew she was on a time crunch and needed to go to baggage claim and meet her Claymont liaison, Julia. She definitely did not want to keep her waiting, first impressions and all. But there was one call she had to make.

Her mom answered.

"Hello?"

"Greetings from Italy," Lyla said, exciting herself as the words came out of her mouth.

"Oh, thank goodness. We're so glad you finally made it there," Mom said and then shouted, presumably at Dad, "Lyla's on the phone!"

Lyla winced from the volume.

"Geez. Was he on the roof or something?"

Mom chuckled and said, "No, he just finished mowing the grass and is about to hop in the shower. I had to shout over the water."

She pictured her Dad just about to step foot in the running water and then hearing the call from his wife, shutting it off because God forbid he adds an unnecessary drop to the water bill, and then sprinting naked across the house to catch his daughter on the phone. She scrunched her face and laughed to herself at the same time.

"At least make sure he's wearing clothes first."

"I can't guarantee anything with your father, dear."

Lyla smiled and shook her head and heard his footsteps enter the room and then his voice.

"Lyla bug?" he asked

She could tell by the slight distortion in the clarity of the call that she'd been put on speaker phone. She pictured the phone sitting on the kitchen counter while they eagerly hovered above it, and it made her realize how much she was going to miss them.

"Hi, Dad."

"Everything good?"

"Yeah, just landed at the Perugia airport."

"Okay, you're six hours ahead of us, so that puts you at 9:01 p.m. over there?"

Lyla looked at her watch even though she knew what time it was.

"Yep. I'm in the future."

"How are you feeling? Are you jetlagged?" Mom asked.

"Yeah, it definitely doesn't feel like night. I'm wide awake."

"Well, hopefully it'll level out in a day or two," Mom said.

"Honestly, I think I'm just excited more than anything. I'm sure once I get settled in, I'll crash. I'm not worried about it."

"So, what's the next step? Did you get your bags yet?" Dad asked.

"No. I didn't want to forget to call you guys before I headed over there. I'm going to do that as soon as I get off here."

She looked at the restroom beside her and just the sight of the female figure beside the door triggered her body, and her stomach rumbled from a day's worth of travel food.

"And you said they have someone waiting for you there to take you to the school?" he asked.

"Yeah, but stop calling it a school," she said too sternly, but she'd told him that ten times already. "It's a writer's residency."

"Excuse me," he said with mock offense. "I assume they have someone waiting to take you to the *residency?*"

"Just call it Claymont," she laughed. "But yeah, Julia, my contact or mentor or whatever her role is. Not sure the extent of her duties yet."

"Better not keep her waiting, then," Mom said. "Go get your bags and call us when you get to the sch—when you get to Claymont."

"Will do."

The rumbling in her stomach was getting worse, and she hoped her parents picked up on the dismissiveness in her tone.

"Okay. We love you."

"Love you, Lyla bug," Dad said.

"I love you, too. I'll call later."

"Okay, bye."

"Bye!"

"Bye," she said and ended the call and hurried into the restroom, reluctantly bringing her carry-on and backpack with her.

She was soon attempting to navigate the airport, having to look for the English on the signs but ultimately resorted to the little pictures and arrows. She found baggage claim and snagged her checked bags, struggling to lift them off the conveyer belt. She stared at the two large suitcases beside the smaller one.

"This is going to be fun," she said to herself.

Enjoy your real-world experience!

She sighed and extended the handlebar and wheeled the heavy load toward the exit sign. Once she got going, it wasn't as bad as she thought it would be. That made her grin as it summed up the story of her life perfectly up to that point.

As soon as she rounded the corner, following the orange exit arrows, she saw a tall, broad-shouldered man in the nicest suit she'd ever seen, standing near the doors, holding a sign with her name on it. The guy was big enough to be a linebacker in the NFL and towered over most passers-by. She was grateful Claymont sent him; he'd be a hard target to miss.

Once she was close enough, she noticed that the sign was thick and rigid like wood. This was definitely not a flimsy piece of posterboard with her name written in black marker. The sign had "THE CLAY-

MONT RESIDENCY FOR WRITERS" printed across the top in gold lettering with the same font and little ink and quill logo that she'd seen on their website. Her last name was written in elegant cursive with the same golden color. Somehow, this tailored sign impressed her more than the first-class flight.

The tall man in the suit regarded her with zero emotion as she approached him.

"Hi, I'm Lyla Robbins."

"Greetings, Ms. Robbins. Welcome to Italy," he said with a voice as deep as the ocean she'd recently flown over. "Allow me to help you with your bags, please."

"Thank you," she said and watched as he effortlessly maneuvered the two large suitcases.

"My pleasure. Now, if you'll follow me, I'll take you to your car."

"Sounds good. What's your name?"

He regarded her like no one had ever taken an interest in him.

"Maurice," he said.

"Do you work for Claymont, Maurice? I like that name."

"Yes, Claymont is a lovely name."

Lyla chuckled and then realized he hadn't been making a joke.

"I meant your name. I don't think I've met a Maurice in my life. I have read a couple of writers with that name though, both brilliant in different ways," she said, noticing that she was doing her nervous rambling that she'd become more self-conscious of since it was pointed out to her in school.

"Oh, well thank you," he said, "But to answer your question, yes, I work for Claymont. I mostly drive Ms. Allard."

It took Lyla a second to remember Allard was Julia's last name. He started to walk toward the exit, and she followed.

"The car is just up here to the left."

As soon as the glass doors hissed open and they stepped out into the night, Lyla paused and took a moment to savor her surroundings and relish in the fact that she'd made it to Italy. She smelled the air as a gentle breeze blew through the warm night. The atmosphere just felt different on this side of the world.

"It's this way, Ms. Robbins," Maurice said.

Lyla followed the large man with the sign tucked in his right arm as he pulled the two suitcases. He was headed to a black SUV. She didn't recognize the make and model from the distance, but she did see a woman leaning against it, smoking a cigarette. She had short, dark hair and wore an outfit Lyla had never seen in America. She looked like she'd just walked off the runway in Milan.

The woman flicked her cigarette across the car when they approached her.

"Lyla Robbins, please meet Ms. Julia Allard."

Julia pushed her shades up her head where they stayed. She smiled and had flawless skin and teeth. More than that, her genuine joy was disarming. Lyla didn't know why she thought this woman would be some strict taskmaster. She guessed she was in her early to mid-thirties, and she carried herself like she was the head of a *Fortune* 500 company.

She still might be. Don't rule it out just because she knows how to put on a convincingly welcoming front.

"Lyla, it's so nice to finally see you in person," Julia said.

Maurice popped the trunk and began loading the bags.

"Likewise," Lyla said, still feeling a bit nervous.

"How was the trip? I bet you're exhausted."

"It was great. I read, got some sleep, met some interesting people, and really enjoyed my experience in first class."

Julia smiled.

"The first of many, I'm sure. We have a large endowment from generous benefactors, and we want our residents to know how valued you all are to us."

Maurice shut the trunk, opened the sliding door, and got in the driver's seat which was on the opposite side of the vehicle from what Lyla was accustomed to.

"Are you ready to begin your journey, Lyla?"

She took a deep breath and nodded.

"I am. I'm excited."

"Good. Hop in and I'll fill you in on as much as I can before we get to town."

"How far is that?"

"Around 40 kilometers. The ride won't take long, and there's something special waiting for you there," she said in her French accent and stepped into the spacious vehicle, sliding over to the window.

Lyla got in, and the door slid shut beside her.

"Are we ready?" Maurice asked.

"Yes, dear. Off we go," she said and turned to Lyla. "I'm sure you have a million questions, so I'll start with the basics, and we can go from there."

"Okay."

Maurice pulled out and drove through the airport parking lots.

"I will be your guide for the first week of your residency and then act as a mentor to you and the other ladies. It's my job to discuss the rules of the facility, expectations regarding your writing performance, and give you a tour of the grounds. You're going to be amazed. If the first-class flight impressed you, prepare to feel like a princess in a new castle, literally."

"Oh, I've seen the pictures. The castle looks amazing."

"Those pictures don't do it justice. Just wait," she said with a smile.

Maurice pulled out of the airport and followed the signs on the road that said, UMBERTIDE, and had little arrows leading the way.

"When I first saw the castle—just the outside—I was awestruck. I moved here from Paris, so it's rare that architecture floors me like that."

"What did you do in Paris?"

Julia raised her eyebrows and considered the question. Lyla noticed that it was a similar reaction to Maurice's when she'd inquired about something personal.

"I am a project manager by trade. You name an industry, and I bet I've worked in it. Whenever an individual or a business has a goal, I develop a strategic plan and help them execute it. I like to think of it as teaching business babies how to walk. I sort of fell into it when my girlfriend started an interior design firm. She was the creative force, and I had to make her vision a reality. Once it took off, so did she," Julia said with a grin.

"That's not cool."

"It turned out to be the best thing that ever happened to me career-wise because people noticed what I did, and I got paid double what I did before to help a small business become a big business. After that, I was naming my price."

"So how did you end up here?"

"How indeed," she chuckled. "I took the Sterlings' offer for my daughter. They hired me a little over five years ago when they wanted to make Claymont a reality. It was a proposal I couldn't refuse. This position is temporary, but it will change our lives. Enough about me, though."

"Will you tell me more about them?"

"They're private people, Mr. and Mrs. Sterling. They tend to stay out of the public eye and use their resources to help others. You'll meet them, though. Don't worry about that. They typically make monthly visits to Claymont, check in with the staff and make sure the program is running how it's supposed to, and meet new residents. I'm sure you'll be seeing them soon."

"Sounds intriguing," Lyla said and looked out the window at the night sky, amazed at how clear it was with the full moon amid a sea of stars. "How did they amass this fortune? What's their motive for funding a creative writing residency of all things?"

"That is their story to tell, and you will find out when they visit," Julia said and leaned closer. "Listen, it's best to not worry about the Sterlings. Your first goal is to get accustomed to the way of life at Claymont and write the best work of your life."

"No pressure, right?" Lyla said with a nervous smirk.

"True greatness requires pressure, motivation, accountability. This is why you are here, right?"

Lyla opened her mouth but didn't say anything. It donned on her in that moment that she had romanticized everything. The castle, the landscape, the town, and the creative lifestyle had taken up most of her focus. Not until Julia said those words did she truly feel the pressure of delivering on whatever potential the powers that be saw in her when they admitted her into the residency. A brief pang of anxiety hit her, but she shut it down immediately.

"Yes," she said. "I want to write something great."

A slow smile formed on Julia's lips.

"I read your submission, you know? As long as you follow proto-col, I know the program will help you achieve that goal."

A cell phone dinged from the front of the vehicle. Maurice looked at the screen dashboard.

"Your final transport is awaiting your arrival," he said.

"Final transport?" Lyla asked.

"It's a Claymont tradition…a lovely way to introduce new resi-dents to the castle grounds. Just remember that it was my idea," she said.

Five minutes later, they crossed a long, green bridge and approached a row of old houses that lined the river, each with glowing lights at their base. Lyla leaned forward to get a better look through the windshield and saw beautiful homes and stores that reminded her of a village out of a fairy tale. She failed to conceal her smile.

"Welcome to the city of Umbertide, one of the most charming places in Umbria," Julia said.

"It's amazing. How far away is Claymont?"

"There's a road just at the base of the mountain on the other side of town. That is where your horse-drawn carriage is waiting to take you to the castle."

SIX

"Oh, my God," Lyla said as they arrived at their stop.

"Here we are," Maurice said and put the car in park.

She stared at the white stallion in front of the four-person coach. A young man about her age sat in the seat and held the reins. He had dark hair, tanned skin, and wore a suit similar to Maurice's. He turned and regarded them like he could see her through the tinted windows. His eyes made Lyla's heart skip a beat. She wondered if he was a local and felt slightly giddy at the prospect of being driven by him to the castle.

The side door automatically slid open, and the two women stepped out. The young man directed his attention to the horse. Lyla watched Maurice round the car, open the trunk, and load her luggage in the back of the carriage.

"Are you ready to go on a ride?" Julia asked.

She looked at the masculine horse and followed the reins to the young man holding them who turned and met her gaze like he could sense her. He smiled before she could look away.

"Hello," he said in an Italian accent.

"Hi," Lyla replied, not really sure what else to say.

"Lyla, this is Leo and his horse, Aldo," Julia said. "They'll be our escorts up the mountain tonight."

Maurice closed the trunk and got back in the SUV. The door slid shut, but the vehicle just idled there. She wondered if he was going to wait on Julia for however long it took her to escort them to Claymont.

"Ready when you are," Leo said.

Julia led the way, walking up the retractable stairs to open the little wooden door on the side of the carriage. The four spoked wheels were almost as tall as she was. Lyla looked back at Maurice's vehicle one last time, but she couldn't see anything through its dark windows. She knew it wasn't possible for Leo to have been looking at her when she'd been inside, but she couldn't shake the feeling that he had.

"Come, come," Julia said, taking a seat and patting the spot beside her.

"Okay," Lyla said, grinning as she walked up the three steps and sank in the comfortable cushion.

"All aboard?" Leo asked from the front.

"Aye, captain," Julia said with a grin and turned to Lyla. "You know, in addition to being our escort for new arrivals and graduates, Leo works with his mama at this little coffee shop just right down the road there. He makes an espresso to die for. You must stop by and try it once you're able."

Once you're able?

She said it like she wouldn't be allowed to immediately leave the grounds.

Leo made a clicking sound with his mouth and jiggled the reins. Aldo, the white steed, trudged forward, carrying the rolling carriage off the smooth asphalt and onto the stone path. The road was bumpy, but the carriage must've been equipped with shocks that reduced the vibration, because Lyla only felt a slight rocking.

She marveled at the sights before her. The higher up the slight incline they went, the more beautiful the scenery became. Trees began to pepper the road on both sides, and soon they were surrounded by lush, forested walls. She looked up and saw the clear night sky again, taken aback by the brightness of the moon and stars. An orange glow in front of her caught her attention. Leo had lit a lantern that hung off the carriage to his right. The flickering glow inside the fogged glass illuminated the road enough for the horse, she supposed. It was certainly not as bright as a pair of headlights, not that they needed them with the full moon shining down on them.

"Okay, time to talk specifics," Julia said with a slightly more commanding inflection. "Claymont operates under a set of rules that have been scientifically proven to improve productivity, creativity, and efficiency. They are designed to help the author flesh out their story as organically as possible.

"Everyone has a story to tell. Some people have a desire to write theirs down. But, for a host of reasons—or excuses—they don't. 'Life' gets in the way. The program eliminates all that."

"I've never had a problem with the discipline," Lyla said, only half-paying attention as she stared at the trees slowly passing by, trying to see how far into the darkness she can gaze.

"We shall see."

That made her turn around. Julia lit a cigarette and smiled at her.

"Rule number one: no cell phones. Ever. There is a communal land-line at Claymont that you can use, but it is a privilege, not a right. It's also for emergencies, of course."

Lyla thought about how weird it would feel to not have her phone on her at all times. No social media, no text messages, no phone calls, no ability to search anything on the internet, no music, and no pictures. The more she tallied up the uses for her phone, the more aware of how tethered to it she actually was.

Her anxiety reared its ugly head with "what if?" scenarios, but she pushed them back down. She was here to write and claimed that she would make sacrifices to do so, and yet she was balking at the first rule. Taking a step outside of herself and doing an honest appraisal like that made her sick to her stomach. She took her phone out of her pocket.

"You don't have to give it to me until we reach the castle," Julia said. "We'll put it in your storage bin in a secured room. You'll be permitted time before we enter to make any final calls if you need to speak with Mommy and Daddy."

Lyla couldn't get a read on Julia. Half the time, she seemed warm and encouraging, but she could quickly veer into condescension with one sharp comment. She just puffed her cigarette and smiled.

"Rule number two: Claymont has a strict in-house curfew of ten p.m. Unless it is for pre-approved reasons, no resident is permitted outside of the castle past this hour."

"Why?" Lyla asked, again regretting the tone in which she asked that question; she felt herself coming off as rebellious, and the last thing she wanted to do was rock the boat on day one.

"Ten p.m. to five a.m. are The Reader's hours," Julia said in a tone so matter of fact that it chilled Lyla to her core.

"What does that mean?"

Leo scoffed and shook his head from the front. He must've felt Julia's glare because he straightened up quickly when she shot him a look.

"The Reader is the Sterling family's most valuable asset. He is the heart of the program."

"Who is he?"

"Even I don't know that, but that's how it's supposed to be. The Sterlings insisted on complete anonymity, or it wouldn't work—this entire creative endeavor. Just think of him as the world's greatest editor, and I'm not using hyperbole when I say that."

"And he only comes out at night?"

"Yes. You will never see him. If you do break curfew, it's grounds for immediate dismissal."

"Wow. Okay. This is really odd, isn't it?"

"Greatness was never achieved by doing the status quo."

They rode in silence for a moment, listening to the click-clacking of the horse's hooves against the stone and the wheels bumping across the uneven terrain.

"Tomorrow, we'll have a discussion and form an individualized plan based on goals you set for yourself. All the luxurious amenities you saw on the website—using the phone, access to the Wi-Fi on personal devices, and even leaving the castle grounds—will be permitted as long as you continue to hit your weekly goals. They are rewards to keep you motivated. If you fail to hit your goal three times, you will be dismissed from the program."

Lyla raised her eyebrows, really feeling the weight of responsibility. *This is no vacation.*

It can be, though. It's teaching you how to balance work and play.

"Don't worry," Julia said, bringing Lyla back to the present moment. "Remember, you set your writing goals. So, when we do our tour of the grounds tomorrow and have our discussion, be sure to think about what a realistic output for you would look like."

"Is it true that we can stay here for as long as we want? As long as we're hitting our goals, I mean."

Julia grinned.

"Your residency at Claymont is active for as long as it takes you to finish your book."

"Almost there," Leo announced over his shoulder.

"Okay, here we go," Julia said and patted Lyla's leg.

Lyla felt her heart flutter. She watched the tree line on the right and saw the corner of a wrought iron gate that ran parallel with the road. As soon as the carriage approached it, the trimmed foliage around the perimeter gave way to a clear view of the castle. Nothing has ever taken her breath away like her first sight of The Claymont Residency for Writers.

A towering structure stood tall above the high fence. Once the carriage moved a bit further up the road, the thick vines clinging to the fence dissipated, giving her a full view of the front of the castle.

"Wow."

"Wow, indeed," Julia replied. "I never get tired of seeing it."

"It's so…magnificent."

"There's over a thousand years of history in those stones. The tall structure at the front right there, that's called The Keep. It was the first part built, functioning as a watchtower of sorts."

Lyla peered around The Keep at the tall stone walls that seemed to run on forever into the night. She admired the gorgeous front doors that looked exactly how she hoped they would—tall arching slabs that parted in the middle. They were big enough for the entire horse and carriage to fit through, and she guessed that was by design, assuming people would ride their animals and caravans right into the castle's courtyard.

"I won't give you the detailed history of each addition to the place. You can look into it when you get the chance. It might make for some inspiration. It will definitely give you a newfound appreciation for it. When you're standing in something that's been there for that long, you realize how small you really are in the grand scheme of things."

Lyla listened but couldn't peel her eyes from the ancient structure. A long walkway cut through the perfectly cut grass and connected to the stone road, right at the spot where the party approached. Leo pulled on the reins, and Aldo snorted and came to a halt. The doors to the main gate perfectly matched the doors to The Keep. A black, metal sign was welded to the right side of the gate. It simply read, THE CLAYMONT RESIDENCY FOR WRITERS, in golden letters and a border that matched the one Maurice held at the airport.

"Are you ready?" Julia asked.

Lyla turned to face her, smiled, and nodded.

"Then let's go."

A whirring sound of tiny gears came from the gate, and Lyla realized the doors were slowly opening outward. Her eyes ran up the path, and she stared at the windows that faced her. There were glowing lights from all but the one at the top—the fifth floor. She peered into the darkness, realizing that was where The Reader resided. Time seemed to pause, and the world around her blurred until only the window remained in focus. The longer she stared, the more she felt someone staring back at her.

She jumped when the castle doors opened the same way the gate's had done. But unlike the open mouth that was the fifth-floor window, light spilled out of the castle's interior. Two figures emerged—both tall, broad-shouldered men wearing suits. They were not only the same height, but they had the same coiffed, dark hair on top with the sides neatly trimmed.

"Ahh, perfect timing," Julia said. "Here come the twins."

Now it made sense to her. Julia was quick to elaborate, though.

"Don't ever let them hear you refer to them as 'the twins,' despite my bad example."

"What do they want?" Lyla asked, feeling somewhat put off by the seriousness of their demeanors and what Julia had said.

"They're going to get your bags for you, princess," Leo said from the front and chuckled.

Lyla felt her face redden the second he called her 'princess.' He wasn't doing it mockingly, she thought. Julia smacked the back of his head. He stiffened and apologized as the handsome twins approached the coach. They looked to be in their thirties, she guessed. Julia leaned over Lyla's lap and addressed them.

"Gentlemen, this is Claymont's newest resident, Lyla Robbins."

They both nodded but maintained the serious expression on their faces.

"Lyla, these dashing men are two of our program monitors and the lifeblood of Claymont. This is Mariano and Antonio Dinardi," she said, gesturing to each one as she said their names.

"Pleasure to meet you, Lyla," Mariano said.

"Yes, welcome to Claymont."

"Hello, I'm Lyla," she said, feeling like she suddenly lost the ability to communicate.

"May we grab your belongings?" Mariano asked.

"Yes, please."

They didn't waste any time with pleasantries and went about grabbing suitcases from the rear of the carriage.

"Thank you," Lyla said.

"Our pleasure," the twins said in unison and then looked at each other like they got annoyed every time they did that.

Once they had everything, Mariano said, "These will be waiting for you in your room."

"Thank you, gentlemen," Julia said in a tone that let them know to take a hike. She turned to Lyla. "And now the hard part."

Lyla didn't know what she meant by that and just studied her face as she waited on an elaboration.

"Now is the time you make any last phone calls, texts, social media...whatever. You can have ten minutes, and then we'll go inside."

Lyla took her phone from her pocket and swiped it open, surprised she had service way out there.

"If you want some privacy, feel free to step out and walk along the gate."

She opened the door and almost forgot about the steps but caught herself just in time to not look like she almost fell.

"I'll be waiting right here," Julia said, lighting another cigarette. "Leo, you can't have one until you're off duty."

Leo just shook his head and smiled as Lyla walked past him and the horse. She smiled and looked at her phone.

All of the little red lights around her social media icons meant nothing to her in that moment. She opened her text messages and clicked the group chat she shared with her WVU cohort. They had been having a long conversation without her over the last day, but she didn't feel like wasting time scrolling up and reading fifty messages. All she did was type, "I just arrived at Claymont in Italy. I won't be active on here for a while. I'll update everyone as soon as I can. Wish me luck!"

She didn't even wait for them to respond before dialing her mom's number and pressing the call button. It rang three times. By the fourth one, Lyla was beginning to get nervous. The last thing she wanted to do was leave a voicemail, but she would if that was her only option. Just as she was about to abandon hope, her mom answered.

"Hello? Lyla?"

"Hi, Mom," she said, fighting the urge to start crying.

"How's everything going? Where are you?"

"I just got here. I'm outside the castle fence."

"Don!" she yelled, causing Lyla to momentarily pull the phone from her ear. "Get down here! Lyla's on the phone! Sorry, dear. I don't want your father to miss this."

"It's okay."

She listened as the audio quality switched to speaker mode.

"Lyla bug, how are you?" Dad asked.

Again, she refrained from crying.

"I'm good. I'm here. It feels like it took a week, but I made it."

"So, tell us about the castle," Mom said.

"It's gorgeous. It's nighttime here, but it's still the most beautiful building I've ever seen. It's like something from another world."

As soon as Lyla said that, she realized the time was after ten p.m. Technically, she was out after curfew even though she hadn't officially checked in yet. But still, wasn't this "The Reader's time" as Julia had stated. She looked up at the fifth-floor window and saw someone take a step back into the shadows. Her heart leapt up to her throat. The Reader had been watching her.

"Send us some pictures!" Mom said, startling her.

"Oh, I uh, don't think I'm allowed to do that."

She looked back at Julia who was smoking and talking to Leo. Aldo the horse appeared to be keeping an eye on her though.

"What do you mean, you're not allowed to do that?" Dad asked.

"They have strict rules here. One of them is that I have to give them my phone."

"Wait, what?" Mom asked.

"Yeah, Julia told me the entire program operates on evidence-based research to eliminate all distractions. To be fair, I can't think of anything more distracting to a writer than a cell phone."

"So, I'm assuming they have landlines then?" Dad asked.

She heard the slight concern in his voice.

"Yes, but I have to earn that privilege." Before her parents had the chance to fully freak out, she said, "I'm meeting with Julia tomorrow to discuss my goals. As long as I'm meeting my weekly writing goals, I'll be able to call you. Plus, I still have my MacBook, so it's not like I'm completely cut off from society. But I do need to hit my goals to use the Wi-Fi. I'll also be able to write you," she said, not even knowing if that was true.

"How do you feel about that?" Dad asked.

"I mean, it kind of freaked me out at first, but I see the logic in it. And the fact that I reacted like that really showed me how tethered I am to this thing."

"People have survived without cell phones for years," he said.

Lyla had lost count of how many times she'd heard her father say that.

"Well, you call us as soon as you get settled in, okay?" Mom said.

"I'll call as soon as I can. Promise."

"We love you, honey. You're going to flourish," she said.

"Thanks, Mom."

A twig snapped across the street. Lyla's eyes immediately shot toward the forest, unable to see in the darkness beyond the tree line. She waited for any other sound, but nothing came. She looked at Julia and Leo, still talking, and seemingly oblivious to the sound. But what really troubled her was the horse. Aldo snorted and kept glancing at the trees. Leo made a sound with his mouth to steady the steed. Julia met her gaze and held up four fingers.

"I only have a few more minutes to talk, and then we're heading in," Lyla said. "Oh, listen to this. This driver in a suit picked me up from the airport. He was waiting in the main lobby with a sign with my name on it. Julia was in the giant SUV waiting for me, and when we passed through Umbertide—which I'll have to tell you about when I have more time—they had a horse and carriage waiting to take us up the mountain."

"Oh, goodness," Mom said. "That sounds so lovely."

"Yeah, apparently it's a tradition for how they welcome new residents."

"That is quite something. I'm so excited for you," Dad said. "Just stay on top of your game, girl. You get me?"

"Yeah, yeah. I get you."

"Well, we won't hold you up any longer," Mom began. "Go have fun. Make friends. Get some rest."

"Okay. I love you guys."

"Love you, too," Mom said.

"Love you, Lyla," Dad said.

"Bye for now," she said and ended the call.

Just when she turned to go back to the carriage, something rustled the earth beyond the trees. Aldo whinnied, and finally got the attention of Julia and Leo. Julia exited the carriage and met Lyla at the gate.

"It's time to go in," she said and held out her hand.

Lyla knew what she wanted and gave her the phone.

Leo urged Aldo into turning the carriage around.

"I'll see you around town, eventually. Stop by the shop. First coffee is on me!" he said.

"Sounds good."

"Goodnight, Lyla. Julia, I'll be waiting out here."

"You better be. I don't intend on spending the night," she said as she looked around the forest and then at Lyla. "Let's get inside."

The two women crossed the threshold, and the gate immediately folded its doors closed behind them. As they walked closer to the ever-growing Keep, Lyla saw no trace of anyone in the fifth-floor window.

SEVEN

A chill hung in the air within the castle walls, but it wasn't entirely unpleasant. Lyla felt the initial bristle, bringing her fully into the present moment and allowing her to take in her new surroundings.

Julia led the way through the arched castle doors that led to The Keep. They walked into the entryway, and the doors closed behind them. Orange lightbulbs illuminated the room, despite Lyla's romanticized notions of candlelight and candelabras hanging from the walls. Still, the artificial light was warm enough to put off that illusion.

"This is the entryway. This is your sign in/sign out log. You will use it any time you leave the property. So, whenever you go get your coffee from Leo and do your best to avoid his less than subtle advances, you will just note the time out, destination, and time in. Got it? Good."

Lyla glanced at the unfolded book atop the tall table pushed against the wall. A mirror hung above it, and she caught sight of her reflection for the first time since the airport and immediately felt self-conscious.

Her brown hair that she'd pulled into a bun was frazzled and hung to the side. The beginnings of dark circles formed under her eyes, and her skin was too shiny for her comfort. And forget about her clothes. She had chosen comfortability over presentability when choosing her outfit for the trip. Her stretchy jeans and faded Edgar Allan Poe T-shirt weren't meant to cast a glorious first impression, but at least it would be an honest one. For better or worse, that's who she was. She did want to freshen up before meeting the other residents, though.

Potted plants stood tall in the corners of the opposite wall, and a large painting of the sprawling land hung in the middle of it with the castle being the art's focal point. She looked down at the tile floor and could tell it was a new renovation. Everything was elegant, and she dared not start calculating the expenses or she would be walking around on eggshells, afraid to sit on a ten-thousand-dollar antique chair.

"Okay, through here we have the commons area—not the technical term, but someone just called it that, and it stuck."

Lyla's eyes couldn't widen any further, and she had to catch her jaw from dropping as they walked into the open area. A long red carpet with intricate golden designs ran the length of the room with stone pillars spaced out every ten feet lining both sides. She followed them up to the painted ceiling. Three evenly placed chandeliers ran the length of the carpet. There was open space serving various functions in the areas beyond the pillars. She looked to her right and saw a door that led to a staircase.

"Ahh, yes. That is the staircase that leads to the five floors in The Keep. The second and third floors are where the residents' rooms are located. Administrative offices and residences are on the fourth, and we already know who occupies the fifth."

Lyla nodded, walking atop the thick carpet, glancing from left to right, trying to take everything in.

"So, we have a lounge area here. Some of our residents choose to sit by the fireplace there to work. On this side is the café. The full kitchen is just ahead, but this is where you can grab a quick snack."

Lyla eyeballed the area that looked like one of the shops at the airport. She was amazed by how much food and drinks were in there.

"And in case you're wondering, there's a wine cellar in the basement," Julia said, with a side-eye and a grin. "Everyone is welcome to it as long as it doesn't interfere with productivity. There is no tolerance for overindulgence at Claymont according to the rulebook. So as long as you don't get shitfaced and make an ass out of yourself, you'll be fine."

"I don't really drink, so that won't be a problem."

"Good. The gym and spa are both through those doors on the left. Both are fully furnished with the latest equipment and cleaned daily. The rec room and arcade are through that door. We're coming up on the laundry room and storage area. And the last door on the right leads to the computer lab. It is also a quiet room, meaning it's treated like a library. Residents are free to use the computers for drafting or research when working. Recreational use is permitted—"

"As long as I'm hitting my weekly goal," Lyla finished.

"Precisely. You're getting it," Julia said and then stopped.

Lyla didn't realize she had until the woman was two steps behind her. She turned around.

"Is something wrong?" she asked.

"No, no. I just want you to know that I understand this all seems like a bit much—the rules, the amenities, the damn castle itself—but I've seen it work firsthand. Some of the biggest names in recent publishing came through here. I obviously can't tell you who; that's up to them. But what I will say is make sure to remember your fellow residents. Depending on their chosen genre, you might see them at the top of the bestseller charts one day."

Lyla felt a rush of excitement as she pictured her name on the front of a book with the words "*New York Times* Bestselling Author" written above it.

Don't get ahead of yourself. You don't even have a story yet.

The submission she had sent that gained her entry into Claymont was just a draft of something she never intended on fully fleshing out. She wanted her time at the castle to inform her project. That was the whole point. But now that she was there, and they were talking about weekly goals and punishments/rewards, she felt her anxiety hovering over her shoulder. She wondered if the other residents came in with ideas in mind or what their processes were like.

"That's amazing," she said. "But where are the other residents?"

"I would guess that a few of them are straight through that door. This leads to the formal dining room and patio. Come on in."

Julia stood in front of two shiny, wooden doors with brass rings for handles. She grabbed one and pulled the door open, gesturing for Lyla to enter first. When Lyla saw the dining hall, she released her second audible gasp of the evening.

"Oh my God. This is amazing."

Two rows of connected tables ran the length of the room with a clear walkway down the middle that led to a stage-like area at the front. Once she got a little closer, she saw there was indeed a podium on the slightly elevated area. Claymont's name and logo were printed on it loud and clear, of course.

"This is where three meals are served at the same time every day. Attendance is optional unless one of the residents is doing a reading. Everyone is expected to attend readings and participate in the Q&A sessions. These don't always take place during meals, though."

Lyla looked to her right at the kitchen which took up half of the wall and was surprisingly deep. The buffet style setup reminded her of a college cafeteria with trays and silverware stationed at the beginnings of the two open windows.

"That's our kitchen. You'll never have a better meal than what's served here. I don't care what the locals in Umbertide say. Once you sample the menu of what our chefs prepare, you'll never want to eat anywhere else."

Just thinking about authentic Italian cuisine made her mouth water.

"You were asking about the residents, and I do see a couple of them out there on the patio."

Lyla turned to her left and noticed a row of glass doors leading to the outside patio. Metal torches burned along what she assumed was the perimeter. She saw a hot tub, lounge chairs, and two circular tables with umbrellas where two young women sat. The burning flames looked so exotic in the night sky, and then she remembered the curfew rule. It was well after ten p.m.

"How are they allowed outside right now?" she asked.

"Oh, you're referring to the curfew?"

"Yes."

"It's a tad difficult to see it from here, but the patio is completely enclosed with glass and netting. We conceded to the fact early on that our residents needed one outdoor space that's open twenty-four hours, and that's how the patio came to be. It's the most recent renovation to the castle."

"But what about The Reader?" Lyla asked, not really sure why.

Julia gave her a curious look.

"The Reader is aware of the arrangement, and his nightly excursions do not interfere with this area. You don't have to worry about having a glass of wine and a smoke in the hot tub at midnight and getting startled by The Reader walking by you."

Lyla hadn't been worried about that, specifically, until she'd just said it. Now, she had a new fear. Just thinking of stepping out there in her bathing suit and not being able to see what was looking back at her from the darkness turned her stomach to knots.

"Would you like to go out and say hello?"

"Sure."

"You'll meet the rest of the residents tomorrow, but I'll introduce you to these two, and you can get a better view of the patio," she said and walked toward the glass doors.

Lyla followed and watched the two young ladies regard Julia with friendly smiles. That reassured her. Julia was a tough woman to get a read on, and the fact that two of her new colleagues lit up when they saw her was promising. Julia slid the door open and stepped out, letting Lyla enter the patio before sliding the door closed.

"Hey, Julia," the dark-skinned girl said in a northeastern accent.

New York, maybe?

One of her college flings was a boy from the Bronx, and this young lady's cadence matched his exactly. The girl sitting at the table beside her, smoking what looked and smelled like a joint, looked to be of Asian descent.

"Hello, Deja," Julia began. "Ladies, we have our newest resident at Claymont. Her name is Lyla Robbins. Lyla, please meet Deja and Linh and ignore their late-night debauchery."

They broke out in a stoned giggle fit.

"Hey, we've been working our asses off all week. We're celebrating," Deja said.

Linh turned around and smiled at Lyla.

"Hi, Lyla. I'm Linh, the best writer here."

Deja scoffed.

"Lyla, everyone in this place thinks they're the best writer here. Don't listen to her," Deja said, as they both laughed.

Julia nodded and looked at Lyla.

"That's a thousand percent true. I've never seen so much condensed ego in one location."

Lyla smiled at the two young ladies who looked like they just got out of the hot tub.

"It's nice to meet you," she said.

"Wanna join us?" Linh asked, teasing her joint.

Lyla glanced at Julia, not that she was asking for permission, but more for her to jump in and remind Linh of the rules that were hopefully in effect now. Julia looked like she sensed her trepidation.

"Sorry, ladies. You know the drill. I still have a little bit of the tour left and have to show Lyla to her room.

Deja sat up straighter like she had something to say.

"Ahh, come on. Look at her. She just traveled halfway across the world. She's exhausted. She *needs* this, Julia. It'll inspire her."

Julia raised one eyebrow like this conversation had gotten a bit too familiar for her liking.

"Deja, you made the same trip from the United States of America that she did a few months ago. Do you recall getting high on your first night at Claymont?"

"No, ma'am."

"Linh, how about you? You flew out from California almost a year ago now. Did your peers lure you onto the patio the second you walked in the door and offer you a joint?"

"No, ma'am."

"No, no, those incidents did not in fact occur because I was the one who walked both of you through those doors and did this very same routine, only then there weren't two residents getting baked on the patio and casting a wonderous first impression on not just themselves, but Claymont as an institution."

No one said anything. The only sound Lyla heard was the bubbling hot tub water and a breeze blowing across the blackness beyond the patio's mesh enclosure. She was afraid to even swallow for fear of people hearing her gulp, despite her throat being desert dry. The two girls looked at each other in that stoned way like they knew they were in trouble but needed reassurance that it was really happening, then they looked back at Julia.

Lyla side-eyed Julia and saw her unsuccessfully trying to conceal her ruse.

"Oh, you are *mean*, man!" Linh said and then started laughing.

Julia smiled and shrugged her shoulders.

"You had me going there for a second," Deja said. "Shit. My heart feels like it's going to explode. I'm too high for this shit."

Once Lyla realized what was really going on—how the residents had this laid back rapport with Julia after being there for a while—she exhaled a sigh of relief and smiled. Deja pointed at her.

"Look! You're going to scare the new girl away with your evil tricks faster than we ever would with a little bit of weed."

Lyla laughed and shook her head.

"No, I'm not going anywhere. I don't scare that easily," she said, realizing it came off more of a brag than an admission that she wouldn't let anything ruin this opportunity for her.

Both girls on the chairs had impressed looks on their faces as they nodded in seeming approval.

"We like this one," Deja said.

"Yep," Linh echoed.

"As do we," Julia said, leaving Lyla unsure of who the 'we' were in that statement, but accepting the compliment, nonetheless.

"Thank you?"

"Before we head off, where are the other six residents, if you know off-hand?" Julia asked.

"Rae and Rachel were in the game room earlier. They didn't want to come out with us. Uh, Kay and Sue just came down for food and went back upstairs. I'm guessing everyone else is in their rooms," Deja said.

"Or, possibly getting some late-night words cranked out in the library," Julia said and turned to Lyla. "Which is the last stop on our tour of the common areas. I'll take you to your room after that."

"Sounds good."

"You girls get some rest."

"That's what we're doing," Linh said, and they both laughed.

"Don't worry, Miss Julia. We won't stay up past our bedtime," Deja said and smiled like an innocent tween trying to get her way.

"Keep up the good work, ladies," Julia said and pivoted to go back inside.

"It was nice to meet you," Lyla said.

"You too," Linh said.

"We'll see you at breakfast, where you'll get to meet the others, hopefully," Deja said.

"Sounds good."

Lyla smiled as she followed Julia back in, making sure to close the glass door behind her.

"We have all kinds of creative types here," Julia said, almost apologetically. "But like they said, they're hitting their goals, so whatever keeps them on track flies."

"Partying was never really my thing," Lyla said, feeling like she was going to be the boring horror girl in a castle full of writers.

"You'll fit in just fine."

They crossed the dining hall and passed the podium to their left. A door adorned with wooden cherub carvings was in the far-right corner on the same wall as the kitchen buffet line, but there was about twenty feet and three expensive-looking paintings separating the two areas.

"Look at that detail," she said, admiring the craftsmanship of the carvings.

"It is quite impressive. I can't tell you how many times I walk through this door, and I take it for granted unless I'm seeing it through someone's eyes for the first time. It reminds me of home."

The longer the two women analyzed the wooden, winged babies, the more unnerved Lyla became. There was something not quite right about the children's faces. Yes, she knew it was art and abstract, almost dreamlike in its depiction, but the cherubs' undefined eyeballs and wide grins looked more demonic than angelic.

Or it's just your morbid view of the world wanting to see the darkness hidden beneath all things.

"Okay," Julia began, breaking the trance as she opened the door. "Let's go. It's getting late, but I have a feeling you're going to want to see this."

Lyla beamed with excitement as she followed her under the arch of grinning faces.

EIGHT

The hallway leading to the library was lined with paintings of famous authors on both walls. Lyla didn't notice that Julia had moved ahead of her because she got caught up in staring at the oil on canvas renderings of some of her favorite authors, some she admired because of their historical significance, others she pretended to read and respect because her professors didn't think one could contribute to the cannon of literature unless you had sampled the classics, and a few authors she didn't recognize. They weren't named or even signed by the artist. And just like the cherubs on the door, the eyes of each subject made her uneasy. They reminded her of the way the Mona Lisa's gaze followed you around the room from the forced perspective. Out of all ten paintings, Edgar Allan Poe was her favorite.

"You like the portraits, I see," Julia said from the end of the hall near another set of arched doors.

"Oh my God, yes. They're beautiful. I feel like I keep saying that, but that's the only word that comes to mind."

"I hope you brought your thesaurus, then," Julia said with a sly grin.

"Who did these? I mean, I'm assuming they're all by the same artist. They have the same style."

"A local painter I discovered. The Sterlings insisted on having this room filled with writers' portraits. It was interesting to watch each one come in as we prepared to open."

"She did each one of these that fast? Geez, I don't know much about painting, but that seems pretty quick to produce something so—"

"Don't say beautiful."

"Detailed," Lyla said with a smile as she continued to walk. "It's curious that she didn't sign her name. Or if she did, I didn't see it."

"I do know the reason for that," Julia began. "She's a humble woman who insisted that the paintings, the pigment, belonged to the land, and she would never claim ownership over such a thing."

"That's a lovely way of looking at the world."

"Are you going to do that with your story? Have it go uncredited?" Julia chuckled.

"Heck no. I'm not even humble enough to use a pen name."

Julia nodded and said, "As you should be. Now, check this out."

She pulled the door open and gestured for Lyla to walk in first. She was awestruck, wanting to look at everything everywhere all at once because it was so overwhelming. The library was a perfect circle and, she now realized, was inside one of the castle's towers. In the center of the circular room, sat rows of empty tables, save for a green desk lamp on each one. A desk, computer, and a commercial grade printer were against the wall directly in front of her. She imagined that was where the residents printed physical copies of their works to submit to The Reader.

"Take a breath, darling," Julia said.

Lyla did as she was told as she gradually looked at the spiral staircase that wrapped along the walls and stretched all the way to the top of the tower. She counted four floors. Each floor had an exit from the main staircase that fed into railed walkways. And, in a childhood fantasy come true, all four bookshelves had rolling ladders connected to them. She'd once been envious of Belle in her favorite Disney film, *Beauty and the Beast*, for having such a luxurious library in the Beast's castle, but not anymore. Yes, this was Claymont's library, but for the foreseeable future, she'd pretend like it was all hers.

"This is amazing."

"I agree."

She walked over to the computer desk and turned around. "Residents are free to use this computer and printer to make hard copies to give to The Reader. That is its only function."

"Okay. So, I'm going to be visiting this room at least once a week then."

"Yes, but judging by your reaction, I'm guessing it will be much more than that," she said as she walked past her, back to the door from which they had just come. "I'm sorry to cut your visit short, but it's time for me to show you to your room. I can only imagine how my chauffeurs are keeping themselves occupied right now."

Chauffeurs?

She then remembered Leo and his horse but also Maurice in his SUV in town.

Was he really still parked there since dropping them off to be driven by the carriage? And he'd have to wait for her to ride back down the mountain. Sheesh.

"You have some patient drivers," she said, exiting the library and entering the hall of portraits.

"They get paid well to sit on their asses all night."

Lyla laughed and walked back through the cherub door and into the dining hall. They turned left at the podium and down the center line to the exit, passing the patio doors in the process. She saw the two girls still sitting out there, talking and laughing like they didn't have a care in the world, and she couldn't wait to settle into their way of life. Deja noticed her and waved. Lyla waved back, but Julia just trudged forward without glancing in that direction.

When they entered the commons area, she saw a girl in the snack area. She had an energy drink in one hand and a candy bar in the other.

"Good evening, Lori," Julia said, startling her so badly that she dropped her candy bar.

"Jesus," Lori said. "You scared the hell out of me."

"Sorry about that. It looks like you have no plans on going to bed anytime soon."

"I've gotta get my words in. I got in a slump the last couple of days and need to get on it. Hey, is this the new girl?"

Sensing that Julia was about to scold Lori, Lyla said, "Yes, my name is Lyla Robbins."

"Hi, Lyla. I'm Lori. I see you're getting the grand tour."

"Well, not the *grand* tour," Julia corrected. "We'll have to cover the grounds tomorrow, but she's seen everything on the first floor, and we're headed to her room now."

"Oh, cool. Nice to meet you, Lyla. Welcome to Claymont. Don't follow my example of procrastination. It works for me but not others."

"Noted. I guess I'll see you at breakfast."

Julia continued walking toward the staircase with Lyla attempting to keep up while responding to her most recently introduced resident. There was something about Lori's confidence that relaxed her. Even though she was stocking up on caffeine and sugar to meet a deadline, she didn't look panicked. She didn't look like her world would end if she failed to meet her deadline.

"I'll be there. Probably without having had any sleep, but I'll be there," Lori said from behind.

The stone staircase looked like it was a thousand years old. Artificial torches were embedded in the walls every few feet that provided just enough light to make it to the next one.

"Be careful," Julia warned. "I've heard stories of sprained ankles and busted tailbones from trying to hurry up these stairs in the dark."

"It probably doesn't help if you're wasted."

Julia laughed, a genuine laugh that seemed to escape despite her best efforts. That made Lyla smile with pride. She'd gotten through to the boss.

Is that what Julia is? A boss? An authority figure? A mentor?

Relax, you'll find out more tomorrow.

They passed the landing for the second floor.

"We have five residents living on this floor, each with their own room and bathroom, of course," she said. "Now, if we keep moving, we'll arrive at your floor."

Lyla regarded the amber glow of each candle as she approached them one by one and couldn't help but be reminded of the opening credits for one of her favorite classic TV shows, *Tales from the Crypt*. It held a special place in her heart because her dad loved it too and even let her watch it with him despite all the language, violence, and nudity. Mom was never thrilled about that, but she also didn't interfere, and Lyla always respected her for that, especially as she got older, more mature.

"And here we are," Julia said. "The third floor."

Soft-glowing chandeliers hung from the ceiling—five of them, illuminating the entire hallway. Just in hearing the hum, Lyla could tell they were the adjustable kind; they could brighten this corridor if they wanted, but the setting they were currently on was perfect, especially for that time of night.

"The chandeliers are on a timer," Julia said, as if she was reading her mind. "The switches are along the wall there if you ever need to adjust them. They can also be set to motion activated. That's how the residents usually have them; that's why the second-floor hall was so dark. But we were anticipating your arrival, of course."

Lyla tried to take in everything as quickly as she could, which had become the theme of the night for her. There were more paintings hanging on the walls, some medieval-looking banners, country flags, family crests she assumed were authentic and kept for historical purposes. All the doors to the rooms were on the left. As they walked down the carpeted hall, she understood why. Directly across from every door was a deep, oval-shaped window.

The first one stopped Lyla dead in her tracks, and she strolled off the path and looked through it. She could see the lights from the city below the mountain and realized it was Umbertide. The sight took her breath away, a sensation she hoped she would never lose no matter how long she stayed at Claymont.

"Quite the view, yes?" Julia said in a quieter tone than she'd been speaking all night, and Lyla guessed that was because there could be sleeping residents in their quarters.

"It's so pretty."

"You can say beautiful again if you want."

Lyla smiled and said, "It really is beautiful."

"The glass wasn't always there, of course. That was part of the modernization. Once the families who lived here no longer had a need for archers to ward off enemy attackers through these windows, the glass went up."

"*Archers?*"

"Yes, you really should research the practicality of why castles were built, this one in particular. It really does have such a storied history, but like I said, it's not mine to tell."

"Then whose is it?"

"The dead," she said so matter-of-factly.

Lyla turned her face, processing what she'd just heard.

"When you do your own research, you learn the truth straight from the source. That's how we keep the ghosts alive—through history, through memory."

"That's so true," Lyla said, never having thought of ghosts in that perspective before.

"Now," Julia said, reverting back to cheerful tour guide mode, "your room is the third door down. Follow me."

Lyla looked out of every window as she passed until they reached her room. Julia withdrew a small key ring and unlocked it.

"Ready?" she asked.

Lyla grinned and entered behind Julia just as she flicked on the light.

"Oh, wow. This is amazing!"

"I knew you would like it. You'd be hard-pressed to find anyone who doesn't approve of our living areas."

A chandelier hung from the center of the ceiling in the square-shaped room. The queen-sized canopy bed stuck out from the left wall. Its massive wooden headboard and carved bannisters made it the room's focal point. Lyla counted at least six lilac pillows atop the fluffy white comforter. Nightstands adorned both sides, each with a lilac lamp. Opposite that wall stood the matching wooden dresser with a large rectangular mirror mounted on the top. Her suitcases and bags were neatly placed in front of it. Two doors were on either side. Julia opened the one immediately to their right.

"This is your closet," she said and turned on the light.

Lyla was wowed again at the height and depth of the walk-in

closet. A custom robe, towels, washcloths, and an extra set of bed linens were stacked on individual shelves to her left. An empty metal bar stretched across the back with all its hangers pushed to the right side. There was a shoe rack and hooks to hang more items than she could ever dream of possessing.

"I don't think my clothes would even fill the dresser out there, let alone this closet."

Julia laughed.

"I know. For our residents' purposes, these closets are a little extravagant unless you travel to town or another province and stock up on local clothes. They were part of the castle. We didn't add them on. You can store your luggage in here once you unpack, at least."

"Yeah."

"Okay, let's check out your bathroom."

They walked past the mirror, and Lyla immediately looked away, not wanting to be reminded of how weary she appeared. Julia opened the bathroom door, turned on the light, and took a step back. She had a smile on her face like she knew Lyla was about to be impressed again.

And for good reason. It was the most extravagant bathroom Lyla had ever seen, better than any hotel suite or beach house. The glass shower with its rain shower head looked heavenly, and the clamshell bathtub adjacent to it was just as inviting. The long marble sink top ran the length of the left side of the room and had glamour lights bordering the mirror above it.

"The drawers are full of toiletries, all local and organic, just in case you forgot anything."

Lyla pulled one open and saw the bottles of various hair products, soaps, lotions, and skin regiments.

"I brought all my stuff, but I don't think I'm going to even get it out of the suitcase," she laughed. "I can't wait to try some of these out."

"So glad you like it," she said and walked out. "The last thing…"

Lyla stepped into the bedroom and glanced at the desk pressed against the wall. A black swivel chair was pushed under it. Notebooks, a cup of pens and pencils, a typewriter, and a stack of white paper sat on top of it.

"Obviously, you can use this desk if you prefer to write in your room, and all of this is just here in case you change your writing method. I don't think any of the current residents use anything but laptops and computers but having these options available was actually The Reader's only suggestion as far as the aesthetic of the building."

Lyla dragged her fingers across the typewriter's keys and then touched the thick paper stock beside it. She felt compelled to sit down and start writing on the spot.

"I can see why," she said. "One useful suggestion I got from a creative writing class was to switch up your methods to keep your writing process fresh."

She looked out her window and saw the moonlit courtyard surrounded by the castle walls. The peninsula jutting out from the center of The Keep was the hallway that led to the dining hall and then the library past that. She could see the patio roof, but the building top obscured her view of the actual lounge area.

"Quite the view, isn't it?"

Lyla turned back around.

"Yes. Everything is just...amazing. This is perfect. I feel like I'm going to wake up any minute now and be back in my parents' basement in West Virginia."

Something kicked on beside the desk, like a little whirring engine.

"Oh," Julia began, "the minifridge. It's right here beside the desk. I don't know if they stocked it or not, but it's there if you need it."

Lyla passed her and saw the black refrigerator that looked to be about three feet tall. She opened it and was surprised to find it full of a variety of beverages, such as water, soda, juices, energy drinks, and a few bottles of beer. It wasn't until she saw the water that she realized how parched her throat was.

"Don't mind if I do," she said, grabbing a bottle and chugging a third of it. "It's been a long day or night. I don't even know anymore."

"I know exactly what you mean. Don't worry. Your body will regulate quicker than you think," Julia said and walked back to the front of the bed before turning around. "Do you have any questions for me right now? We'll talk about the program tomorrow, of course, but is there anything that you can think of that I haven't covered?"

After a moment of trying to get her overstimulated and fatigued brain to function, she finally said, "No. If I think of any, I'll just ask you tomorrow."

"Well, all right then. If there's nothing else, I am going to head out."

"Okay. I appreciate everything you've done for me, Julia, sincerely. I think I'm just going to get unpacked and test out that tub. I'm beat. Thank you for being such a great host."

Julia waved her off.

"It's my job. And my pleasure. I'm just glad you like it so far. There's so much more to see in the daylight. In the meantime, I'll leave you to it," she said and almost made it to the door before stopping. "I almost forgot. Here's your room key. I'll just set it right here," she said and placed it on the dresser.

"Oh, thanks."

Julia just smiled and grabbed the doorknob. Right before she shut it, she looked back one last time.

"Have a good night, Lyla Robbins. Welcome to Claymont."

NINE

Lyla stepped out of the tub feeling like she'd washed thousands of miles of accumulated sweat and grime off her body. The products she'd used from Claymont's selection made any shampoo or conditioners from back in the States pale in comparison. She dried off and wrapped her wet hair in a towel, staring at herself in the steamy mirror and then wiping a streak of moisture away to get a clearer view.

Even though she knew better, she couldn't help but only see what she considered to be imperfections. A lifetime of social media had taught her to compare herself to others, creating an unattainable ideal. That negative voice in her mind wouldn't shut up, despite what her conscious mind knew to be true. She stepped out of the cleared portion of the mirror and rendered herself invisible once again.

Julia had only opened one of the bathroom drawers earlier, so Lyla decided to check out what else was in there. She opened one of the lotion bottles and smelled the floral scent, which was intoxicating. After rubbing it on her body, she grabbed the robe she'd brought from the closet (along with all the towels and washrags) and draped it over her shoulders, tying the front and immediately feeling like she was wearing something well out of her price range. She rummaged through a couple of the other drawers and found an essential oil disperser and a variety of scents.

"Why not?" she said to herself and brought it to the nightstand nearest the minifridge.

The lavender vial she'd chosen released its fragrance as soon as she removed the lid. Just that first little smell calmed her mind, matching her relaxed body. She plugged in the machine, added some water to it, and put a few drops of the oil in until whisps of vapors spurted out intermittently. After blow-drying and combing her hair, she put on her pajamas—shorts and an oversized *Scream* T-shirt—and removed the pile of decorative pillows on the bed, leaving just two fluffy ones to sleep on and a firm body pillow to hold.

As she climbed under the sheets and slid her legs down, the sheets tightened around her feet like a taut linen pocket. She positioned her pillows, gave the room one final look over, and turned off the lamp on the left side nightstand.

A giddy, tingly sensation overcame her as the reality of having made it there and potentially marking a turning point in her life. Starting tomorrow, she would wake up as a professional writer. She repeated the mantra in her head, trying to manifest it into existence. Thoughts of doubt, of everything that could go wrong, tried to creep in, but she found her way back to the mantra.

I am a writer. I am a writer. I am a writer.

Within five minutes of being cocooned by the comforter and memory foam mattress, she fell into a deep and dreamless sleep.

———

TAP. TAP. TAP.

Lyla's eyes shot open. She had no idea where she was or what woke her up. The dark room was not her parents' basement. As her mind settled back into reality, she took a calming breath.

Claymont. You're in Italy.

She sat up and rubbed her eyes, looking at the room with a renewed sense of recognition. A sliver of moonlight shone through the crack in the mostly closed curtains. She stared at the dresser in front of her, studying its shape in the darkness. Her eyes drifted to the right where she saw the closed closet door, and then the bedroom door, which remained shut as well. She peered along the wall beside her until she was looking at the nightstand with one of the two matching lamps. A small digital clock that she hadn't noticed before was angled toward the bed and displayed 03:17 a.m.

Lyla turned back to the front of the room and paused on the open closet door. She tilted her head, telling herself that maybe it hadn't been shut when she looked at it just moments ago. Her gut knew better. The door had been shut or else she wouldn't be looking at the shelves right inside the doorframe. The light provided just a peek into the darkness, but it was enough for her to see someone standing there.

The shadowy figure took a step back and disappeared completely. Lyla backed up as far away from the closet as possible, pressing herself against the headboard as she shuffled to the other side of the bed and turned on the lamp. She looked back at the open door and could see deeper in but not all the way. There was no one visible from her vantage point. In her instinct to distance herself from the door, she'd neglected to turn on the other lamp—the one on the nightstand directly facing the closet.

Lyla didn't want to move to the other side of the bed. She wanted to scream for help, to pound on the walls and hope one of her roommates would rush in to help her.

Wait.

Her panic subsided. She remembered back in college how she got pranked by other girls in her dorm during her freshman year, but then she got to return the favor as an upperclassman.

Is that what's happening here?

She thought about Deja and Linh getting high on the patio earlier. Clearly, Claymont was not all work and no play. If they were testing "the new girl" by playing creeper in the closet, she'd be damned if she was going to let them get the best of her. Apparently, they didn't know what her chosen genre was. Even if they did manage to scare the shit out of her now, she'd come up with something much more sinister to get them back.

Lyla cracked a smile and slid as quietly as she could to the other side of the bed. She tilted her head and still saw the shadowy end in the closet. Turning on the lamp would illuminate what was left of the darkness. She reached for the lamp, touched the little piece of plastic, but couldn't bring herself to push it.

What if it's not them?

Who else would it be?

She thought about Julia, the twins who brought her luggage to her room, the carriage driver, the chauffeur, but most of all, she thought about The Reader. A cold chill rattled her, and without wasting more time thinking about it, she pressed the button.

The light didn't turn on, and the lamp on the other side of the bed went dark.

Oh, shit.

Lyla kept her hand on the lamp. She heard movement in front of her and immediately pressed it the other way, hoping she'd just turned the lamp on her left off through faulty wiring. The light came back on, and she breathed a sigh of relief. She turned back to the closet. The door was shut.

"Okay, fuck this."

She needed to get out of there. If her new roommates were playing a practical joke, they won. She swung one foot off the bed and was about to step down when she heard weight shifting behind the closet door. She stopped and stared, wide-eyed. The bedroom door was just a few quick paces if she wanted to make a run for it.

Or you could just scream for help. Who gives a shit if they think you're nuts? Feed them some bullshit story about having night terrors or something.

Before she could decide which course to take, she heard the original sounds that woke her up.

TAP. TAP. TAP.

Lyla stared at the closet.

TAP. TAP. TAP.

She looked at the crack under the door and saw two pale feet. The hairs on her neck stood on end.

Lyla swallowed and said, "Who's there?"

Nothing. Just the hum of the refrigerator and her panicked breathing.

"I said—"

TAP. TAP. TAP.

She leapt from the bed.

Just make it to the hallway…

As soon as her bare feet touched the floor, the lamp behind her switched off, and she stopped in complete darkness. The sliver of moonlight that had previously been bright enough to give her a good enough view of the room was useless now that her vision had grown accustomed to the light that just went out.

Hallway. Hallway. Hallway. Move.

Lyla took one step forward and heard the creak of the closet door slowly opening. She sped blindly in the direction of her exit. Her hand reached out and grabbed the cool door handle.

"Lyyyyy-luhhh," a raspy voice whispered from the closet to her left.

She jerked the door open and ran into the hallway faster than she'd done anything in her life. The warm glow of the chandeliers greeted her as she hurried to the window before turning around. She was trembling as she peered in the open bedroom doorway. Her pulse throbbed, and she took a deep breath to quell her hyperventilating.

Lyla looked to her left and right and saw that she was alone. If she'd woken any of her neighboring residents, they weren't coming out to check on her. She could run to the closest door and tell them what just happened.

You'd look like a psycho.

So what? Someone is hiding in your fucking closet!

And your plan is to get Deja or Linh to go investigate? You don't know what's in there.

She looked at the door to her left and decided to risk looking like the overreacting newbie by waking up whomever was in there. Before she could even take a step, she heard a window opening. Her eyes darted back to her room to see the breeze blow the curtains back.

They just went out the fucking window.

But you're on the third floor…

Lyla forced herself to cross the hall and stopped at the threshold to her room. She took a quick breath and reached inside, feeling the wall until she found the switch. With one quick flick, the chandelier filled the room with light. Her window slammed shut. She gasped and stumbled back as two legs climbed the outside glass.

A door opened to her right, and she let out a startled scream. Linh leaned out from her room. She hurried over to her confused neighbor.

"Lyla?" she asked, still sounding half-asleep or half-stoned or both.

"Yeah, holy shit. Someone was just in my room."

She looked back, making sure she was still alone in the hallway.

"What do you mean someone was in your room?"

"Can I come in, please," Lyla said, not waiting for Linh's permission to enter as she brushed past her and turned the light on.

"Come on, man," Linh said, shielding her eyes as she shut the door.

"Will you lock that?"

"My door?"

"Yes, I'm fucking telling you someone was just in my room, and I'm pretty sure they climbed out through the window."

Linh laughed.

"Huh?"

"Someone was hiding in my closet, tapping on the door. I ran out, and they climbed out the window."

"You saw them?"

"I saw…feet. Or legs, I guess. I don't know. It happened so fast. But there was definitely someone outside. What was it that woke you up?"

"You, opening your door and freaking out, I think."

Linh walked further into her room and sat on the bed.

"So, do you want me to call the twins up here? It'll give them something to do other than watch shitty movies all night."

"Yes!" Lyla said, feeling her panic subsiding. "Wait, how can you call them?"

Linh pointed to the phone mounted to the nightstand on the left side of the bed.

"You have a phone?"

"Yeah. You don't?"

"No. I thought the only phone was downstairs."

Linh chuckled and said, "Oh, these don't dial out. You just pick them up and it automatically rings the main office/security room/whatever the hell you want to call it. That's where the twins are supposed to be, at least. Monitoring the cameras. They just watch movies though. Lori caught them one night asleep with some *Transformers* movie playing.

"Okay, yeah. Call them, please."

As Linh walked toward the nightstand, Lyla had a moment of dread and said, "Wait!"

Linh jumped as she turned around.

"God, what is your deal? You scared the shit out of me."

"Don't call them."

"Why?"

A flurry of scenarios played through Lyla's mind, each one causing more anxiety than the last: the twins coming to her room and finding nothing, Linh telling Deja and Deja telling someone else and so on and so forth until the entire residency was talking about the new girl who had a panic attack her first night in the old castle, and being branded as the weirdo for not only writing horror but being a real-life headcase as well. Her fear of what people thought of her overrode her "better safe than sorry" philosophy that her dad instilled in her from an early age.

"I don't want to cause a big scene," she admitted.

"But do you really think someone was in your room, though?"

When Lyla was in her early teens, she went through a phase of what the doctors referred to as sleep paralysis: she would lie in bed, not sure if she was awake or not, and see things. Most of the time, the hallucinations were shadows of people or floating abstractions, and they would disappear once she fully regained consciousness. On top of that, she also dealt with sleepwalking and night terrors for a few years. To say she worried her parents sick would be an understatement. She remembered waking up to her mom and dad asking her what she was doing standing by their bed in the middle of the night.

You're jetlagged. You're exhausted. It's possible that what just happened, only occurred in your mind, right?

It's possible.

But if she did relapse into night terrors, this was the most bizarre one yet because there was no distinct period where she remembered waking up except for when she'd heard the first round of tapping. She let out a deep sigh.

"I used to have night terrors in my teens. I haven't had one in forever. I'm sitting here asking myself, what's more likely: did an intruder somehow sneak into my room while I slept and woke me up just to toy with me and then climb out the window of a third story building, or did I have a jet-lag-induced night terror?"

Linh looked at her with sympathetic eyes. She didn't look put off or bothered by being woken up in the middle of the night anymore.

"I get it, man. Do you want me to go check out your room with you? I don't mind. I'll fuck a bitch up."

Lyla laughed out loud. She couldn't help it. Not only did Linh reassure her that she had at least one friend in this new place, but she would go to war with her. It felt like a genuine sisterhood. She wasn't alone. It felt familiar. It felt like being back with her friends at WVU.

"I feel dumb, but yeah, that would mean a lot if you did."

"Are you calm now?"

"Calmer."

"Okay, good. Because you just had me lock my door a minute ago."

"I know. I'm good…I think."

"Fair enough. Let's go."

The two of them walked into the hall and looked at Lyla's closed bedroom door.

"Was that shut when you came in my room?" Linh asked.

Lyla forced herself to focus on her breathing.

"No."

"Want me to call the twins now?"

Lyla didn't know where the urge came from, but she stormed forward, opening the door and stepping into the brightly lit room. She immediately looked to her right at the empty closet. She turned on the light in there and walked inside, just to make sure. Her palms were sweaty, but her fists were clinched.

"There's nothing in here," she said, turning around to face Linh still standing by the door.

"Damn, what's gotten into you," Linh asked as Lyla breezed past her and entered the bathroom.

"Tomorrow is supposed to be the first day of the rest of my life, and I'm not going to let my anxiety fuck it up."

Satisfied that the bathroom was empty, she approached the bed and looked under like a parent on the hunt for monsters, but there were none to be found.

"Technically, tomorrow is going to be the first day of the rest of your life no matter what, so you really can't fuck that up. It's like, physics."

"Help me get this window."

The two girls pushed the weighty window up and a slight, warm breeze blew in. They looked across the courtyard and the surrounding forest that adorned the mountain. The moon held a yellow hue like a cheap flashlight trying to illuminate too wide an area.

"Didn't you say you saw someone crawling on the window?"

"Yeah," Lyla said, unable to hide the embarrassment in her tone.

Linh leaned out and looked up.

"Jesus, be careful. This window could chop your head off."

"Well, hold it then. I'm the one looking for wall-crawling perverts out here," she said, taking her time to look all around. "I don't see anything. This fucking guy would have to be Spider-Man to scale this wall. There's literally nothing to hold onto."

Lyla wasn't sure if that made her feel better or worse. The rational side of her brain was relieved, but the writer side—the one she used to conjure up the horrors in her imagination—was inventing all kinds of terrifying scenarios.

"How far up is the next window?" she asked.

"The fourth floor? There isn't a window there. I don't think there's a bedroom above you. I think it's an office."

"What about the fifth?" she reluctantly asked.

Linh leaned out even further.

"Be careful!"

"I got this. Chill out. Just hold my legs and don't let that window come loose."

After a few seconds, Linh said, "Yeah, there's a window on the fifth floor. Straight above."

Lyla somehow knew it, but that didn't numb the sting of the shock.

She nearly let go of her friend's legs before snapping out of her worried state.

"Help me back in."

Lyla kept one hand on the window and grabbed Linh's outstretched hand with her other. She didn't breathe a sigh of relief until she was safely back inside the room.

"I gotta be honest," she began, "I don't see how anyone could climb up that wall."

Linh shut the window. Lyla turned her back to her and rubbed her temples. She looked at the clock and saw that it was almost four in the morning. She wanted to get up for breakfast in a few hours and had an important meeting with Julia in the afternoon.

"Are you good?" she asked from behind.

"Yeah. I mean, it's not how I wanted my stay here to start, but I don't think anyone crawled in my window just to scare me from the closet and then climbed back out."

Once Lyla actually said her concerns out loud, she believed it for the first time. The thought was ridiculous. But then again, she wasn't alone, and all the lights were on. It was much easier to be brave. Still, she decided that what she'd experienced was a combination of her previous condition and her jet-lagged state of mind. Yes, it felt real, and if she were to take a lie detector test in the minutes that followed the encounter, she was convinced she would pass it. Now that she was fully awake and saw the situation from a broader perspective, a wave of relief washed over her.

"Alright then," Linh said. "I'm going back to bed. Let me know if you need anything. But please don't need anything because I'm fucking tired and have to get up early."

Lyla let out a soft laugh, fully relating to what she was saying.

"Thank you. Sorry for waking you up and if I freaked you out."

"It's all good. Talk to you tomorrow."

"Okay. Goodnight."

"You want me to shut this door?"

"Please," Lyla said.

She listened to her neighbor open and shut her door and angled her ear so that it was pointed at their shared wall, just to see how clearly she could hear Linh, if at all. Aside from a mild thump from what she assumed was the girl falling back into her bed, there was dead silence.

Lyla stood up and quietly paced her room, still trying to keep the doubting thoughts at bay. The minifridge caught her eye. It was too late for one of those beers because she definitely did not want to walk into her first breakfast looking *and* smelling hungover, so she grabbed a water, made sure the window was shut and locked, closed the closet, and double-checked that Linh had shut her bedroom door all the way. Satisfied, she turned on the lamp beside her bed before walking back to the chandelier light switch by the door and turning it off.

The room darkened, and shadows grew with just the lamplight glowing. She took a drink, put the water on the nightstand, and crawled back in bed, propping herself up on a stack of pillows and lying on her back. Her eyes naturally drifted to the closet and then down to the crack under the door where there was nothing but darkness, no shuffling feet, no lingering presence, no big bad wolf knocking for a little pig to let it in.

Lyla took a deep breath, reached to her right, and turned off the lamp. Nothing jumped out from the darkness. There was no more tapping. Everything had returned to normal, except for the fact that she was still awake. She closed her eyes and took long breaths, forcing herself to forget everything that just happened so she could get a couple more hours of rest. And just when her wandering mind was about to shut off, a chilling thought caused her eyes to open.

A rope.

Linh had said someone would need to be Spider-Man to crawl up the castle walls. She was wrong. A rope dangling from the fifth-floor window would do just fine.

TEN

Lyla woke up right at 7:25. She'd set her alarm for 7:30, but it was one of those days where she willed herself awake. She got up, brushed her teeth, got dressed, and brushed her hair, rationalizing everything that had happened only hours ago. The one hole in her night terror/jet-lag theory was the open window. Even if the flickering lights and the closet door opening and closing at will were part of a night terror, someone had to have opened the window when she ran out of the room.

Or did you do it?

She reflected on the moments when she supposedly stood in shock.

Did the window even open at all? It slammed shut, but Linh didn't hear it. Neither did anyone else. Both of you strained to lift it. How could someone open it from the outside while hanging from a rope?

The thought seemed ludicrous in the bright light of day, and she rationalized the strange occurrence away with logic. She thought of her mom and dad, her safety net. She imagined her dad laughing at such a tale, and it brought a smile to her face and rejuvenated her enthusiasm for the day.

Finish getting ready so you're not late.

Normally, she was a shower in the morning girl, but the bath she'd taken the night before still had her feeling fresh. Plus, she didn't want to deal with drying her hair. She put on her shoes and headed for the door but stopped.

Did Julia say to bring anything to their meeting? Had she even set a time for their meeting?

Lyla looked at her laptop and briefly considered bringing that but ultimately decided against it.

You're just going down there for breakfast. You're not going to work…yet.

She opened the door and stepped into the hallway. The sun shined through the small windows. She looked down the hallway at the rays beaming in like headlights against the wall of doors. With the chandeliers hanging down and muted in their glow, the sight was enchanting enough to be a postcard or at least the background display on her laptop.

"Okay, let's do this," she muttered and began her walk toward the staircase.

The closer she got to it, the more she thought about going upstairs, creeping past the fourth floor and then stealthily peeping in on the fifth. She wondered if it looked like her hallway but immediately dismissed the notion when she pictured the design of the architecture from the outside. The fifth floor wouldn't have a hallway. It would just be the one big floor at the top of The Keep.

The penthouse suite.

Or a dungeon…

Stop. You know what's real and what isn't.

Time and daylight made her initial interpretation of the events from last night seem less believable. She'd settled on night terrors brought on by a disturbed sleep pattern and intensified by her exotic new surroundings. Clinging to that truth allowed her to continue on with her day without being in a perpetual state of dread.

Just as she approached the spiral, stone staircase, she heard footsteps on the stairs above her. She stopped and waited until a man who looked like an even broodier version of Javier Bardem stopped on her floor and glared at her. He wore jeans with a T-shirt and an open black blazer. The fabric looked light and breathable, like it was tailored to his body and could be worn in any weather. She didn't know why she got this interpretation, but the man just looked effortlessly cool. If she had to guess, she'd say he was in his early forties. He cocked his head and squinted like the light hurt his eyes.

"Who are you?" he asked in a gruff voice with a thick Italian accent.

"Lyla Robbins. I'm a new resident."

He peered over her shoulder like he was looking at her bedroom.

"You're Ann's replacement?"

"Was Ann in room three?"

"Yes."

"Then I guess so."

He nodded and gave her one last glance before turning around like he was going to go downstairs.

"Wait. Who are you?" she asked, not meaning to sound rude, just curious.

He stopped and shook his head as he faced her.

"Forgive me. I'm awake, but it appears my manners are not," he said, forcing a smile.

She could see that he was tired as he approached her and extended his hand.

"My name is Dante Farina. I am the Program Director."

Lyla shook his hand, feeling imposter syndrome creeping up on her.

"Nice to meet you. Sorry for bothering you. I haven't had my coffee yet either," she said and shrugged her shoulders.

"Were you on your way down for breakfast?"

"Yes, I am, actually."

"Come, come. I'll escort you there."

"Okay."

Dante walked with a long stride, taking two steps at a time for every one of hers.

"So, you arrived last night?" he asked without looking back.

Lyla had to speed-step to keep up with him as they approached the second-floor landing.

Two girls were talking near the end of the hall. They looked when he passed by, but he didn't acknowledge them. Lyla gave them an awkward wave, and they just returned blank stares, probably wondering who the hell she was.

"Yes. Kind of late, actually."

"And how was your travel from America?"

"It wasn't too bad. The horse and carriage ride to the castle was definitely the cherry on top of a long trip, though."

She heard him chuckle but only saw his back as they kept descending.

"That's good to hear. I'm sure Julia relished every minute of your reaction."

"Why do you say that?"

"She didn't tell you? She was the one who put this all together, our prime facilitator. I didn't come on until they had already finished with the renovations and had the residency guidelines in place."

"Yes, she did tell me that."

"I knew it."

"So, if she designed the program, what do you do as Program Director?"

Dante laughed and pointed a finger.

"Now that is a good question," he said. "Program Director is just a fancier title than manager, I suppose. I oversee basic operations and make sure everything runs like a well-oiled machine."

He stepped onto the first floor and entered the commons prior to the dining hall. To her surprise, he stopped and turned around and waited for her.

"But enough about me. You're the new resident at Claymont. How was your first night in the castle?"

Lyla pictured the legs crawling up her window.

"Relaxing," she lied.

His eyes lingered a little too long for her comfort, and then he just nodded and said, "Good," and resumed his trek.

They walked to the red carpet, passing the mostly deserted area. One young lady exited the door to the fitness center and looked like she'd had a good workout. She was patting her face with a white towel when she noticed them.

"Good morning, Brittany," Dante said with a little more enthusiasm than when he'd initially greeted Lyla upstairs.

Maybe the jog down the staircase woke him up a bit.

"Good morning," Brittany said.

Lyla gave the same awkward wave that she did to the residents on the second floor, and Brittany just nodded her head, probably having no idea who she was. So far, the only residents who seemed at ease since she'd arrived the night before were Deja, Linh, and even Lori at the snack bar, despite admittedly being behind schedule. Everyone else didn't know how to react to her.

Lyla kept up with Dante without making it look like she was a suburban mom out for a Sunday powerwalk.

"Can I ask you something?"

He regarded her and said, "Always. It's in my job description to answer questions."

"What happened to the girl who was staying in my room before me?"

Dante raised his eyebrows.

"Oof. How about we save that question until we've had our first cup of coffee. It's not exactly light walk and talk hallway fodder."

The response piqued her curiosity. Something scandalous had happened or else he wouldn't have said it that way. If she'd simply finished her novel and moved on, why the raised eyebrows? Why the tabling of the question? She wondered if Ann had been kicked out and then began thinking of the various rules she could have broken to warrant such a punishment. There were so many of them, after all.

But what if it's worse than that?

Worse like how?

Lyla heard the tapping on the closet door in her head. *TAP. TAP. TAP.* She suddenly began to feel like the narrator of "The Tell-Tale Heart." The mystery intrigued her as much as it intimidated her, and she couldn't get to the dining hall fast enough.

"Sure, no problem," she said.

Dante grinned as they reached the end of the hallway. He paused for just a moment in front of the arched doors.

"First breakfast at Claymont. I do hope you like it. I'll be forced to beat the kitchen staff with their own spatulas if you don't."

"Is that also in your job description?"

"More of a perk than a duty," he said with a grin and a wink and pushed the doors open.

Sounds, movement, smells—the dining hall was alive and bustling with sensory overload compared to the dead silence of the previous night. The workers in the kitchen—Lyla couldn't see exactly how many there were back there, but counted at least three—were cooking, stirring, setting food trays on the serving line, and communicating in Italian. The closer they got to the breakfast buffet, the more her mouth watered.

"Breakfast officially begins at eight and remains open until nine-thirty. Lunch is at twelve and runs until one-thirty. Dinner is from five to six-thirty. The staff normally cleans up and clears out by eight, but you can always get anything you want from the snack bar in the other hall. I'm sorry if Julia told you all this already."

"No, this is good. Thank you," Lyla said still scanning the room.

Two girls she hadn't met yet sat at the end of one of the tables with their drinks. They hadn't noticed her. She looked at the patio and saw a tall, thin resident smoking a cigarette while leaning on the railing that overlooked the courtyard and the trees that grew above the castle gates.

"Lyla," Dante said.

"Hmm?"

She whipped her head back at him.

"Coffee is this way," he said, pointing to the beverage station that began before the buffet line.

"Oh, okay."

She followed him over there and stared at the row of stainless-steel beverage dispensers beside shelves of mugs and cups. A container of single-serving sugars and creamers of every sort was on the opposite end. Honestly, she thought the beverage station didn't look any more impressive than a continental breakfast display at a Holiday Inn. He must've been able to see the lack of enthusiasm on her face.

"Do you not approve?" he asked.

"Oh, no. It's fine. This looks just like places back home."

He smiled and nodded.

"I believe Julia did that intentionally. We have all kinds of residents, you see. Some ladies come here and want to sample our cuisine and beverages, while others are more content with the comforts of back home—like this, for example. If you want a regular coffee with some store-bought single-serving enhancements, well, there you go. If you'd rather eat a burger and chicken nuggets, that's always on the buffet line at lunch."

She made a face, and he laughed.

"However," he said and put a hand on her shoulder like he was trying to sell her a car, "If you're craving the real deal, all you have to do is step over here and place your order."

Her eyes widened as he led her to the last window on the buffet line, greeting each kitchen staff member as they passed. Lyla looked over at the girls sitting together and saw they were watching them. She'd been spotted and was relieved there was no gawking and giggling, not that she really expected it at this stage in her life, but something about the scenario felt like high school. And the high school girls she dealt with sucked.

They stopped and stared at the menu hanging above the coffee and espresso machines she'd only seen in movies. She stared at the sealed jars of coffee beans, blenders, cream dispensers, and so many other things and had to force herself to look at the man approaching them.

"Lyla, this is Pete. He can make you the best beverage you'll ever taste."

She thought he sure didn't look like a Pete. He was short with olive-colored skin and thick hair, slicked back.

"Hi, Pete," she said.

He didn't say anything, only nodded and with no expression whatsoever. Dante shook his head in amusement and looked at Pete while talking to Lyla.

"Pete doesn't speak. He's a born and raised local."

Lyla failed to see what those two facts had to do with one another.

"He doesn't speak English?" she guessed.

"Hell, if I know. He won't even speak Italian to you if you tried it.

Pete's not even his real name. I just call him that because I know how much he likes it."

Lyla felt a growing hostility and leaned toward Dante.

"Can he talk?"

"Oh yeah. He can correct me any time he pleases, but he won't. He can talk. Just prefers not to, especially to you. Well, not you specifically, but the residents and anyone associated with Claymont for that matter."

Before Lyla could ask why, Dante said, "But he will make you the best damn mocha latte on God's green earth if that's what you order."

There was a sternness that eased its way out, a shift in tone from congenial to fuck-around-and-find-out in the span of a sentence.

"So, what are you having?" he asked like that tense moment never happened.

Pete's emotionless eyes shifted from Dante to her. She tried to read the stout man's eyes, but he had the poker face of a seasoned card player, neither friendly nor irritable; he was just *there*.

"Oh, I..." she said and quickly glanced at the menu. "I'll just take an iced coffee with a double shot of espresso."

Pete nodded and began making her drink.

"And while he's doing that, I'm going to go get mine," Dante said, walking back the way they came.

She watched as he stopped at the beverage station and poured a cup of black coffee and mixed in three little packets of sugar. He looked at her and smiled.

"What can I say? I'm a man of the people."

Lyla truly didn't know what to make of Dante. He had the confidence and charisma that just radiated charm, but he could flip a switch, like she just witnessed, and become a formidable force of nature with just a subtle look. He seemed to get along well with the residents and was in a trusted position, most likely appointed by the Sterlings. She couldn't help but become somewhat enamored.

Pete's sudden presence in her peripheral made her spin around to face the expressionless man. He was a bulldog with a mustache and eyes that told no story. She looked down at the ring on his finger as he slid her drink across the counter.

Someone loves him, and if he's married then he loves someone back or at least did at one point.

"Thank you," Lyla said.

Pete nodded and went about his business just as Dante approached her with his Styrofoam cup and plastic lid. He looked at his watch.

"The other ladies should be trickling in any minute now. Do you want to grab a plate and sit down? I can introduce you to everyone."

She looked at the two girls still drinking coffee at the table and saw the third one outside extinguishing her cigarette in the ashtray on the patio.

"I think I'll have my coffee first."

"No problem. Do your thing. I'm going to grab a bite and chip away at my to-do list. Enjoy your morning and your breakfast. I think Julia will be around shortly to do the first-day stuff. Nice to meet you, Lyla," he said and was about to turn around before she stopped him.

"Hey, Dante."

"Yes?"

"Why doesn't Pete talk to us?"

"Pardon?" he said, mid-sip.

"You said he's a local who doesn't talk to anyone associated with Claymont, but he works here. What's his deal?"

"His *deal* is a shared point of view by a sizable percentage of locals toward this institution."

She waited for him to elaborate.

"They weren't thrilled when the Sterling family bought the castle and the land. To them, a family of wealthy Americans turning these grounds into a writer's residency was not exactly sacrilegious, but more of a slap in the face. This castle stood empty for decades. It wasn't like it was being used for anything other than to lure tourists who would also frequent the shops of Umbertide. And even then, some of the elders didn't like it."

"Geez. I didn't realize that."

"I bet you're wondering why he's working here if he hates it so much."

"For his family. He doesn't let his pride get in the way of supporting them."

Dante took a step back and looked at her from a new lens.

"Are you a Sherlock Holmes type of mystery writer? How did you come to that conclusion, detective?"

"His wedding ring."

He rubbed his scruffy chin.

"I am impressed. You're very perceptive. I mean, most of the writers here are, by nature, I suppose, but that was something out of an Agatha Christie book."

Lyla felt herself blushing, despite her best efforts. She longed for Pete's poker face skills at that moment.

"Is that the kind of writer you are, though?" he asked.

She blinked away her awkward response to compliments and focused on answering the question.

"No, I write horror mostly, but I guess there are mysteries in my stories. Nothing like Agatha Christie, though."

"Horror," he bristled. "I don't do the scary stuff. No offense."

She shook her head.

"None taken. I get it. You don't know how many times I've heard that response."

Deja and Linh entered the hall, and Lyla saw a few more ladies behind them walking down the red carpet. Dante looked back and waved at them.

"Well, it looks like a morning crowd is forming. They're all down here a little earlier than usual," he said, facing her again. "I guess they want to meet the new resident because they're certainly not here for me."

He took another sip of coffee and turned toward the door.

"Have a lovely first day, Lyla Robbins," he said loudly with his back to her.

That caused the rest of the residents who weren't looking at her to immediately start looking at her. She made eye contact with Linh who was heading her way.

"Hey, new girl," she said. "Want to get some breakfast and meet the rest of the coven?"

ELEVEN

All ten residents sat around one table, some eating breakfast, some just sipping coffee, but all of them were probing Lyla, "the new girl." They'd been sitting there for about twenty minutes asking her where she was from, what kind of writing she did, who were her biggest influences, how much of her novel did she have written, did she have a boyfriend back home, did she like to party, why didn't she go to grad school, and so on and so on.

Upon Deja's insistence, Lyla sat at a chair Linh scooted to the end of the long table. The other nine girls sat on the benches, four on one side, five on the other. Lyla had adamantly objected to this interrogation, but they all had been so insistent and quick about it that she was facing them like a matriarch at the dinner table before she had a chance to protest. Each time one of them asked a question, they would say their names and told Lyla they were going to test her memory when they were finished.

Even though the entire situation shoved Lyla headfirst out of her comfort zone, she gradually began to appreciate it and see it for the ice-breaking, borderline team-building exercise that it was. None of them officially said it was part of the program, and maybe that was planned, but this type of introduction was not just getting her out of her shell, but smashing it with a mallet until she was bare and exposed. And the longer it went on, the more comfortable and confident she became. It was a brilliant tactic, she had to admit, albeit torturous in the beginning. They were revealing more about themselves than she felt she was in answering their line of questioning.

"Okay," Deja said, sitting directly to Lyla's left. "Quiz time. Starting with me, go clockwise around the table and say everyone's name and something personal about them."

"Something personal?" Lyla laughed.

"We all revealed at least one thing," Linh said with a mischievous grin.

The patio door slid open, and Julia stepped halfway in, looking like she'd just walked off a runway back home in Paris. Her other half held a cigarette outside that she took a drag from and blew away from the building. Her presence confirmed Lyla's suspicion that this was all a coordinated effort, undoubtedly another one of Claymont's (Julia's) traditions.

"Morning, ladies," she said.

The residents all addressed her at the same time in different ways that came out as an indistinguishable legion of greetings. They looked at her like she was going to say something else, but she just took another puff and said, "Don't let me interrupt you."

One by one, the ladies turned back to Lyla, who was starting to feel the pressure of the hot seat again now that Julia was there. She looked at Linh and then to Deja.

"We're waiting," Deja said.

Lyla took a deep breath and spoke as quickly as she could.

"Your name is Deja. You're halfway through your romantasy novel, but your true passion is poetry," she said and moved on to the next one without waiting for a reaction.

"You're Rae. You're from Texas, and your great American novel sounds like it needs a little work to not be so Steinbeck derivative.

"Becky, you are the shortest resident here, but you have the highest IQ, which comes across in your vocabulary and analytical questioning; however, you overthink and second-guess yourself which is why your weekly writing goal is most likely the lowest in our cohort—oh, sorry, *coven*.

"Lori, you're even more introverted than I am, and I bet it made you more uncomfortable than me when you had to pretend like you were casually asking me questions. You're almost finished with the first draft of your book, but it didn't turn out exactly as you'd hoped, but that's okay because you're in a safe space where you'll learn that's part of the process."

Lyla swiveled in her chair to face the other half of the table who were all staring at her with bewilderment, which only fueled her confidence as she continued to shatter the power dynamic.

"Hi, Sue. You're from Maine, and you claim that you're immune to horror because you grew up in Stephen King territory, and nothing can faze you, an overexaggeration to say the least because you shuddered when Deja asked me what I thought about *The Exorcist*.

"Kay, you write about loss and grief because your mom, a published author, got you into writing and would've been so proud to see you get accepted into Claymont, but she passed away during your freshman year of college. I'm guessing cancer since that's what your protagonist is facing. Also, some unsolicited advice about writing through trauma: be careful. It can be cathartic, but it can also take you down a dark hole. I've seen it happen to one of the best writers I know.

"Hello, Brittany. This is your fourth year at Claymont, making you the most senior member among us. You have turned in five different drafts of your manuscript and have yet to be given the stamp of approval. It's not your editing ability that's holding you back; it's your resentment against The Reader. You don't agree with his suggestions. No, wait. Sorry, judging by that face you just made you *do* agree with his suggestions, but you address them half-heartedly, and it continues to spiral your narrative.

"Rachel, you're an early riser, and you arguably smoke more cigarettes than Julia. Not only are you the tallest of the ten of us, but you're the only one whose operating on a Plan B. We all wanted to write, but you wanted to be a model and work in fashion. You picked up the pen only after realizing that older guy you were dating your senior year was not the big shot in the fashion world that he claimed to be. Luckily for you, that sprawling narrative of feminist rage that you wrote in less than a week earned you a seat at this table. Bravo, truly."

Lyla turned to Linh, sitting directly to her right, looking like a deer caught in the headlights—a look Lyla had seen on literal deer hundreds of times growing up in West Virginia.

"And last but certainly not least, my next-door neighbor, Linh. As evidenced by last night, you work hard, and you play hard. But you get away with it because you're such a naturally talented writer. You had a full academic scholarship to Florida State, and if it wasn't for your dad being a distinguished alumnus, you would've been kicked out when you were caught with your boyfriend's weed stash in your dorm. Boyfriend got punished, and you graduated summa cum laude. You're currently writing a political satire that honestly sounds like it could win the fucking Pulitzer, and the reason it's so scathing is because of your personal history that you bring to it. Without reading a word written by anyone here, I would bet my spot at this table that you might or might not get published first, but you will have the most successful writing career and certainly be the most celebrated. But you still love your weed, and nothing is going to change that."

Lyla ran out of breath on the word. She looked at her peers, trying to gauge their reaction. No one said a word. They all had their eyes fixed on her, some more shocked than others, some impressed, others embarrassed, but they had set her up to do this, and she gave them exactly what they'd asked for. She could've gone much deeper, but she wasn't trying to be mean or alienate herself on her first day. Her only intentions were to prove she was worthy of being there—as much to herself as to them—and to establish that she was not a doormat. If there was any cliques or a hidden hierarchy she didn't know about, she had to let them know she wouldn't be kept on the lowest rung, despite being the new girl.

After a few moments of silence passed, her fellow residents looked away from her and exchanged glances with each other as if they were trying to determine a verdict of being angry or impressed. Lyla felt her heart pounding and the sweat forming in her palms. Did she take it too far? It wouldn't be the first time she completely misread the room. At her twelfth birthday party, she had a sleepover and chose to show her friends *Suspiria*, thinking they would find it just as insanely cool as she did. They didn't make it past the first twenty minutes before demanding it be turned off.

Is that what's happening now? Did you just show a room of twelve-year-olds Suspiria *again?*

"Bravo," a voice said that broke the unbearably awkward silence.

It took Lyla a second to realize the voice had come from outside of their makeshift gathering.

"Bravo, indeed," Julia said from the patio door.

She took one final drag from her cigarette and tossed it in the ashtray.

"I have to say, out of all the residents I've seen go through this little get-to-know-you exercise, that was the most entertaining one to watch. And the most accurate, if I'm being honest. Judging by the looks on some of your faces, the truth hurts. It was fun to watch though," she said as she approached the table and sat down the opposite way on the bench so that her back pressed against the table, and all she had to do was turn her head to the right a little bit to see everyone. "Ladies, does anyone disagree with Lyla's assessment?"

The other nine residents acted like they were waiting on someone other than themselves to speak first, but no one did.

"Really?" Julia said and then looked at the end of the table. "Lyla, I think this means you passed the test."

Julia's approval felt good, but it was shadowed by the discomfort she'd just caused. Maybe she did come on too strongly. She didn't know what to say, but that didn't matter because Julia broke the silence again.

"Like I said, that was the most impressive cold reading I've seen since my time here. There's no doubt you're skilled at reading people, picking up on things others would dismiss or pay no attention to. But here's the real test, Lyla, and one I hope will level the playing field: can you turn that unflinching lens around and focus it on yourself?"

Julia had a downright sinister glee in her eyes. Lyla knew there was only one way out of the scenario, and that was to give her exactly what she wanted. She also knew if she did it right, it would, as Julia said, "level the playing field."

"Fine," Lyla began, "I'm Lyla Robbins. I'm from Charleston, West Virginia in case you detected any Appalachian accent. I went to West Virginia University, and even though it's in my home state, it's four hours north of where I grew up. When I got there, I met people from all over the country—the world. And that's when I really became self-conscious about how I talk. Even some of the native West Virginians didn't have the 'hillbilly twang.' It really bothered me because I thought people assumed I was stupid, and a lot of them probably did. So, I tried to lose it, but on my best day I still sound like Jody Foster in *Silence of the Lambs*."

A few of the girls looked at her with confused looks, obviously not getting the nearly thirty-five-year-old reference. She had to remind herself that not everyone in the world knows movies like her, especially horror movies.

But that's a classic. It should be required reading and viewing at some point in an English or Film Appreciation course.

"So, aside from that, I would say my biggest insecurity is that I write genre fiction."

Deja cocked her head.

"So? What's wrong with that?" she asked.

"I write horror."

"Some of the most celebrated works of literature fall into that genre," Linh said, in a tone that gave Lyla the impression that maybe she wasn't harboring any ill-will about her comments.

"Yeah," Kay said. "*Frankenstein, Dracula*, all of Edgar Allan Poe's stuff."

A few of the girls nodded like the issue had just been resolved, but Lyla knew better. She's had this conversation before, gone down this road before, and it always tends to end on an "agree to disagree" note.

"Guys, I know the classics, and I appreciate what you're trying to do, but I don't write literary horror. I'm not Shirley Jackson or Anne Rice, and I'm not trying to be."

Lori leaned forward to chime in.

"So, are you saying that you're more transgressive and unapologetic?" she asked.

"I mean, I'm not *trying* to be, but—"

"Because you can walk into any Barnes and Noble right now and find *American Psycho* in the classic literature section, and that book was straight-up boycotted when it came out," she continued.

"Yeah," Sue began, "I think the author was even questioned by the FBI, and the original publisher refused to release it. I can see why, though. I couldn't get through the book, but the movie was okay."

Lyla had to bite her tongue and pause before she proceeded.

"I get your point. Even one of the most controversial books of the last forty years can find its audience, but that's not exclusive to horror. I guess what I'm really getting at is that I don't have any intention of trying to win any literary awards. I don't care if what I write offends people. I'm not trying to embed my prose with social commentary even though horror is arguably the best vehicle to do that with."

Linh opened her mouth like she was about to say something, but Lyla wasn't finished.

"I just want to scare people, that's all. Yes, I want to write commercial fiction. I want my shit to get made into movies. As cliché as it sounds, yes, I want to be the next Stephen King even though that's impossible."

"Hey, he dealt with his fair share of criticism. It wasn't until later in his career that most literary critics started taking him seriously," Lori said.

Lyla looked at Julia who just had a satisfied smirk on her face, obviously pleased with herself because of how well her team-building exercise was going. Even though she was pissed at having been pushed into the spotlight, Lyla didn't feel as timid or awkward around them. In the short time since breakfast, she felt like she gained nine sisters, albeit having to go through some growing pains to get there, but maybe there was a method behind the madness.

Claymont would hardly be as exclusive as it is if it wasn't working.

"You're right," Lyla conceded. "I'm just so used to being the only horror writer in the program and not taken seriously because of it. My professors—god, I can't tell you how many times I heard the word 'potential'—they'd say that I have so much potential, and I should explore different literary topics. I know that's why I didn't get into any of the MFA programs I applied to. It's bad enough that I was just writing to entertain; add horror to the mix, and who's going to take a chance on me? I'll never be a Stephen Graham Jones. I felt like everyone looked down on me, and obviously I came here thinking the same thing. I can't even begin to tell you how shocked I was when I got the acceptance letter. I'm not going to lie and say that I'm not sitting here with imposter syndrome."

Lyla let out a deep breath and sat back in her chair, wishing she could just sink into it and out of existence.

"Nicely done," Julia said.

Lyla looked up.

"How do you feel now?"

Lyla looked around at the friendly faces and took another deep breath.

"I feel like I just unloaded all my personal baggage on this table for everyone to look at."

"You did," Julia said and stood back up, slowly walking toward the end of the table. You exposed all your fears. Your insecurities. Your biases and preconceived notions. You took it all and dumped it on this table, just like your sisters here had to do. Claymont—the ladies of Claymont—are more than just residents; you all are sisters. They've all heard me give a version of this same speech, and you will too the longer you stay. But in doing what you just did, you rid yourself of ego. You're a blank slate who's no longer bound by those mental restraints. You are a vessel."

Lyla considered that word choice: vessel.

"A vessel for what?"

Julia walked behind her and placed her hands on the top of Lyla's chair.

"Ladies," she said, "care to answer that for her?"

Deja smiled and said, "Inspiration."

They went around the room, each giving their own responses.

"Creativity," Rae said.

"Originality," Becky said.

"Productivity," Lori said.

"Motivation," Sue said.

"Fearlessness," Kay said.

"Truth," Brittany said.

"Oh, I like that one," Julia said, still standing behind Lyla.

"Serenity,'" Rachel said.

Linh was the last one, and it looked like she was putting serious thought into her response.

"Well, come on. We don't have all day," Julia said, making everyone else chuckle.

Linh grinned and said, "Divinity. Yeah, that's the one."

"A vessel for divinity? Like God?" Lyla asked.

"Whatever you want to call it. I was thinking like divine inspiration, but whatever."

"Maybe take a break from the peace pipe for a while, sweetie," Julia said, causing everyone, especially Linh, to share in the type of laughter that hurt your belly.

Lyla couldn't remember the last time she'd laughed so hard. And as she looked around, sharing the joyous moment with her new sisters, she finally felt like she was home.

TWELVE

"I hope I wasn't too hard on you back there," Julia said, ashing her cigarette as the two of them exited the patio through the side door near the hot tub.

Lyla followed along the stone path that wrapped around the enclosed patio and headed toward the open courtyard.

"I think you had to be, right?" she said.

Julia gave her a smug look.

"You're a bright one, kid."

Lyla admired the castle walls that towered over her to the left.

"So, this is the pool area on your right."

"Wow."

The infinity pool was on the outside of what must be the library. It was surrounded by concrete and littered with chairs, tables, a hammock, and loungers.

"Everyone is welcome here until curfew, so long as—"

"We're current on our goals. I got it."

"Good."

The path turned and connected with the pool area. They were walking on freshly cut grass that rivaled any golf course Lyla had seen on TV back when her dad actually used to watch the sport. From that point, she had a clear view of the rest of the castle grounds and the fence that kept people out or kept them in or both. She smiled at the thought, not necessarily minding if she was trapped in paradise. The only remaining structures were the two towers on the corners straight ahead and what they referred to as the "guest house" in the back. The stone building was bigger than her parents' house.

A row of trees ran along the left side of the wall, and Lyla noticed the wooden bench strategically placed between two of them, perpetually shielded from the sun no matter what time of day it was. Julia was headed there.

"So, let's have our little chat over here. I find it quite peaceful."

"Is this where you establish plans with all the residents."

"Yes, as a matter of fact, it is."

"You're big on traditions and routines."

Julia seemed to be pondering the statement as she approached the bench.

"I suppose I am. Do you know why?" she asked and sat down, scooting over to give Lyla plenty of room.

"Um, I think the easiest answer is control. The traditions and even the rules are meant to keep us in line and on task."

Julia stared at her, unblinking.

"But that's only part of it."

"Oh?" Julia said. "Then what's the rest?"

"I once read that Albert Einstein had several sets of one outfit and would wear the same thing every day because he didn't want to waste any time and brain power trying to decide what to wear in the morning."

Julia nodded along like she was acknowledging that Lyla was on the right track.

"If everything about the program is planned out, you don't have to waste time fixing something that isn't broken, and we know what to expect every day. The routine allows us to save just a little more brain power to focus only on our writing."

"Very good. Now, speaking of that. Let's get to it," Julia said and reached in her bag, coming out with a rolled-up piece of parchment that was tied in the middle with a green ribbon.

"What is that?"

Julia didn't say anything; she only untied the bow and let the paper unroll. The twelve-inch paper only had two words written on it at the top: LYLA ROBBINS.

"This is your formal contract," she said, withdrawing a fine point pen. "Here, take this."

Lyla took the pen.

"The paper, too. It's your contract, not mine."

"Why am I getting an Ariel and Ursula vibe right now?"

"Seriously? That makes me Ursula in this scenario. I'm not *that* much older than you, and I damn sure don't look like a sea witch."

Lyla stretched the paper out across her thighs. Before she could ask what she was expected to write, Julia began her instructions.

"I'm going to ask you some questions, and you're going to answer them on the paper, after we discuss them of course. That's one tradition that didn't stick past the first few residents."

"What happened there?"

"I didn't help them with their plans, and they gave themselves overly ambitious contracts. Both of them burnt out and failed to keep up with the goals they set. They barely lasted three months between the two of them."

"Oh, well I definitely don't want that to happen."

"I have a feeling it won't with you. Let's begin. Are you a pantser or a plotter?"

"Uhh, I guess it depends on what I'm writing. I've written a bunch of short stories. I used to just wing them with no outline, but my professors said they started off strong and ended too abruptly. So, I realized I had to at least know the ending of my short stories before writing them."

"And what about your longer work like the one you sent in…was it outlined?"

Lyla thought about the piece she'd submitted. It was the same one she'd sent to all her dream MFA programs. The story revolved around a couple in their late twenties who decide to get married and have a baby. After a few pages of what she considered to be solid character development she did a scene break and picked up a few years later, and they now have a young daughter. Lyla wrote the daughter with enough personality to make her believable. She wrote a scene where she is in her bedroom at night, and her dad is reading a book with her. The little girl keeps getting distracted by the tree that stands next to her window, described as a two-story giant who stared at the little girl while she slept. She told her dad she was scared of it and didn't like it there, but he said it was an old tree and there was nothing they could do about it, assuring her that it was harmless, even telling her to think of it as an old guard standing watch at her window.

The little girl didn't buy it. Through more scene jumps, Lyla gradually increased the tension by having its branches start scratching her window on windy nights. It was especially menacing during thunderstorms. The girl was convinced that she'd witnessed it change shape whenever the lightning would flash across the sky.

As months passed, the tree continued to terrify the girl, and she pleads with her parents to have it cut down. Neither one of them seemed to take it as seriously as she thought they would. They just explained to her that they didn't feel right about cutting down a tree so old and assured her that it was not a monster, despite her telling them it was getting closer every night. The scene ended in a big fight where the girl told her parents that they'd wake up one morning, and she'd be gone, and they'd be sorry because they didn't do anything to stop it.

During the climax, the girl is in her bed with the curtains drawn shut, sleeping soundly until she hears the *BOOM* of thunder. Her eyes dart open, and she turns just in time to see the lightning reveal the shadow of the monstrous tree through the curtains, and it was moving toward her.

The final sting in Lyla's story occurred when the parents are woken by what they think is an earthquake. The foundation of their house wobbles, and everything shakes, causing the mom to fall off her side of the bed. It abruptly stops, lasting less than ten seconds. They don't know of any earthquake that happened like that and immediately go check on their daughter. When they approach her bedroom, they see the door is bowed out as if an incredible force had slammed against it.

The dad pries it open, and branches that had been leaning on it jut forward. He calls for his daughter, but she doesn't answer. He climbs the branches and looks in the room only to discover that the old tree they had cherished too much to cut down was blown over by the wind and crashed through their daughter's bedroom. It ends with the mom screaming at the sight of her daughter's broken arm sticking out from under the trunk, as a pool of blood forms around it.

Lyla knew it was a particularly mean-spirited piece, but she felt that it showed off her skills at building tension, character development, irony, and delivering a satisfyingly shocking conclusion. If readers wanted to derive themes of how parents should listen to their kids and how the real dangers in the world are often more terrifying than made up ones, well, that was fine with her. What was important to Lyla was that she didn't start that story with a theme in mind. She had no plans of writing about a kid getting neglected and not being taken seriously and how that led to her untimely demise. When she started it, she genuinely wanted to write something about a sentient tree that was terrorizing a little girl. It would play on the childhood fear she knew everyone had at one point in their lives: the thought of something scratching on your window while you sleep. She led with this premise which ultimately built up the tension in those night scenes and made her fears seem credible because she was writing with that ending in mind.

Once she realized it would be more shocking to have the girl die by the tree falling over from natural causes that could have been prevented if the parents had bothered to check on the state of the tree, she felt like she'd subverted expectations and was quite pleased. It was during her rewrite that she really fine-tuned everything to make sure she jerked the rug out from under the reader's feet. It had the scares in the beginning and middle, but the fact that the death happened because they didn't heed the girl's warning was what would truly haunt the readers after they put the story down. And above all else, scaring, shocking, and haunting the minds of her readers was the ultimate goal.

So, even though she didn't feel like it was her best narrative or showcase her ability to write longform, she hoped the selection committees at the schools to which she applied would see the craft hidden beneath the obscene.

Just when Lyla realized she was caught up in her own head and not engaging in the conversation, movement by the library wing of the castle across the courtyard caught her eye. A head peeked around the corner and was smiling. She was a resident, but from that far away, Lyla couldn't tell who it was.

Kay, maybe?

She turned to Julia.

"Who is that?" she asked and pointed back to the castle, but the person was gone.

"Where?"

"Someone was looking at us from behind the library."

Julia glanced at the area and back at Lyla.

"Well, I don't see anyone there now, but I'll keep my eye out. The girls know better than to interrupt me during a planning."

"I think it was Kay."

Julia looked annoyed, like she was ready to move the process along.

"I will ask her about it when we go back inside. Now, back to our conversation. The longer piece you sent in, did you do a detailed outline of that, have basic plot points, or just wrote blindly?"

"I just started with the premise of a little girl scared of the tree by her window. It turned into what it turned into once I started writing and figured out what the heart of the story really was."

"Okay. How long did it take you to compose the first draft?"

"Four days, I think."

"In hours, dear. How many hours did it take?"

"Oh, I think about eight or nine at the most. I only wrote a few hours every morning."

"Okay, so the word count was approximately thirty-five thousand."

"Right."

"Is that how long you plan to spend writing each day while you are here?"

"Yeah. Anytime I try to push beyond that, you can see the fatigue in the work. Why, is that too low?"

"Lyla, this is your contract. You are setting your own pace. But I will say that that's about average for our residents. One of our current writers has hers set at five hours per day but her weekly word count would still come out around the same as yours because you write faster."

"Okay, so if I plan on three hours per day and aim for two-thousand words, that'll set my weekly goal at fourteen-thousand words per week."

"Correct."

Lyla pondered the number before she said anything.

"Keep in mind," Julia began, "the hours are not the requirement. If you magically wrote fourteen-thousand words Friday and submitted them, you would still be in compliance with your goal. The hours are a guideline to help you stay on track. Most of the residents break up their writing sessions throughout the day, anyway. Don't feel like you have to tether yourself to a chair every day and not get up until you hit your goal."

Lyla nodded and said, "Okay. I think that will work for me."

"You're positive? You can go lower if you like but think about why you came here in the first place."

"What do you mean?"

"You had time to sit around and write that many words in your parents' basement, but you didn't. To me, it seems like you need to push yourself to thrive, just don't set yourself up for failure."

"Fourteen-thousand words a week. I can do that."

"If you've settled on that, write it on the contract."

Lyla looked down at the unrolled parchment that had her name on it and nothing else.

"What exactly do you want me to write?"

"You can keep it simple and just write 'weekly word count: 14,000.'"

"Okay."

Lyla gripped the pen and positioned the paper on her thigh, careful not to puncture the contract, and wrote exactly that in one line scrawled near the top under her name.

"I think I already know the answer to this, but do you have an estimate on how long your novel will be?"

"I looked online at my favorite horror books, and most of them are around the one-hundred-thousand-word mark, unless it's written by Stephen King."

Julia chuckled.

"Do you have any idea what it's going to be about?"

"No, but I will tomorrow once I start writing."

"Very well. Write an estimated word count and make sure to note that you don't have an outline. You can mention that you're a pantser if you want."

"Just write that in my own words right here?"

"Yes."

Lyla wrote, "My novel will be approximately 100,000 words long, and I won't be using an outline."

She sat back, and Julia checked what she wrote.

"Write that you don't have an idea for your novel yet."

Even though she thought this whole process was off, she did as she was told and wrote it.

"Okay," she said, awaiting more direction.

"That's it," Julia said. "Now all you have to do is sign the bottom and mark it with your blood."

Lyla slowly glanced at her. The businesswoman from Paris couldn't keep a straight face and let her laugh slip out. Lyla laughed too, but it was more out of relief than anything.

"Sorry," Julia said, still chuckling, "I thought a horror aficionado would appreciate that joke. I don't normally say that during the signing."

"I'm glad to be the outlier," Lyla said. "It means I'm special."

She signed her name and looked back up just in time to see Kay staring at her from around the corner of the building again. From that angle, her smile looked unnaturally large and stretched out.

"There! Look!" she said, pointing at the now-empty area.

"What?"

"Kay was back there again. I just saw her. She had this creepy smile on her face."

Julia took a deep breath but didn't say anything.

"I'm going to give her the benefit of the doubt and say that maybe the girls or even just her wanted to watch you officially sign your contract and weren't up to any shenanigans."

"Have they done that before?"

Julia looked toward the corner of the castle and then turned her head to the right until she was staring at The Keep, specifically, the top of it.

"Yes."

"Okay, so I'm free for the rest of the day?"

Julia quickly looked away from the castle, and for just a second, Lyla thought she saw fear in her eyes. If she had been scared, she turned it off with no more effort than flipping a switch.

"Almost. We're going to walk around the other side of the castle. There's one more thing over there that I think you'll find enjoyable. And then we're going to deliver your contract."

Lyla had been so intrigued by the first part of that sentence that she nearly disregarded the latter half.

"Wait, we're going to the fifth floor?" she asked.

Julia scrunched her eyebrows, but her wrinkleless forehead didn't move.

She definitely has Botox in there.

"I'm going to show you The Reader's submission box which is located on the fourth floor," she said and stood up. "Let's go."

"Okay. Here, do you want this?" Lyla asked, offering the signed contract.

Julia recoiled as if Lyla had offered her an ice cream cone full of shit.

"No, no. That's all yours now. Here's the ribbon. Go ahead and roll it up and tie it back on. It'll be your first official drop off to The Reader."

Lyla tied it and stood up, still a bit perplexed by Julia's reaction to touching the contract. She watched her walk forward.

"Come, come," she said like she knew Lyla hadn't taken a step.

Lyla followed as they crossed the courtyard and rounded the castle where Kay(?) had been watching them, but no one was there.

"Check out this area," Julia said pointing to a wooden porch with a standing fire pit circled by chairs and torches.

A string of unlit twinkly lights adorned the four-foot fence.

"This is nice," Lyla said.

"Wait until the sun goes down, and they get the fire going. The lights and torches turn this whole area golden. Sometimes the residents will meet out here and have drinks or make s'mores and tell campfire stories. God knows what else," she said with a chuckle.

Lyla noticed the absence of a full enclosure like there was on the patio with the hot tub.

"I'm guessing this area is off limits after ten?"

"You guessed correctly. The Reader supposedly likes to take walks and rest in this area because it's the most secluded outside area within the castle walls."

"It's lovely."

"I'm glad we've moved on from just 'beautiful.'"

Lyla grinned.

"Follow me to the front of the castle. We'll go in through The Keep and drop that off," she said, gesturing with her head to the contract in Lyla's hand.

They entered The Keep and walked directly up the stairs. Lyla glanced at each passing floor as she crossed the landing, taking careful note of her own hallway on the third level. As soon as she placed her foot on the first step to go up to the next floor, she felt a flutter in her belly like she was doing something wrong. The air got progressively cooler the farther up they went. She wanted Julia to slow down. Some part of her for reasons she couldn't mentally articulate did not want her to go up there. But before she could or would protest, Julia reached the landing and turned to wait on her.

"You'll definitely get your steps in while staying here," Julia said. "Not that you have any need to worry about that. You're fit as a fiddle. That's a saying in America, yes?"

Lyla didn't even try to hide the fact that she was winded.

"Yes," she said, catching her breath. "That's a saying, but it doesn't apply to me. I'm not used to these steps yet."

She reached the landing and looked down the hallway that was different than the residential rooms below. The residents' halls were decorated the same. No door was different than the next. The archer's windows and chandeliers were in the same spot on both floors. The fourth floor didn't have chandeliers and looked more like a place of business.

Tall lamps lined the outer wall, along with thin wooden desks adorned with vases full of fresh flowers that Lyla could smell from where she stood. The first door on the left had a wooden sign on the stone wall beside it that had Claymont's standard lettering and symbol with the words PROGRAM DIRECTOR printed across the top and the name Dante Farina written underneath.

"As you can see, this is Dante's residence. It's more of a suite, really. He's an odd duck, that one. His office is through the door, but there's a connecting room for him to stay whenever he wants."

"So he stays here only part of the time? I can't imagine sleeping at work," Lyla laughed.

"You must understand something. Claymont has a barebones staff. We have security, the kitchen employees, and one local company to maintain the grounds and another to serve in a janitorial and all-around general maintenance role. And then there's Dante who controls the chaos and makes sure everything is running smoothly. That just leaves me, and I've already told you enough about what I do."

Lyla nodded and looked at the other two doors down the long hallway.

"What's down there?" she asked.

"The first door is Mr. and Mrs. Sterling's office and the second is their living quarters for when they come to visit. There's nothing for residents down that way, so that's it for this floor."

"Where do I put this?" Lyla asked, holding up her contract.

"Right behind you, my dear."

Lyla turned around and noticed a black metal cube mounted on the stairwell wall.

"Oh, I didn't even see that."

Julia stepped over to the box which was about chest-high and gripped a knob on the top, opening it like a cellar door.

"You put everything you want The Reader to see in this box. Make sure your papers are in here by Friday night, The Reader will review them over the weekend, and they will be returned to you first thing

Monday morning. You can go ahead and put that in here," she said, closed the lid, and took a step back.

Lyla regarded her with an ire of suspicion. She had a look in her eye like she was watching some monumental moment taking place.

It probably is to her. She scouted you out and got you here. Turning the contract in is probably a big goal for her.

Lyla felt a sudden appreciation for Julia, liaison to The Sterlings and mentor to the residents. She approached the box and touched the brass knob, raising the lid, surprised at how heavy it was, dropped the rolled-up contract inside, and released the knob. The lid slammed shut, sending an echo down the hallway and causing Julia to flinch.

"Sorry," Lyla winced.

"Nothing to be sorry about," Julia said and gave a quick glance toward the staircase that led up the fifth floor. "What's done is done."

She turned back to Lyla.

"Now you can enjoy the rest of your day. Relax, hang out with the girls. As of right now, you have all the privileges that come with being in compliance with your goal. Don't stay up too late, though. Your work begins tomorrow."

"I'm looking forward to it."

"Good, let's go back downstairs," she said and turned around without waiting to see if Lyla was following her.

Lyla hurried to her as she listened to her footsteps descend the stairs, but she stopped as soon as she entered the spiral staircase. She watched Julia disappear around the corner and was about to catch up with her, but she got the overwhelming sensation of being watched. The hair on the back of her neck stood on end as she sensed something leering at her from behind, crouched down on the steps in the dark. She quickly looked over her shoulder just in time to see a face in the darkness disappear around the turning staircase.

"Lyla?" Julia said and gripped her forearm.

She nearly screamed. Her reaction caused Julia to jump back.

"What is it?" Julia asked.

"I thought I..." Lyla began but cut herself off when she thought about the figure in her closet and how it climbed up her window.

"You thought what?"

Realizing that if there was something nefarious going on with the recluse living on the floor above, she didn't want to say anything there that he might hear.

"I'm just curious is all," she said, trying to play it down.

"Well, get that out of your brain. Don't even look up there unless the Sterlings give you permission. Now let's go."

"You make it sound like we're in danger," Lyla said with a forced chuckle as they began their descent.

"We will be if I don't get a damn cigarette in the next two minutes."

They stopped at the third floor.

"I'm going to head to my room for a bit. I might take a nap and explore all the rec areas on the first floor. Maybe see what the rest of the girls are doing for the rest of the day."

"Okay. I don't know where I'll be when you make your way downstairs, but I'll be around until dinner if you need anything."

"Thank you, Julia."

"Of course," she said and started to walk to the next floor before Lyla remembered that she did need something.

"Hey, Julia," she said.

"Yes?"

"I talked to Linh earlier, and she said there was supposed to be a phone in my room to dial the main office or downstairs or something?"

"You don't have one?"

"No."

"That's odd. I'll let Dante know, and we'll get that squared away in no time."

"Okay. Thanks."

"You're welcome. Now go get some rest."

After the night she'd had and the busy morning and afternoon, rest was exactly what her body was demanding. She hoped her anxious mind would permit it.

THIRTEEN

Lyla woke from her afternoon nap to someone knocking on the door. She immediately remembered the closet.

No, it wasn't a knock on the closet; it was a tap.

"Lyla, are you in there?" a male voice asked from the hallway.

She recognized the Italian accent and the firmness of his tone. It was Dante.

"Yes," she said rubbing her eyes and making sure her hair wasn't too crazy in the mirror. "Just a second."

"Take your time."

She grabbed her shorts off the floor and slid them back on as she walked barefoot to the door. The peephole in the center was something she hadn't noticed before. Out of habit, she looked through it before she unlocked the door and opened it.

Dante did a double take but tried to play it off like he didn't. He probably didn't expect to find her standing there in her pajamas, though there wasn't anything special about them. Maybe it was the oversized t-shirt that hung down almost past her shorts that had caused an illusion of her not wearing any pants. Regardless of what it was, something about her had caught his eye. And even though she'd found him attractive in that rugged, older guy kind of way, not to mention his accent and the confident energy he effortlessly exuded, the fact that she had just disarmed him made her face flush.

He looked at her unmade bed and drawn curtains.

"Sorry to wake you," he said. "Julia told me to install the new phone in your room."

"Oh, I didn't think it would be that fast."

"Well, when Julia says that one of her girls needs something, I have to snap to it. Plus, this has been on my to-do list since Ann—" he began but stopped himself like he had to consider exactly what to say next. "Since Ann left. That was months ago, and I meant to do it before you got here, but the damn new phone just got buried in the supply closet."

"It's no problem. I'll get out of your way."

He smiled and nodded and squeezed by her and crouched down beside the nightstand on the left side of the bed. There was already a plastic mount screwed into it, but it was noticeably broken from where she stood. Dante took a power drill off his belt and removed the case with three quick zips. He pocketed the screws and unboxed the new phone.

"So, Ann stayed in this room for her entire residency?" she asked, still standing near the open door.

His hands stopped moving inside the phone's box for just a second, but it was long enough to give Lyla red flags. He knew something.

"Yeah, she did."

"What's her last name? Is she on the bestseller's chart now?" Lyla said with a smile.

Dante looked up.

"She didn't finish the program," he said and positioned the new phone mount to the nightstand.

"What happened?"

Dante fired up the power drill over her question and whizzed in the three screws.

"It's not really my place to talk about previous residents," he said and put the new phone in the case.

"Did she not finish her book or something? I'm not trying to be nosey, really. I don't want to make the same mistakes. I just have a feeling that I'm going to mess up."

"She died."

Dante attached the new cord to the phone and then the wall jack, behaving like what he just said wasn't a big deal.

"I'm sorry, what?"

He picked up the phone and put it to his ear and hung it back up.

"Your phone's working," he said and stood up, gathering his supplies and putting the drill back in his belt.

"Yeah, thanks."

Is this guy seriously just going to walk out of the room after dropping that bomb?

"Hey man, you can't leave me hanging like that. How did she die?"

Dante stopped at the doorway with his back to her. He turned to the closet. She saw his fist clench and relax.

"I told you, it's not my place to be talking about former residents, especially when it's something sensitive like this."

"She didn't die in here, did she?"

"Why do you ask?"

Lyla furrowed her brow.

"Because I'm staying here now. I'd kind of like to know if someone died where I sleep."

"This castle is a thousand years old. Hundreds of people died in this place," he said before stepping into the hallway.

"Hey, wait," she said a little too sternly than she meant to.

He turned around, looking frustrated.

"Look, I've got other stuff to do. I told you, it's not my place to talk about it. Ask Julia."

"I can walk next door and ask Linh. What's really going on?"

That seemed to get his attention. He bit his lip and stepped back into the room, shutting the door behind him. She got that queasy feeling in her gut. She didn't know this guy. He could whip out that power drill and turn her into Pinhead in five minutes if he wanted to. Now she was alone in a room with him.

"Is it part of the program for the director to be alone in residents' rooms with the door closed?"

"You want to know what happened or not?"

He wasn't trying to intimidate her. He was trying to protect himself. Lyla could only nod.

"She tried to leave. Like flee this place in the middle of the night. I don't know why or where she was trying to go, but I saw the video of her sneaking out of here. She made it to the gate, but you can't see anything past that, especially on a rainy night. She just disappeared into the blurry footage."

He paused like he was considering whether or not to proceed with the story.

"It was just a tragic accident. The taxi driver said he didn't see her until it was too late. She didn't survive the hit."

"Jesus Christ."

He nodded and clenched his jaw.

"Yeah. I'm only telling you because if you ask the girls, they're bound to tell you rumors."

"Like what?"

"Like she killed herself."

Lyla's eyes widened.

"Yeah," he said. "Ann was having a rough week leading up to that night, but I don't think for a minute she would've taken her own life."

"So, she just, what? Fell? Slipped during the storm?"

"Or she was running."

"Running from wh—"

The door opened, and Linh stood there with a baffled look on her face like she just walked in on her parents fucking.

"Your phone's good to go," Dante said and switched back to that charming façade, giving Lyla a pat on the shoulder as he walked away. "Let me know if you need anything else." He stopped at the door. "Linh, everything good with you?"

"Yeah," she said awkwardly looking back and forth between the two of them.

"All right then. Have a productive day, ladies," he said and disappeared into the hallway.

Linh stepped in and then looked back, making sure he was gone before opening her mouth.

"What's really going on here?" she asked with a grin.

"What? Nothing. He just installed the phone. Why are you grinning like that?"

"Oh, I don't know. Dante in your room with the door closed and..." she looked at the messy bed.

"Shut up. Eww. He's like in his forties," Lyla said, really playing up her repulsion.

"So, I fucked one of my professors. She was older than Dante."

"Oh...that's nice."

"Yeah, you didn't pick up on that during your little table read did you?"

"Guess not."

"M'hmm. I'm just saying, don't get close to him. He's nothing but a distraction that you don't need, especially this early in the program."

"Don't tell anybody I told you this. Deja is the only other person who knows. But I'm pretty sure he had something going on with Ann, the girl who had this room before you."

"What makes you think that?"

"Let's just say these walls aren't as soundproof as they seem. Plus, I saw him sneaking out of her room a few times."

"When did Ann leave?" Lyla asked as naively as possible. "Did she write something great?"

"Look, Lyla. I don't want to freak you out, and I'm kind of surprised that Julia didn't tell you this already, but Ann's room only became available because she died. She called a cab in the middle of the night and didn't tell any of us what she was doing. But the weird thing about it was that she didn't pack anything. All of her stuff and her suitcase were still in here. Why would she call a cab and leave her stuff?"

"I don't know what to think."

"Well, we think she killed herself—Deja and I. She was acting weird the last week she was here. Really withdrawn. She stopped writing. Sounds like a broken heart to me."

"You think she killed herself over Dante?"

"We're writers. We can fill in the blanks," she said with a sigh and a smile. "But I didn't come in here to talk about all this depressing stuff."

"Good. I don't want to be depressed. What's up?"

"A few of us are making a run to town. Do you want to go or do you need me to bring you back anything?"

"Oh, umm, I don't think so. I'm pretty sure I have everything I need. Thank you though."

"Okay. Well, I can't wait to take you to town when you're allowed. It's beautiful, and there are some lovely locals—ones who are younger than Dante, at least."

Lyla forced a laugh.

"Sounds fun. I think I'm going to explore the castle a little more before dinner."

"Okay, we'll be back before then," Linh said and opened the door. "I'll see you later. Don't go getting into trouble on your first day."

"I don't think I could if I wanted to, but you all have fun. I'll be here."

When Lyla was finally alone, she shut the door again and tried to process everything she'd just learned. Her desire to socialize and explore abated, and now all she wanted to do was go grab some junk food from the first floor and stay in her room and read, hoping some inspiration would strike.

———

Lyla ate dinner as soon as it was served. The meals seemed to be getting better and better. She thought she'd had authentic Italian cuisine before, but nothing compared to the chicken alfredo, salad, and fresh bread she scarfed down while sitting alone on the patio. She looked at the tree line above the gate, watching the sun gradually descend into the forest.

When she finished eating, she returned her tray and ventured into the library. Linh had said she and the rest of the girls would be back before dinner, but obviously that didn't happen. Lyla belched against her will, feeling the effects and regrets of overeating. She knew she'd have to monitor her diet at Claymont. Lounging around, eating, drinking, and writing all day would pack the pounds on little by little. She opened the library doors, and the view was just as stunning as before. More than anything, she wanted to find the nearest shelf ladder and go for a ride.

The idea of looking at all the books seemed insurmountable. Even if she spent an entire week in there, she doubted she could read the titles of every book on each level. But she had to start somewhere, so she turned to her right and began perusing the shelves, trying to determine what section she was in. After scanning the spines of a few of the tombs written in Latin, she surmised she was in some rare, antique showcase display. She kept walking around the tower's circle of books until she found a map of the library layout, marked floor by floor.

The fiction section comprised the fourth floor. That was her first stop because she had to know what kind of horror selection she'd be dealing with for the foreseeable future. Her expectations were low, but her hopes were high. She ascended the circular staircase that lined the walls and stepped off when she reached the top. The dinner in her belly didn't do her any favors during the climb. She huffed and puffed a little too much for her standards.

Mental note: check out the exercise area and form a game plan.

Lyla glanced to her left and then to her right, feeling small amid the large circumference of literature. She turned around and looked straight across at the other side of the circle and then, against her better judgement, leaned over the railing and peered down. Vertigo instantly warped her vision. She spun back around and stood as closely as she could to the books with her eyes shut until the feeling passed.

What the hell is going on?

Normally, heights didn't bother her. She'd hiked up the mountains by the New River Gorge in West Virginia with her friends and stood on the edge of a cliff just to get the right shot with the sunset and the gorge in the background. The dorms at WVU had certainly stood taller than four stories, especially the notoriously steep basketball coliseum, and none of that ever triggered a reaction like she was having. Her mind cut back to what she was looking at exactly when she peered over the edge. It had not just been the steep drop, but the spiral staircase. The elongated and twisty loop must've triggered some kind of dizzying effect.

Lyla opened her eyes and turned her head slightly. Her vision wasn't lagging, and the nausea had left her gut. She took a deep breath and shook it off. After randomly choosing to walk to her right, she began scanning the titles. She was in the classics section. It transitioned into general fiction, and she slowed to see if they had any of her favorite contemporary authors.

A door opened and shut below her. She stopped and approached the railing, mentally preparing herself for the warped view, figuring that if she knew what to expect, it wouldn't have the same effect on her. The center of the first floor was empty except for the tables with their glowing green lamps. She was about to turn away when she realized that those table lamps hadn't been on when she first entered the library.

Lyla stayed where she was and stared below, waiting for any sign of movement.

"Hello?" she finally said, her voice sounding louder in the tower chamber.

No one responded. She listened for any sound. Any footfall. A cough. Anything.

"Is someone down there?" she asked, louder that time.

Still nothing.

Maybe one of the staff came in and turned on the lights for evening hours and went back out?

The thought didn't carry much weight. Something felt off. Just like her first night in her room, she didn't feel alone. Her flesh warmed like she was being watched. From her vantage point, she kept scanning the open first floor for someone hiding under the second level walkway. Satisfied that no one was there, her eyes darted to the beginning of the staircase and followed it up to the second floor. She slowly dragged her eyes around the ring of books, having to lean over the railing to see directly under her, and she still couldn't see everything below her. There was room for error and plenty of blind spots, but she continued scanning each level until she reached her own.

Lyla didn't see anyone. She didn't hear anyone. All she had to go on was the sound of the doors opening and closing and the lamps. The physical sensation of being watched could've just been triggered by her heightened sensory awareness. She forced herself to take calming breaths and stepped away from the railing and went back to looking for a book.

A metal-on-metal rolling sound screeched below her. Her heart leapt to her throat, but she hurried back to see. The bookshelf ladder on the first floor shot around the room like someone just pushed it. Lyla was about to scream at whomever was messing with her when she heard the same sound, only louder this time. The second-floor ladder flew on its track in the opposite direction as the one below it.

"What the fuck?" Lyla muttered and hurried along the landing, hoping to see the people doing this hiding in her blind spot, but there was no one there.

"Who's there?" she shouted, hoping to sound more frustrated than fearful.

No one responded. She watched the ladder on the first-floor pass by as it slowed.

Something vibrated below her feet and shot off to the right. She knew what it was without seeing it, but in two seconds it appeared on its track, zipping along the third floor. As badly as she wanted to run, she couldn't. The realization that who or whatever flung that ladder was directly below her rendered her motionless.

This has to be a joke. This has to be some hazing bullshit that the other girls are doing. Maybe it's connected to what happened in your room and that wasn't just a night terror. Maybe they really weren't late coming home from dinner. They were planning some way to freak you out and took full advantage of you going to the library by yourself. For all you know, they were watching you eat dinner on the patio, just waiting to make their move.

But what if it's not them?

The ladders had been pushed one by one, moving up a floor each time. The only one left was attached to the wall about fifteen feet to her left. She slowly turned her head and stared at it.

She held her breath and waited. The little wheels in the track looked like they were shaking as if some invisible presence had just gripped the ladder. Her eyes widened.

The library doors opened, and Lyla screamed louder than she ever had in her life. The only still moving ladder slowed to a natural stop.

"Who's up there?" a female voice called from the first floor.

Lyla realized she was hyperventilating and still staring at the ladder near her. It didn't budge.

"I heard you scream! Who's up there?" she repeated.

Lyla was still flattened against the wall of books, too scared to move, but her body chemistry was gradually regulating.

"It's Lyla," she said, barely loud enough for herself to hear it.

She took a breath and walked to the railing and saw Kay and Rae looking at her.

"What's going on up there?" Rae said with a little slur in her voice.

"Yeah, why'd you scream?" Kay said, chuckling.

Both of them were noticeably fucked up even from four floors up.

Just as Lyla was about to reply, she looked at Kay and remembered her face peering around the outside of the library tower earlier when she was meeting with Julia. There was no evidence of that grotesque smile on her face now. She looked like she did the first time Lyla met her.

But she was at the library earlier looking all fucking weird, and now she's the first one on the scene in the library?

"I was looking for a book, and the door just scared me. I'm coming down."

She walked down to the first floor, casually glancing at all the shelf ladders that weren't moving in opposite directions now.

The two ladies stood at the bottom of the staircase, glossy eyed and smelling like wine and weed.

"Where's your book?" Kay asked.

"Well, I was going to get one, but you all scared the shit out of me. Now, I don't even want to read."

Rae laughed and held up an unopened bottle of wine that just looked like it cost hundreds of dollars.

"I got this from the cellar. Want to chill in the hot tub?"

"What's the occasion?" Lyla asked.

"Uhh, we're living in a castle in Italy, and everything is free. That's the occasion," Kay said with a grin. Plus, Rae hit forty-thousand words today."

"Oh, congrats," Lyla said, still feeling flustered from the experience. "Yeah, I'm down for a drink."

"Sweet. Let's go," Rae said, leading the way.

Lyla followed and looked back at the tower of books. She watched as one of the lamp bulbs flickered off and quickly hurried out.

FOURTEEN

The hot tub worked wonders, as did the alcohol. Lyla's nerves were as relaxed as they had been when she first pulled up to Claymont in the horse carriage the evening before. Being with the other two girls, and the rest of the residents who filed in the snack bar since the dinner buffet had shut down for the night, made her realize that she wasn't wandering around a mysterious castle all by herself.

As soon as she had company, the effect of whatever supernatural presence she felt simply lost its power. It was so much easier to be brave when surrounded by a group of carefree, like-minded souls. But she couldn't outright dismiss the incidents. A lifetime's worth of horror movies and scary books had taught her better. She'd be damned if she, the heroine of her own story, would go down the same brush-it-off-like-nothing-happened-until-it's-too-late route that so many protagonists in her genre repeatedly did. No, she wasn't going to downplay what happened, and right then, she had all the liquid courage needed.

"Hey, guys. Have you all ever experienced anything weird since you've been here?" Lyla asked while Kay and Rae were in mid-conversation about "hot locals."

They both turned their heads and looked at her like she just asked them what the meaning of life was.

"Huh?" Rae replied.

"Like hearing things or seeing things that couldn't possibly be there."

"Like what?" Kay asked, sounding like she took the question a little more seriously.

"I'm just going to put this out there because I don't know how else to say it. I thought I saw someone in my room last night."

"Wait, what?" Rae asked.

"Yeah, my closet to be specific. And then weird shit started happening with the lights, and I got all freaked out and got out of the room, but then I saw someone outside my window."

Rae stared at her and let out a slow laugh like she knew she was fucking with her.

"I'm serious. It wasn't just that either. This afternoon," she began and then looked at Kay who was hanging on every word, "This afternoon, I was meeting with Julia in the courtyard. We were sitting on the bench by the trees creating my writing plan, and I look up and see someone staring at me from behind the library tower."

"Who was it?" Kay asked.

If Lyla had been sober, she knew she could've deduced more from the tone of Kay's question, but right then, her detective powers were dulled. Her mind was operating at a slower speed.

"I swear on my life that I'm not making this up. It looked like you."

Kay shook her head.

"Me?"

"Yeah, and you were smiling, only it wasn't a normal smile. It looked like two fishhooks pierced the corners of your mouth and stretched it out into this freakish grin."

"Eww," Rae said.

"Well, I can assure you that I wasn't spying on you and Julia this afternoon. I was writing."

Lyla continued like Kay's comments meant nothing.

"The really bizarre thing is that I saw your face again."

"This is crazy," Kay said.

"That's what I thought. I mean, I definitely saw someone. There's no debating that unless I'm just randomly hallucinating."

"Did Julia see her?" Rae asked.

"Don't say 'her' like you're talking about me. I wasn't there. I was fucking writing. I already said that."

Lyla studied Kay. She looked genuinely unnerved by the line of questioning. It was almost like she doubted her own story.

"What'd you write today?" Lyla asked.

"Huh?"

"Quick, without thinking. What did you write about today. Surely, you must remember."

"I finished a scene in my novel that I've been trying to crack for days."

"What's happening in it?"

"It's too hard to talk about out of context. It'll sound stupid," Kay said. "And by the way, it's none of your business what I write in my book."

"Okay, I believe you. Chill. Take another drink. I wasn't trying to piss you off. I just had to ask because if it wasn't you, that means it was someone else, and I need to figure out who that person is."

"Or," Rae began, "you can fucking chalk it up to a million different reasons why you thought you saw something and get to work on your story."

"I definitely will, but there's one more thing that happened that's going to make me sound even crazier. We've come this far, so who cares?" Lyla said.

Kay and Rae were all ears.

"You know when you all came in the library and heard me scream?"

They both nodded.

"It wasn't because I was just startled while looking for a book. I originally went in there to find something to read, but once I made it to the fourth floor, some really weird shit I can't explain happened and just thinking about it right now freaks me the fuck out."

The seriousness in her tone must've been evident because the two girls suddenly seemed more invested in the story.

"What happened in the library?" Rae asked.

"You know the bookshelf ladders? Well, I started walking along the landing, looking for the horror section, and I heard one of them spin around on the first floor."

"No way," Kay said but not in a dismissive manner.

"I looked over the railing and saw it literally spinning around the room, but there wasn't anyone down there, unless they were hiding under one of the tables or somewhere else down there."

"That's freaky," Rae said. "You're positive no one else was in there?"

"No, that's what I'm saying. I have no idea if someone was fucking with me or if there was some kind of…" she said, trailing off.

"Some kind of what?" Kay asked.

"Presence."

"Like a ghost?" Rae said.

"I didn't want to use the word, but yes, something like a fucking ghost because all the other ladders started spinning one by one until you guys randomly burst in."

"Dude, are you messing with us?" Rae said.

"No! I thought you all were messing with me. But that's why I asked if you'd ever experienced anything weird here."

"You mean other than living with an unseen recluse who gives us a curfew for the fucking castle we live in?" Kay laughed. "No, other than that, I can't say that I have."

"That makes me feel even worse."

"Why?"

"Because it either means I'm losing it, or something here is targeting me."

Rae and Kay looked at each other and then back at Lyla with skeptical glares.

"Wait a second," Rae said. "You're a horror writer, and on your first day, you're legit saying ghosts are haunting you?"

Lyla rolled her eyes.

"Jesus. Forget it."

"It's a little coincidental," Kay admitted. "I mean, I'm all about living through my characters, but this is some method writing shit."

Lyla was already getting out of the hot tub.

"Just don't tell anyone else, please," she said as she wrapped herself in a towel.

"Get some rest, Lyla," Rae said. "It's a school night."

The remark confused her for a moment until she realized her orientation was over, and she was expected to start writing the next day. But rather than feel intimidated, she looked forward to creating a new world and jumping into it. It might take her mind off the weird shit happening around her.

Lyla passed Linh and Deja going out as she was coming in.

"Lyla," Deja began. "Where are you going, girl? The night's young."

"Yeah, I'm just not feeling it tonight. I ate and drank too much. I'm going to go crash. You all live it up though."

She didn't even bother to slow down and see their reactions.

"Okay. Let me know if you need anything tonight," Linh said.

"Thanks," Lyla said as she headed toward the dining hall doors.

The hall of columns had a few other residents. Rachel and Sue were in the snack area, and she heard Becky laughing from the rec room. Everyone else seemed to be having a good time. They were all close, or they all had at least one close friend. She was once again the outsider after just feeling like she had nine new sisters earlier that day.

Stop with the negative thoughts. They've been here longer than you and formed deeper bonds. Give yourself time.

Lyla flinched when The Keep's front door swung open and two big men entered, but her nerves steadied when she recognized the twins.

"Evening," Mariano said, and Antonio nodded.

"Hi," she said, and she must've had a concerned look on her face because Antonio offered some reassurance.

"Just doing our evening rounds. Call down if you need anything."

"Thank you. Have a good night."

"You too," they said at the same time, which made Lyla cringe.

By the time she'd walked up the three flights of stairs, she felt like she was going to throw up. She shut her door and, despite having full intentions of relaxing in the bathtub, she just took off her bathing suit and slid into an *Evil Dead* T-shirt and shorts. Her bed was calling for her, but she forced herself to go brush her teeth and wash her face. She stared at herself in the mirror.

"A writer's retreat," she said to herself like it was some kind of epiphany.

But that's how it happened with her stories. Random thoughts or images or lines of dialogue would pop in her head like a seed and germinate. She thought of Linh, Deja, Kay, and Rae and how she could take tidbits of their personalities and use them as the basis for four out of five characters in her novel, with her being the protagonist, of course. Before the idea fluttered into the ether, she hurried out of the bathroom and over to her desk. She grabbed a piece of paper from the stack and a pen and jotted down random notes, just enough to jog her memory in the morning.

She wrote, "Five friends from college go on a writer's retreat in a secluded somewhere. Castle? Cabin? Yacht? Mansion?" Then, she scribbled those four ideas out and wrote "Airbnb lake house" and underlined it. She felt euphoric. Having the premise was all she needed to make a start in the morning. She placed the pen on top of the paper and was halfway turned around when the title appeared in her mind's eye like a glowing marquee. She snatched the pen and scribbled, "WRITE BY MOONLIGHT," and stared at it for a moment.

"Write By Moonlight. Write By Moonlight. Write By Moonlight," she said over and over, hearing the cadence, testing out the sound of it.

Satisfied, she nodded her head and said, *"Write By Moonlight."*

She had a title and premise, and now she just needed a good night's rest. Right before hopping into bed, she made sure both doors were shut, and the window was covered with the curtain. The relief she felt overrode any fears from earlier. Still, she turned the bathroom light on and cracked the door. She'd work her way back up to sleeping into total darkness in a few nights.

It didn't take Lyla long to fall asleep. She dreamed of wandering the castle, through endless hallways lit only by torches on the walls. No matter how far she ran, she couldn't find the exit. The doors moved and the rooms to which they led constantly shifted. And each time she thought she'd found a way out, she'd end up back in the hallway.

Claustrophobia and panic clawed through her brain. Something in the back of her mind was telling her this wasn't reality. This was a dream—a nightmare—but she'd eventually wake up. She willed herself to wake up to no avail. It was as if her feet were covered in quicksand, and the harder she tried to break free and run, the more the hungry floor pulled her down. She writhed and screamed, desperately trying to break the confines of her subconscious and wake up back in her bed.

"Lyyyyylaaaaa."

She froze, waist-deep in the mushy floor that should've been solid stone. For a split second she saw someone standing at the end of her hallway. The silhouette was tall and thin. It twitched as it began to creep toward her.

"No!" Lyla screamed.

The torchlight above the figure extinguished, and there was once again only darkness. But Lyla still heard the thing approaching, twisted step by twisted step. As soon as one of its legs would appear in the light of the next torch, the flame would instantly blow out. There were only two torches left, separating Lyla from the incoming stranger.

"Lyyyyyyyyyyylaaaaaaaaaa."

Its voice was strained and sounded like someone trying to speak while struggling to take a breath. The raspy, dead moan made her body shiver with dread.

Another torch extinguished.

Lyla could smell it now. She desperately tried to free herself from the hold the floor had on her, and to her surprise, she managed to pull herself up by gripping the stones on the wall. Just as two legs appeared in the final light's orange glow, she jerked free and got to her feet again. She smelled the rotting thing right beside her.

"LYYYYYYYLAAAAAA!"

Was there desperation in that voice?

The last light blew out. Lyla sprinted back the way she came, down the endless corridor she knew led to nothing but more walls and torches and darkness. It didn't matter though. The dead thing's smell invaded her nostrils. She felt its warm breath on the back of her neck. She ran at full speed, yet somehow this terror behind her continued to close the gap despite Lyla not hearing its footfalls anymore.

Two bony hands gripped her shoulders, but she kept running. The cold claws slid down her biceps and forearms and burrowed into her hands. Lyla felt like her arms had just been plunged into ice water. A heavy breeze blew through the hallway and took the light with it. Lyla felt the thing on her back, fusing to her. The same frozen sensation shot through her spine and legs.

The shape of a head poked over her shoulder, but Lyla was too scared to look at the ghastly thing, no matter how dark the hallway was. She tried to call for help, but her mouth locked in place as soon as she'd opened it. The pale face slid more into her periphery, and she could do nothing but wait for it to reveal its true visage. Her bowels constricted.

"Tell me a story, Lyla," it hissed. "Tell me about *Write By Moonlighttttt.*"

Lyla lost control of her bladder and felt warm urine fill her pants and run down her thighs. The sensation was enough to pull her out of the dream.

"TELL ME A STORY!"

Lyla's eyes shot open, and she sat straight up in her bed. Her heart still thumped like it was trying to break out her chest, and she was covered in a cold sweat. It took her a second to realize she had indeed peed the bed. Her legs were saturated, and she sat in a spreading puddle of warm dampness.

"Oh, my god," she said to herself, still trying to find her footing back in the real world.

She looked around the room. Nothing had followed her out of the nightmare. Everything was exactly how she left it when she went to bed however many hours ago it had been. The bathroom light still kept the room aglow. The time display read 3:17 a.m. She sighed as the dream that had felt so real only moments ago receded back into her subconscious. As the seconds ticked away, so did the feeling that she was actually in any sort of mortal danger.

TAP. TAP. TAP.

Lyla's skin bristled. She looked at the open closet, but nothing was there. The tapping sound had come from that direction though. She stared at the closed bedroom door, imagining what stood on the other side of it.

TAP. TAP. TAP.

The glare of the phone mounted to the nightstand caught her eye, and she slowly turned to face it. She thought about the twins and how they'd told her to call if she needed anything.

TAP. TAP. TAP.

Lyla reached for it, and the bathroom light cut off. She stopped midway, frozen, as she listened to the rings on the window curtain rod slowly scrape on the left side of the room. Moonlight spilled in as it was pulled open. Her eyes found the door, still shut. Whatever had been out there was inside the room with her now.

You're dreaming. This isn't real. It's not possible.

Pick up the fucking phone!

Her hand instinctively shot forward and put the receiver to her ear. Within two beeps, one of the twins said, "Front desk."

"This is Lyla Robbins. Someone's in my room! Please come right now!"

"We're on the way."

The line went dead, and Lyla forced herself to look over her shoulder and face whatever stood behind her. She stared at the window with its curtains drawn, allowing the moonlight to fill the center of the room. There was no one there. She looked behind the curtains, expecting to see some shadowy figure watching her with a demonic grin on its face, but she didn't. She looked in the open bathroom but didn't see anyone there either. The closet and hallway doors were both shut as well.

You are fucking losing it.

Bones snapped under her bed. Lyla froze. Something bumped the bottom of her mattress. She heard claws dig into the floor as whatever was below her cracked and crawled its way toward the foot of the bed. Her comforter slowly slid off her body and fell to the floor, leaving her exposed and shaking in the middle of the bed.

Lyla wrapped her arms around her legs and waited for whatever was at the foot of her bed to jump out and attack her. The tension and stress wrought her insides like someone trying to twist the water out of a washcloth. She was so focused on that one spot she barely noticed the upside-down face outside her window. The bedroom door flung open, and the lights turned on. The twins entered; their faces were all-business like they wished someone would be stupid enough to break into Claymont on their watch.

When Lyla looked back at the window, she saw the remaining whisps of black hair pull upward.

"Out there!" she said, pointing to her left. "Someone's outside."

Mariano opened the closet door as Antonio hurried across the room and raised the window.

"Clear in here," Mariano said and then moved to the bathroom, giving it the all-clear as well.

Antonio stuck his head outside and looked down and across the yard.

"No," Lyla said. "Up."

Antonio gave her a hesitant look, and the fact that he appeared to be scared freaked her out even more. Still, he did his job, struggling to twist his massive frame in order to look up at the top of castle's exterior.

"I don't see any—"

The window dropped and went straight through his neck. Antonio's headless body slid down the wall as squirts of dark red blood erupted from his neck stump.

Lyla's eyes widened, and her jaw dropped.

"Antonio!" Mariano shouted and rushed to the body which still spasmed like it didn't know it was dying.

Linh screamed from the hallway, startling Lila out of her shocked state as Mariano, still getting coated in crimson, rocked his decapitated brother's corpse.

FIFTEEN

The next morning, every resident sat in the dining hall around the table with their breakfast. Some were eating, others just played with their food like they had no appetite, but Lyla didn't bother getting a tray. All she had was a cup of black coffee, and she couldn't even drink it without thinking of the warm fountain of blood ejaculating from Antonio's neck.

Julia and Dante were near the dining hall doors, speaking to the town's local law enforcement who had been there all morning. The two policemen had spoken to Lyla in her room when they'd first arrived. Dante had to assist with some translating because they barely spoke English. She recounted the event exactly as it had happened, saying that she heard weird noises in her room, and then she'd called the twins for help. She swore she saw someone outside of her window who hid when they entered the room. They looked around—Mariano searched the room while Antonio looked outside. That's when the window unlocked and killed the man.

Every time she paused to let Dante translate, he would look at her like she was crazy. That's how she felt, at least. Once she was finished with her statement, Julia arrived and entered the room. They all spoke Italian and gestured to different parts of the room, the window, the body, and then they all turned to look at Lyla who hadn't left her bed since the "accident."

Accident? Is that what it was.

When they finished their little powwow, Dante told her the police were going to investigate the outside area, and the authorities were on the way to clean up the body. He escorted her out and took her into Linh's room before eventually moving everyone to the dining hall.

Lyla felt her eyes getting droopy and lifted the mug to her lips, forcing herself to take a sip and block out the gruesome memory. Mariano had been sent home by Dante after giving his account of what happened which corroborated with Lyla's. She pictured him at home and wondered what it would be like to lose not just a brother, but a twin brother. And he had watched it happen. Would he ever even be able to return to this place? She knew she couldn't.

The doors squeaked open, and all the girls watched Dante escort the policemen into the hall that led to the front door of The Keep. Julia waited a moment like she was considering what to say and then walked over to the table.

"Ladies, you have the day off. The Sterlings have been made aware of the situation and are en route as we speak. You will not be expected to work today unless you want to. That is entirely your choice. I think it would be best for you all to spend the day in town while everything here cools down.

"If you choose to remain at Claymont and not go to Umbertide, we ask that you do not go beyond the first floor until The Sterlings arrive. You'll be granted one hour, starting now, to shower or get whatever you need from your rooms before going to town. They should be here before dinner; at which time they will address you all, so make sure to be back before then. I truly am sorry that this happened and for any potential inconvenience to your work."

Lyla took a drink of her coffee and then another gulp. None of what Julia said made sense to her. It all felt wrong. She took another drink even though it burned her throat.

"Where's The Reader?" Lyla blurted and then downed what was left in the mug.

The room got quiet. Julia looked like a wire short-circuited in her head.

"I'm sorry, what?"

"The Reader. The mysterious guy upstairs with a window two floors above mine. You know, the window that cut Antonio's head off?"

Several residents gasped or raised their eyebrows or looked at Lyla in disbelief, but the question and her tone elicited a visceral reaction out of the other nine girls.

"The Reader is in his quarters in The Keep, Lyla. Why do you ask?"

"Why does he get special privileges? Why isn't he down here talking to the police? Did they even question him?"

Julia cleared her throat.

"The Reader doesn't need to talk to the police because he was not involved in the accident."

"What if it wasn't an accident, though?"

Deja and Linh looked at each other and then at Lyla.

"Of course it was an accident. A very tragic one that you and Mariano both witnessed. What are you getting at with this, Lyla? Where is this coming from?"

"I'm getting at the fact that I've been seeing weird shit all over this place since I got here. But you know where things get especially weird? My room. And like I said, it's directly two floors beneath The Reader's window. I'm telling you I've seen someone at my window twice now. I saw the person right before Antonio stuck out his head. It's a bit coincidental that the window would drop right when he turned around to look up. Both times I've seen him at my window, he's been going up. I think he was waiting out there, and when Antonio saw him, he dropped the window."

Linh shook her head.

"Lyla, the windows close from the inside. That's not possible," she said.

"Read 'Murders in the Rue Morgue,' bitch. Windows can be rigged. Anything is possible."

"That's enough," Julia said. "If you don't feel safe here, you're free to leave at any point."

"Am I?"

The other girls watched their exchange like they were following a ball in a tennis match.

"Of course you are. What is that supposed to mean?"

Lyla didn't want to bring up Ann, but that was what caused her to ask that. She refrained from publicly going down that rabbit hole.

"Lyla…chill," Linh warned.

She felt everyone's eyes on her, especially Julia's. Maybe the best thing for her was to play nice for now and go to town with the girls. She could find that cute boy with the horse at his coffee shop and possibly get the locals' perspective on what's really going on at Claymont. Dante had said they hated the Sterlings and the writing residency even being in the castle. Perhaps some outside perspective on the Sterlings and the history of the castle would give her some more probing questions to ask Mr. and Mrs. Sterling when they arrived that evening.

"Forget it. I'm sorry. I just wasn't prepared for all this," Lyla said.

"You arrived at a very strange time, Lyla," Julia said. "This is not how we normally operate. I understand your frustrations. Whether you choose to visit Umbertide or stay here, come back and meet the Sterlings. Maybe they can provide more answers than I can to put your mind at ease."

Lyla nodded.

"Okay. I can do that. Sorry I called you a bitch, Linh."

"I am, though. It's cool."

"Thank you, ladies," Julia said and then directed her attention to the entire group. "Now, you all have an hour to get ready or grab anything out of your rooms. Dante and I will be around if you need anything before we close off the upper levels. Go enjoy your day off, as best you can."

Julia forced a smile, turned around, and headed for the door to the front of the castle. Once she was gone, Rachel said, "Well, that was super awkward."

Deja stood up.

"I'm assuming everyone's going to town?"

No one objected.

"Meet in The Keep in forty-five?"

The rest of the girls nodded and agreed.

Lyla didn't say anything. She stood up and walked to the door, listening as the rest of her supposed sisters followed behind her. When they entered the hallway to The Keep, none of them spoke or stopped at the snack bar. They just marched in a somber procession toward the spiral staircase and went to their rooms.

As Lyla approached her door, she hesitated, wondering what condition her room would be in. The last time she'd seen it, Antonio's corpse was still lying beside the window. She took a deep breath and opened the door.

To her surprise, the room had been detailed. There was no more blood on the wall or the windowsill. The rug that was saturated beyond repair had been removed entirely. It looked as though nothing had happened, which was fine with her. She guessed she'd have a new room-sized rug in the next day or two.

SIXTEEN

"You know what's funny?" Lyla said to Deja as the two of them walked the path to town.

The rest of the residents were broken up into different groups, all making small talk as they made their trek downhill.

"What's that?" Deja said.

"I was so excited for today. I thought of an idea for my book."

"No shit?"

She nodded.

"I know Julia said not to worry about writing today, but I need the distraction. Plus, the story excites me, and I kind of feel like doing the opposite of what Julia wants me to do right now."

Deja laughed and shook her head.

"Julia really is a good person. She's right about this being a weird time at Claymont. Everything is normally so chill."

"Must just be me then."

"I hate to break this to you, but you're not that scary for a horror writer."

Lyla smiled, and then the memory of the window guillotining Antonio's head replayed and erased her happy expression. Deja put her hand on her back. Lyla flinched, and she immediately removed it.

"Woah," Deja said. "I was just going to say everything's going to be okay."

"Sorry. My mind is in a million places right now."

Deja began walking faster and then turned around, stepping backwards as she talked.

"Then I guess we better hurry up and get your mind on something else. I have just the right café for you."

"Does a certain guy with a horse work there?"

"Ha! Only part-time. Maybe we'll get lucky today."

Lyla looked beyond Deja and the groups ahead of her and saw the end of their stone road and the beginning of Umbertide.

"It's so pretty," she said.

Deja turned and faced the city.

"Yes, it is. Just don't take it personally if anyone gives you the stink eye."

"I'm well-aware of how the locals view us."

"It's not us, necessarily. And it's definitely not all of them. There are some awesome people here who are totally down with the program. It's the Sterlings and what they represent that rile up the old guard, I guess."

"I get it."

"They sure don't mind when taking our money when we come to town, though. The tourists and the residents keep the wine flowing and the bread baking."

"Speaking of wine...are we really doing the whole winery tour thing?"

"For sure. What else are we going to do? Go back to Claymont early and sit by the pool?"

Lyla was already sweating from the walk downhill. Imagining trudging around the city and then exploring the vineyards and winery was making her feel exhausted already.

"Actually, that sounds pretty awesome, though. I've never been in an infinity pool."

"It's cool, but the novelty wears off in ten minutes. Besides, did you even grab a bathing suit from your room?"

"Nope."

They stepped onto the main road where the rest of the ladies had congregated near a fountain in the roundabout. Linh had her hands on her hips like she was trying to figure something out.

"What's going on?" Deja asked.

"Everyone wants to do something different," Linh said.

Kay, Rae, Sue, and Rachel stood in one cluster.

"We're going shopping and hitting up the chocolate shoppe first," Sue said.

"We're going to the bookstore," Lori said, referring to herself, Brittany, and Becky.

"Really?" Lyla asked. "With the library we have up there, you're still going to a bookstore?"

"Deja, bring your girl up to speed," Lori said.

Deja grinned and turned to Lyla.

"So, the bookstore has a couple of hotties working there, one of which seems to have taken a shine to Brittany. And now Becky and Lori are vying for the other one."

Lyla didn't have room to talk. She just nodded and thought about Leo possibly being at the café.

"Well, we're going to see a boy about a cup of coffee and chill there for a little bit."

"So, do we all want to meet at the winery in, what, like two hours?" Linh asked, doing her best to corral the crew.

"Sure," Becky said, apparently speaking on behalf of her delegation.

There were other indistinguishable utterances of agreement, and then they all went their separate ways.

After another mile and a half walk, they arrived at a small coffee and pastry shop on the corner of a row of colorful, aging buildings. A black fence wrapped around the outside, forming a patio with three tables filled with patrons sipping drinks and chatting, some in English, but most in Italian or other languages. A smiling female server who appeared to be about their age, if not younger, walked out of the shop and brought a platter of pastries to a trio of women who were the embodiment of tourists enjoying their retirement, each wearing pins, buttons, or hats from different European countries.

"Jackpot," Deja said.

"Huh?"

"Look. No, wait. Don't look. He's in there, but I think he just saw me point him out to you. Act cool when we go in."

Lyla was already so flustered by her potential faux pas that she just pushed her legs forward and followed Deja into the café. The intoxicating aroma of freshly brewed coffee beans and espresso mixed with the sweet scent of pastries, was overwhelming. It was like picking all of her favorite candle flavors and smelling them one after another.

That should tell you the extent of your life experience. Any frame of reference for authenticity reverts to a condensed and manufactured reproduction of its essence. You're here to capture the essence itself.

Leo did a double take when he saw the two ladies enter. He stood behind a wooden coffee bar that separated them from his collection of brewing machines, ovens, and hanging utensils. He smiled and waved them over.

Lyla led the way, cutting through the packed café until she reached the bar where there happened to be two vacant seats.

"Hello, ladies of Claymont!" Leo said.

An older woman who resembled Leo ran the register. She shot him a look like he should know better, then she glared at them and went back to completing a transaction.

"Hi," Lyla said.

"Good morning..." he said but trailed off.

Lyla was about to remind him of her name, but he cut her off.

"Lyla! Lyla Robbins. Good morning. And Miss Deja, it's always a pleasure to see you in here."

"They're not here for your coffee, son," Leo's mom said, eyes darting between the two of them.

Deja giggled and caught herself. Lyla had to turn away because of how red her cheeks were getting.

"Hi, Leo," Deja said. "What's on the menu today?"

"The joke wasn't funny the first time," Leo's mom said.

"Mama, mind your business. The till will come up short again if you get too distracted in affairs of others," he teased.

"The affairs of my son are my affairs, thank you."

"I don't get it," Lyla said. "What's the joke?"

"We've had the same menu for thirty years. Mama refuses to adjust anything on that sign up there, even the prices. We're going to go broke because of her," he said and turned to his mom. "Mama, these smart girls are here to teach you about inflation."

"And I will teach that big head of yours a lesson in deflation when I start telling stories. Don't press your luck."

Lyla could tell that their rapport was genuine, but there was a playfulness there. The mom didn't hate them. She obviously loved her son and had no problem with Claymont residents being in her establishment, even though Lyla thought she saw a couple of locals get up when they walked in.

"Just two espressos, please," Deja said.

"Sure, sure. Coming right up," he said and turned around to start the bells and whistles of what looked more like a church organ than an espresso machine.

In just a few minutes, he presented them with their gourmet drinks like an artist showing off his new masterpiece.

"Voila," he said. "You two enjoy those while I prepare a couple of other orders."

"Take your time," Lyla said and then whispered so Mama couldn't hear anything, "But there is something important I'd like to talk to you about when you get a minute. Just between us."

"Okay…" he said, eying her with an equal measure of caution and curiosity. "I'll take a smoke break in ten minutes."

As soon as he went back to making drinks, Deja turned to her.

"What was that about?"

"I just want to talk to him alone and get his perspective on Claymont and the Sterlings."

"What do you think he knows that we don't?"

"I don't know that he knows anything we don't. That's why I want to talk to him."

Deja squinted at her.

"Bullshit. That's just your excuse for getting him to talk to you," she said with a grin. "Lyla likes Leo."

Lyla blushed because Deja wasn't entirely wrong. She did want to ask Leo about Claymont. The fact that she found him attractive was beside the point. Plus, he was a local with ties to the residency, albeit in a small way, by driving the carriage up the hill. He didn't directly work for them like the kitchen staff, Dante, or the twins. If all he did was lend out his horse, he was just a contractor and would probably be less worried about what he said. He was also her age, and if he liked her, then he wouldn't hold anything back.

Before Lyla could respond, Deja nudged her.

"I get it. He's a hottie."

"Fine. You've got me pegged."

"You want to get pegged…by Leo," she laughed.

"Jesus."

Deja started to get up from the bar.

"Where are you going?"

She downed the rest of her espresso and said, "I'm going to the bookstore so you can have your moment."

"Wait, what?"

"Meet me there when you're finished. Turn left when you leave here and it's literally a ten-minute walk. You'll see the book sign."

"I didn't want you to leave."

"This is me fast-tracking you out of your comfort zone. You're welcome."

Deja winked and headed toward the exit.

"Really?"

She watched a few people glare at Deja as she passed them and then they automatically looked at her. Lyla swiveled back around and faced the bar, feeling eyes on her back whether they were really still staring at her or not.

"Where'd your friend go?" Leo asked, startling her.

"Oh, um, the bookstore." Before he could ask her why she didn't go, she said, "Hey, don't make it obvious, but are there people still staring at me?"

Leo did a quick fake stretch and looked around the café.

"Indeed, there are."

"Why? Is it just because I'm from Claymont?"

She saw the change in his happy-go-lucky demeanor.

"People heard about the accident last night. So, aside from them already not liking you, they're dealing with another Claymont accident."

"What do you mean 'another'?"

He sighed.

"Mama. I'm going for a smoke break."

"No, I need you in here, and you shouldn't smoke."

"All the orders are caught up, and Rico is in the back sitting on his butt. He can cover me for a few."

"Rico!" she yelled.

Less than three seconds later, a scrawny little teenager popped out from the back room.

"Yes, Mama?"

"Cover for your brother so he can go smoke cigarettes with American girls."

"Okay, Mama."

"I only smoke because you do," Leo said to his mom. "You shouldn't have left your cigarettes sitting out at home. I used to sneak them all the time."

"Then you work for a week for free to pay me back."

Leo laughed and untied his apron as he walked around the bar.

"Come on. Let's go."

Lyla got up and caught Leo's mom shaking her head in disapproval, but not a look of disdain like the other locals had given her. The woman had a sense of humor, and Lyla liked her immediately.

Leo exited through a side door and Lyla followed. They were in a tight alleyway between two buildings. He took out his pack of cigarettes and offered one to her. She shook her head, and he shrugged his shoulders and lit one for himself.

"So, where's Aldo while you're at work?" she asked.

"He's living his best life at home. We have a little farm just outside of town. We used to have two horses, but one died shortly after my father did."

"Oh, I'm sorry."

"It's fine. He drank and smoked too much and had a heart attack. You can see that I learned my lesson from his example."

She shook her head as he grinned and took a puff.

"So, what did you want to ask me about?"

"You work for the Sterlings. I know most of the locals hate them and the fact that they modernized a thousand-year-old castle, but are there any other things I should know about this whole situation?"

"I don't understand what you're asking. And I don't really work for the Sterlings. I've never even met them. I get paid every time I wear a suit and give a new girl a ride. That is all."

Lyla didn't know how to ask what she really wanted to ask without sounding crazy.

"Look, this is my third day in this place, and I'm already feeling like I need to catch the first flight back home. They're supposed to come to Claymont tonight, though."

Leo raised his eyebrows as all levity left his face.

"Wow. Is this because of the accident?"

"Believe it or not, the guy getting his head chopped off in my room is on the lower end of the spectrum of weird shit I've experienced since I got here."

"What's going on?"

"Fuck it, I'll just say it. I think the castle is haunted."

Leo took a long drag on his smoke.

"Why do you not look surprised?" she asked.

"Because of who you stay with at the castle."

"What's that supposed to mean?"

"Your friends. They like to play jokes on each other. I've seen them do it in here. Mama almost banned two of them because they left the third girl in their party at the table. They said they had to go to the bathroom and left her alone to pay the bill, only she didn't have money to pay. Mama called Claymont, and they paid her and assured her it would never happen again."

"Okay, yeah, that's messed up, but that's hardly the same thing as getting up in the middle of the night to play elaborate pranks on me. I mean that's commitment. And the things I've seen…I don't even think they could do them."

"Like what?"

"Lights turning on and off by themselves," she began but saw his smile.

"Okay, that wouldn't be hard to do, but doors in my room opened and shut, and I heard voices."

"And you don't think it's humanly possible for that to be done?"

She shook her head, getting frustrated, but not because he didn't believe her—in fact, he hadn't written off her claims yet. It was because he was making her doubt herself.

But the window and the library.

"Okay, try this then, myth buster. I was in the library by myself. Have you ever been in there?"

"I've been to the castle many times before it was Claymont and have visited that tower, but I've only seen the renovated library once, and that was when I had my initial meeting with Julia. I haven't been inside since."

"But you know the layout of the library, right? With its spiral staircase and bookshelf ladders?"

"Yes. I don't recall the ladders, but I remember the layout."

"Well, there are those sliding ladders on the bookshelf on each floor. I was in the library by myself, and someone slammed the door and then the fucking ladders started spinning on their own, one floor at a time."

He studied her.

"You saw them move by themselves? Like just sitting still and then moving without being touched?"

Lyla waited as long as she possibly could before responding.

"No. I just heard them. There were blind spots."

"I'm not totally convinced yet," he said with a smug smile. "But I am intrigued."

"Fine. This is the one that freaks me out the most. Two nights in a row, I saw figures in my room. Okay, you can rationalize that as my roommates messing with me even though I don't know why they would. But here's the kicker: someone was outside my window. My room is on the third floor. There were no ladders. Someone would either have to climb three stories up a castle wall or—"

"Or just come from the room above," he finished.

"Yes. That's what I think happened. The first time I saw feet crawling up the window and the second time it was someone's face hanging upside down. All I know is that the person had long hair. I couldn't tell if it was a man or a woman."

"Are there rooms on the fourth floor?"

"Yes, but it's just Dante's office/room and the Sterlings room for when they visit."

"Does Dante stay there very often, because I know the Sterlings don't come to Claymont more than once a month."

"I honestly don't know. When Julia gave me the tour, I think she alluded to the fact that he sometimes stayed overnight."

"So, if your friends knew he wasn't there, they could get into his office and mess with you from the window above you, right?"

"Sure, I guess. I don't know how or why they'd go through that much effort. Not to mention it's dangerous as hell."

"They could've put some kind of doll or mannequin or mask or something on a rope and lowered it down."

"But the legs? How would they do that?"

"Easily. Two girls would lower one girl down and pull her back up."

"But why?"

"That I don't know."

He had talked so long that he let his cigarette burn to the filter without even smoking it that much. He lit another one.

"There's another possibility," Lyla said.

"What's that?"

"The Reader."

"Oh yeah. The mysterious editor of Claymont. We've heard so many weird stories about that. Who stays locked up in a tower all day and only comes out at night?"

"I know. It's weird. But their whole philosophy and program is based around thinking outside the box, and that definitely qualifies."

"What if there is no 'The Reader', and it's really someone like Julia. Did you ever think of that?"

"Or Dante."

Leo coughed as he laughed.

"No. It's not Dante. I've known him for a while, and he's friends with my mom. If the person on the fifth floor is actually reading books and providing feedback, it's not him."

"Eww, what if it's the Sterlings themselves, and they never leave Claymont?"

"It's not them."

"How do you know?"

"Because they fly in on a helicopter. Did you not know there's a helipad behind the castle?"

"No, I didn't."

Leo nodded his head and took another drag.

"It's outside the rear wall. I know we can scientifically explain everything away even if we don't know the motivations, but it doesn't feel like that's the answer. Even if my night terrors and sleepwalking episodes are coming back because of being jetlagged, I still feel like something weird is going down there."

"Fine. I'll talk the supernatural angle with you. There are lots of people in town who all say that old castle is cursed from all the death that happened on those grounds throughout its history. There's also the 'umber' theory."

"What's that?"

"Umbria and Umbertide both got their names from the umber in the area."

"I feel like I should know what umber is," Lyla said, shaking her head.

"It's a mineral that's mined from this province. It's used as a dark pigment in stuff. But if you want to add to the cursed land theory, the Latin word umbra means shadow. So, you've got all the war and bloodshed on land that's full of literal darkness."

Lyla nodded, taking it all in.

"I personally don't believe in any of that paranormal stuff, but I will admit that there have been quite a few 'accidents' there in the short time since the Sterlings bought it," Leo said.

"What have you heard?"

"Well, aside from Antonio last night, three residents have died in the last five years. The last one was just a few months ago."

"Ann."

"Yeah, her. She got ran over by a taxi right outside the gate."

"Wait, you just said three? When did those happen?"

"I heard one girl committed suicide and another one was drunk and broke her neck falling down the cellar stairs."

"Holy shit. Why didn't any of the other girls tell me about them?"

"That was in the first year of operation. Maybe they just don't know. If I was running that place, I certainly wouldn't advertise something like that. Would you?"

"I guess not."

"Leonardo!" Leo's mom yelled from inside the building.

"Break's over," he said, dropping his cigarette and snubbing it out with his shoe.

"Shoot. I feel like I have even more questions to ask now," Lyla said with somewhat of a smile.

Talking with Leo and hearing what he'd said had made her feel less alone, less frightened.

"Well, I don't work every day. I know you all have strict rules and curfews, but I wouldn't mind sitting down with you and chatting again."

Lyla felt her face flush, and the realization only made it worse.

"I'd like that."

"Cool. Just let me know when, and we'll figure it out."

"Okay."

He turned to the door but stopped.

"And Lyla, don't leave. See what the Sterlings have to say tonight. Maybe even talk to them about your concerns."

"I think I'll do that."

"Good. I like to read scary stuff, you know. If it's not against their rules, I'd love to read anything you write."

"That'd be really cool. I appreciate it."

"Have a good rest of your day. And ignore any dirty looks from any of the townspeople. Some of them don't have anything better to do than gossip and complain."

"I'll try. Thank you, Leo."

"Leonardo, get your behind back in this kitchen right now or find new job!" his mom barked from behind the side door.

He went wide-eyed and said, "Gotta go."

Lyla smiled and turned away, walking back to the main street to turn left and hopefully find the bookstore.

SEVENTEEN

Lyla had managed to lose herself in the day, and for that, she was grateful. After catching up with the girls at the bookstore and checking out various shops in Umbertide, they all took the tour of the local vineyard, some of them sampling way more than she did. In those moments of walking through the vines with the sunshine on the back of her neck and the gentle breeze that rustled the plants, she felt fully in the present moment. The events at the castle might as well have happened a hundred years ago and a million miles away.

They finished the day in the vineyard's sunroom, sampling different cheeses—some great, some not so great—and sharing their final bottles of wine. Lyla was laughing again. She wasn't thinking about returning to Claymont or writing her story. She wasn't thinking about the strange things she'd experienced or even about the man who had died in her room. No, the intoxication of her surroundings and their collective joy overpowered any anxieties that might have other-wise plagued her mind. The thought of leaving the residency was a distant memory.

One of them, Lyla couldn't remember who had actually been the responsible one in the party, broke up the revelry and reminded them that they only had two hours until dinner was served. They needed to be back at the castle before dinner because the Sterlings were coming. The sobering realization of why the philanthropic couple were making an emergency visit came flooding back to them all, and they trudged up the hill with the sun beating at their backs and their bellies full of cheese, wine, and pastries was quite different than the giddy mood at the winery.

When they reached the castle gates, the sound of a helicopter whirring in the distance made them all look toward the tree line to their left.

"And here come the Sterlings," Linh said.

The rest of the girls kept walking along the path to the entrance to The Keep, but Lyla stood still, staring at the source of the noise that continued to get louder until the helicopter finally flew over the forest and hovered above the castle. It was all black and smaller than she figured it would be until it began its descent. She watched it grow bigger and bigger until it disappeared behind the castle, and she was left staring at the top of The Keep.

A dark-haired figure stood in the fifth-floor window. Lyla gasped. Was that The Reader? She didn't know. She wanted to shout at the group of girls in front of her, but they'd already entered The Keep as evidenced by the crescent-shaped door closing behind them, causing Lyla to flinch. But she didn't break her gaze from the person staring back at her. The Reader, who didn't look like a man at all, just watched her, motionless. She couldn't see much of the figure, even in the setting sun. Long black hair draped over a white face and what looked like the top of a white dress. Shadows concealed the rest.

In that moment, Lyla somehow knew that this was the person who had been in her room the last two nights. Lyla got a cold chill that made her body spasm involuntarily. The Reader mimicked the motion.

"What the fuck?" she whispered, and if she had better vision, she would've sworn the person in the window's mouth moved as well.

Lyla tilted her head to the side and watched the figure do the same. She moved her head the other way, and the dark-haired head in the window moved with it. It was as if she was looking in a mirror. She took a step forward, but the woman—yes, it was definitely a woman— took a step backward. Lyla didn't anticipate that, and she didn't want to lose the moment, whatever the moment was, so she took a step back. The Reader did the same.

She decided to take this little experiment a step farther and raised her hand. A pale and thin arm appeared in the darkness of the window. Lyla waved, and the elongated hand did the same. The sight of the skeletal fingers made her stomach turn.

"Lyla, what are you doing?"

She jumped and looked at Deja standing at the front doors, hanging half in and half out.

"I…" she said and immediately glanced back at the dark window. *Shit!*

"Were you waving at the helicopter?" she laughed.

Lyla let her gaze drift back down to her friend. She blinked and tried to compose herself.

Just walk and breathe.

"I thought I saw someone wave at me from the helicopter," she said as she headed to her friend, occasionally glancing up but seeing nothing.

"Hurry up. We're allowed in our rooms now, and we have like an hour to get ready."

Lyla approached the door.

"Get ready for what? The dinner?"

"Yes. You have to dress up."

"Wait. What?"

"Oh, I guess I shouldn't have phrased it like that. You *get* to dress up. Check out your new wardrobe when you get up there. We get all these fancy outfits and dresses to choose from when the Sterlings arrive. I swear, each one must be over a thousand dollars. They're all designer clothes from France that Julia curates."

"Wow."

"Wow, indeed."

"I'm kind of shocked that Julia didn't mention that part of the program. She told me everything else."

"Probably the same reason why she doesn't tell you about the carriage ride to the castle…the element of surprise."

Deja and Lyla walked upstairs and went to their rooms. Lyla

approached hers with an air of caution, reaching for the doorknob and then hesitating. She took a deep breath and walked through. Aside from everything being clean like a five-star hotel's room service just blew through, nothing seemed out of the ordinary. She shut the door behind her and looked to her right.

The closet light was on, and true to Deja's word, a completely new wardrobe hung from one of the metal bars. She looked at the five gorgeous dresses and then over to her clothes hanging beside them and felt two inches tall. Her graphic T-shirts and what she considered to be her fancy clothes looked like clothes Goodwill wouldn't accept compared to what the Sterlings had purchased for her.

It's just money. They're not better people than you. You deserve to be here.

Lyla let her hands drift across each dress, feeling the different fabrics and materials. It was uncanny that the dresses were exactly her style. If she had the money to purchase whatever fancy dresses she wanted, she suspected they would look like these.

How did they know that? How did they know your measurements?

"Fuck it," she said and grabbed one of the hangers to take the dress she liked the most into the bedroom and gently laying it on her bed.

She knew she needed to try it on, but she didn't dare with the long day of walking and sweating that she'd had. Just as she began to undress, she noticed the shoe rack also contained some new footwear. It was like the Santa Claus of fashion had visited her room while she'd been away.

"Wow."

She picked up a black pair of high heels and put them on the floor beside the bed. They complimented the white dress with its black satin trim.

White dress.

An image of the woman at the window two floors above her broke the momentary high she was riding while checking out her new items. She looked around the room from a completely different lens. The negative feeling—the impending doom—was palpable. A blanket of dread dropped on her like an unexpected downpour.

Someone knocked at the door. Lyla spun around and hurried across the room, grateful just to have an encounter with another human being to break up the nightmare circus in her mind.

"Lyla, it's Linh."

She opened the door.

"Hey! Oh, I see you already found your goodies. That dress is gorgeous," she said as she walked in the room. "Do you care if I look at the rest? I'm a sucker for fashion, and I just love looking at everyone's new clothes when the Sterlings arrive. 'Sterling Day,' I guess you could call it."

There was something cheerfully upbeat about Linh's enthusiasm. Normally, she was pretty chill and laid back. Lyla had never seen her this excited about anything, not even weed.

"Sure. Have at it," she said, but Linh was already turning toward the closet.

"Holy shit! These are killer dresses. Gorgeous. And they totally fit your personality, too, you know?"

"Oh yeah?" Lyla chuckled. "What's my personality?"

"Well, you're a horror writer, so you deal a lot of good and evil type of themes I'm guessing?"

"I mean, yeah. Sometimes. I guess if you boil the conflicts in the horror genre down to one central theme it's light versus darkness."

"Exactly. Hence all the stark white and black contrasts in these three dresses and the one on the bed. But there's more to you than just what you like to write about, and we can never fall victim to the belief that we are what we write, so that brings us to these golds and yellows."

Lyla put her hands on her hips, genuinely curious about where Linh was going with this. "You're reserved, but not in an antisocial way. You have an observant nature, but not a judgmental one—what happened at our first breakfast aside," she said with a laugh.

Lyla nodded.

"You're a reluctant optimist," Linh said.

"That's an interesting phrase."

"You're not naïve, though. You're a realist but not cynical, despite your best efforts. Deep down you have faith in the goodness of people.

And despite your chosen genre—or the one that chose you, rather—you believe in happy endings."

Lyla suddenly felt like she had underestimated her neighbor's emotional intelligence. She had never felt so seen or understood. Everything she said was right, when Lyla really thought about it.

"I gotta admit, I'm impressed. That's pretty spot-on. How did you determine all that just from a few dresses?" Lyla asked, shaking her head.

Linh turned away from the clothes and faced her. She smiled and held the smile. She didn't blink. It was like someone just hit the pause button on her.

"Earth to Linh," she said.

Her smile expanded. She finally blinked.

"Do you believe in Heaven?" she asked, still with that awkward expression.

"What?"

"Heaven," she said, taking a step closer to her. "Do you believe that's where we go when we die?"

"Why are you asking me this right now? Does it have something to do with the color of my clothes?" Lyla asked, with a nervous chuckle.

Linh didn't respond, only stared with that emotionless smile.

Has she always had blue eyes? No, there's no way. She had brown eyes that matched her hair. How the hell are her eyes blue?

"Are you wearing contacts?" Lyla asked.

Linh shook her head.

Lyla cocked her head, analyzing her friend. Linh mirrored the same motion. Lyla's blood ran cold. She pictured the woman on the fifth floor doing the same thing.

Right before Lyla could say anything, there was an audible *WHOOSH* in the room, and Linh's expression dropped. Her entire demeanor changed. She looked confused like she didn't know where she was.

"Linh, are you okay?"

Linh startled and stared at her like Lyla had an explanation for her odd behavior.

"Lyla? What are you doing in my room?"

Lyla was about to correct her, but didn't have the chance.

"Wait, this isn't my room. Why am I in *your* room?" she asked, shaking her head.

"I don't know. You just knocked on the door and said you wanted to look at my dresses."

"I did?"

"Yeah. You gave me a full psychological breakdown on the colors of my dresses and how they matched my personality, which was surprisingly accurate. You really don't remember that?"

"No," she said, rubbing her temples. "The last thing I remember, I was in my closet, looking through my clothes. And now I'm over here. What the fuck, Lyla?"

Lyla shrugged her shoulders.

"Did you smoke anything today?"

"No, I'm not high. And even if I was, I wouldn't completely lose time like this."

"You drank a lot earlier, and we walked and hiked for miles. Maybe you're dehydrated or something. I don't know."

"Shit. What time is it?" she asked but didn't wait on Lyla to answer.

She glanced at the clock and seemed relieved.

"Okay, we've only been back for like twenty minutes. It wasn't as bad as last time."

As soon as she said that she looked like she wished she hadn't.

"What do you mean? This has happened before?"

All of this could explain what's been going on in Lyla's room. If Linh had some kind of condition like narcolepsy where she zoned out and didn't remember anything, she could be the mystery figure she's been seeing.

But what about Kay looking at you from the side of the library tower? She had that same smile on her face.

You don't know that for sure. You were too far away. And why would that matter anyway?

"It's happened once," Linh finally said. "Back when Ann had your room. I never told anybody, and neither did Ann."

"What happened?"

"It was a few nights before Ann left. I went to sleep in my room and woke up to her yelling at me. I was so confused. I didn't know where I was. Plus, I was standing up. When I saw her in bed, I realized I'd somehow walked into her room and had absolutely no memory of doing it."

"Why was Ann screaming?"

Linh looked down and clasped her hands and immediately unclasped them like she was trying to act natural and failing miserably at it.

"Linh, what happened?"

"She said I was talking in my sleep, and I woke her up. She said my eyes were open, and I kept saying her name and asking about her story. How freaking weird is that? Like, I've never been a sleepwalker in my life. And then I come here, and I've done it twice now? To this room? What's that all about?"

"Twice that you know of."

"Huh?"

"These two incidents are just the times when you woke the person up. Well, I wasn't asleep, but you know what I mean."

"Do you think I've done it more than that? This is giving me the heebie-jeebies, man."

"You? I'm the one whose room you came in. You didn't think to tell me this when I told you that I thought someone was in my room the first two nights here? Jesus fuck, it was you, Linh!"

"No," she said shaking her head, refusing to accept it. "Didn't you say you thought the person was outside your window?"

"Yeah. And your window is right beside mine."

"Oh, so you think I sleepwalked across the outside of a castle? I'm literally the most uncoordinated person that I know. I can't tell you how many times I've nearly tripped walking downstairs."

Lyla thought about Kay's smile and how it matched perfectly with Linh's. She thought about the figure on the fifth floor.

"Linh, have you ever seen a woman upstairs?"

"What do you mean 'upstairs'?"

"The fifth floor. The Reader's floor."

"No..."

"You've never seen anyone at the window on the front of The Keep?"

"No. Have you?"

Lyla hesitated to say anything. A sudden realization that someone could be watching or listening to her at that very moment unsettled her. She looked around the room for hidden cameras and microphones but didn't see anything suspicious.

"Because if you have," Linh began, "You wouldn't be the first one to have spotted The Reader, if that's who she even saw."

"Who?"

"Ann."

"Ann saw The Reader?"

"I'm saying that Ann saw someone in the window on her way back from a walk one night. She was by herself though. That's why none of us believed her. And she had been acting really weird the last week before she left."

"Weird like how?"

"Like paranoid. She kind of withdrew from all of us. That wasn't how she was when I first met her. She was like really happy-go-lucky and totally on top of her shit, but the days leading up to when she... died, it's almost like she knew something bad was going to happen to her. My theory is that she had her thing with Dante, and one of them ended it. I'm guessing it was him, and she just went into full-on depressed writer mode."

"Depressed enough to kill herself by jumping in front of a taxi?"

"I don't know. Maybe."

"Seems like an odd way to do it, especially with a perfectly good window to jump out of," Lyla said and immediately regretted phasing it like a dark joke.

She also thought about what Ann must've felt, if she really did get dumped by Dante, to have to leave the residency. She was apparently so ashamed that she did it in the middle of the night. Maybe she had parents like hers who she knew she would let down if she flew back to the States, having dropped out of the residency. Maybe, just maybe, she called for that taxi with every intention of going home, and the guilt and shame she felt at seeing the cab arrive set in. She must have felt so trapped, too ashamed to go forward and too prideful to turn around. Perhaps she made an impulsive decision, living up to the old adage of suicide being a permanent solution to a temporary problem. Maybe she just jumped into the light and ended it all.

But what about what Dante told you? He said he saw camera footage of her running like she was being chased. He said that he knew Ann, and she wouldn't ever do a thing like that.

Do you really trust a guy like Dante though? An attractive man in a position of power at a residency full of young women who was only made hotter by the fact that he had no competition in the building other than the kitchen staff. Even if he was seeing Ann, that's completely unprofessional and would've gone against everything the program stood for as far as not having any distractions. There's no way Julia would've allowed him to keep his job if she knew about it.

Holy shit! What if Ann was going to tell someone? What if Dante was scared that he would lose his job if she talked? What if he had something to do with Ann's death that night, and everything he'd told you was a lie?

"Jesus, I can't deal with this shit," Lyla said and rubbed the sides of her head. "So, Ann said she saw The Reader. What did she say he or she looked like?"

"She said she saw a woman up there. Everyone knows The Reader is a dude, so we didn't know what to think when she told us that."

"Why does everyone assume The Reader is a man?"

Linh seemed to think about that for a moment.

"Well, all the people who work at Claymont refer to The Reader with male pronouns, even the Sterlings."

"Shit," Lyla said. "The Sterlings are here, and we need to get ready and go downstairs. We'll continue this conversation later."

"Yeah, okay," Linh said turning toward the door. "I'll meet you down there. And Lyla?"

"Yeah?"

"Please don't tell the other girls about this...like any of it, but especially about me somehow sleepwalking in here when I wasn't even asleep. I don't want people looking at me like I'm a freak."

"I won't. Don't worry."

Lyla knew the feeling all too well.

EIGHTEEN

Lyla stepped out of her room and met Linh waiting on her. A few of the other residents talked from the staircase, all of them seeming to be headed to the dining hall at the same time.

"You clean up well," Linh said, eyeballing Lyla from head to toe. "I really love those shoes on you. I couldn't pull them off, but you do."

"Thanks. You look nice, too."

"Okay, we better get going."

"Lead the way," Lyla said.

After a few paces her heart began to beat faster, and she felt her mouth getting dry. They reached the staircase, and her hands were doing that clammy thing she hated. She suddenly felt hot, and worried she would start sweating from nervousness and the fact the spiral staircase just had an extra blanket of humidity that only intensified the earthy, floral scent of the freshly cut flowers tucked in vases mounted to the walls.

When did they do that? It must've been while we were in town. Is it some kind of weird memorial to Antonio?

"I don't know why I'm so nervous all of the sudden," she said, knowing from past experience that vocalizing her fears always soothed her anxiety and took some of its power away.

"You don't need to be nervous. The Sterlings are lovely people. Seriously, they're like the sweet parents you wish you had."

Lyla laughed and said, "But I have sweet parents."

She wished she hadn't said that as soon as it came out of her mouth.

"Well, both of mine are total assholes, so consider yourself lucky. They haven't forgiven me for switching majors and that was over five years ago. It's fair to say that they hold a grudge."

They approached the second-floor landing where Deja was hurrying down the hall.

"Hold up!" she said, doing a little speed walk to the staircase.

"Don't trip on your dress. We have plenty of time."

"So what was your original major?"

"Huh? Oh, they had my future laid out for me to go to med school and follow in the family footsteps of being a doctor. Mom is a neurologist, and Dad is a plastic surgeon."

"Wow. Those are big shoes to fill."

"Eh, sometimes. I guess to other people they're heroes, but unless I had a stroke or needed a tummy tuck, they never paid much attention to me anyway."

Deja finally met them.

"Hey, guys. Oh, my gosh. You both look so pretty," she said.

"Thanks," Lyla said. "I love your hair."

They resumed their descent. Linh stopped and turned around, addressing Lyla.

"Okay, I was going to tell you this before we came down here, but you started talking about being nervous, and I didn't know if I should, but I don't want you to be caught off guard, so just know that when the Sterlings visit, they always greet us at the bottom of the stairs."

"What?"

"Don't worry about it," Deja said. "They're people just like us. If you start to feel intimidated, just remember that everybody shits. Some just do it on ten-thousand-dollar toilets."

Lyla muffled her laugh as they rounded the final curve into the lit portion of the stairs from the chandeliers of the hallway. And true to

Linh's word, there they were. Both of them were supposed to be in their sixties but looked twenty years younger.

Generational wealth is good for your health. That should be a bumper sticker. Note that as a quote for later.

A tall man with a blue suit, matching bowtie, and a head of perfectly coiffed salt and pepper hair stood beside a woman with such a regal posture, Lyla didn't know if she should bow or curtsy in her presence. The woman's dress was ruby red and sparkled under the chandeliers' lights. Her hair was styled in a way that reminded Lyla of Grace Kelly, one of her favorite actresses ever since she watched *Rear Window* with her dad when she was in middle school. She didn't want to guess how much the necklace on the woman's surgically enhanced chest cost, nor the diamond earrings that hung down like little reminders that there was rich, and then there was wealthy.

Both of them had radiant white smiles, greeting Rae and Brittany as the two of them walked on the red carpet toward the dining hall. Linh was the first to step off the staircase. She slowed her pace until the Sterlings turned back in her direction.

"Good evening, Linh," Mr. Sterling said with a voice as deep as it was soothing.

"Hello."

"Linh, you are looking radiant as always," Mrs. Sterling said.

"Thank you, and you as well."

"Oh, you're too kind, darling. We'll see you in the dining hall," she said, and Linh kept walking.

Once Linh passed them, she turned back to Lyla who was approaching the couple, and mimed like she was sucking a dick. That instantly broke the illusion and brought out the absurdity of the entire situation. She did her best to keep from cracking up, which she hoped came out as just a friendly smile as she looked into Mr. Sterling's eyes for the first time.

"Why, hello. You must be Lyla Robbins. My name is Lester Sterling, and this is my lovely wife, Regina. We're so pleased to finally meet you," he said and extended his hand.

"The pleasure is all mine," Lyla said nervously as she shook both of their hands.

She didn't know why she said that. She'd never said it before. It just seemed like the right thing to say in fancy situations.

"I do appreciate you coming. It's always exciting and inspiring to meet a young new writer on her way to greatness," Regina said.

Lyla blushed.

"Oh, I don't know about that. I just hope to get my novel written."

"You will," Lester said with a nod. "That's why you're here. We read your submission."

"Brilliant," Regina said with a warm smile.

"Oh, wow. Thank you."

"Dinner will be ready soon. You better go grab a seat," Lester said.

Lyla realized there were a few girls lined up behind her and got the message that she needed to move it along.

"Yes, thank you both for accepting me. I love it here."

She wasn't sure why she said that either. She didn't love Claymont. She loved the idea when she'd first discovered it, but the last few days have been anything but a relaxing writer's retreat.

"It's our pleasure," Regina said and ushered her toward the dining hall doors that were propped open.

The closer Lyla got to the massive hall, the more she was overcome by the smell of whatever heavenly dish was being served that night. As soon as she stepped inside and saw a few of her friends sitting at the candlelit tables with nothing but empty plates in front of them, she knew something was different. She looked toward the kitchen and saw that the metal buffet windows were pulled down, but a sliver of light shone along the crack at the bottom. People were preparing food. Normally, the kitchen staff made quite a racket while they worked— talking, barking orders at each other in Italian, clanging and washing dishes—so she assumed that the retractable windows were down to eliminate any distractions from the Sterlings' presentation.

Lyla walked across the hall to the table on her left where Sue, Brittany, and Linh had already been seated. Classical music played from unseen speakers at just the right level. She sat beside Linh and looked at the door to see Deja coming in with Rachel behind her. Once everyone filed in, five girls sat at one table and five at the other. The muted chandeliers and tabletop candlelight illuminated the large stone room and its elegant paintings, banners, statues, and what Lyla assumed was a family crest on the wall.

The kitchen doors opened, and a line of servants wearing the finest uniforms Lyla had seen since her arrival marched while carrying covered plates, platters of side dishes, and bottles of wine and water. In a whirl of synchronized servantry, all of their glasses got filled and plates with sterling silver lids appeared in front of them with rolled cutlery.

The dining hall doors opened again, and the girls turned to see Dante, Julia, and the Sterlings enter the room and approach a square shaped table that had recently been put there and must only be used for occasions such as this. They stood by the already prepared table. Lester faced the residents and smiled.

"Well, don't let us keep you waiting. Dig in, ladies. Dinner is served!"

They sat down and began talking, which seemed to give the cue for the residents to do the same. The servants came by and removed the plate covers one-by-one, revealing a breathtaking plate of steak, lobster tail, asparagus, and a side salad. Lyla looked at the dishes in the middle of the table and saw breadsticks, corn on the cob, bowls of noodles, and condiments and dressings. She'd been so nervous walking downstairs that she'd almost retched, but now all that fear was gone, and she'd never been so hungry in her life. The girls smiled at each other and began to dig in.

Lyla had never had such delicious food in her life. She thought she had when she sampled the first offerings Claymont served, but she figured they must really break out the good stuff when the Sterlings were there. She ate everything on her plate, as did most of the other girls, and they were now all on their second or third glasses of wine and savoring the merriment.

Everything was perfect and almost distracting enough to make her forget that a man had been decapitated in her room earlier. She felt a pang of guilt, looking around for Mariano but knowing he wouldn't be there. She wondered if he'd ever return to the job. God knows she wouldn't want to work at a place where a loved one died.

A low whirring sound came from Lyla's left, where the main stage was.

"What the hell is that?" she wondered aloud and saw the source of the sound as soon as she asked the question.

A white screen that rivaled the size of any she'd ever seen in a theater slowly descended from its dispensing bar near the ceiling until the bottom of it stopped a few inches before touching the stage. The same THE CLAYMONT RESIDENCY FOR WRITERS logo that was on the front gate filled the blank canvas.

"What's going on now?" Lyla whispered to Linh.

Linh turned back toward her and said, "You're about to learn a little bit more about Lester and Regina Sterling."

A somberness lingered in Linh's tone. Everyone had been so cheerful and was having a good time. She knew the reason why the Sterlings moved their monthly visit to today, and she was already feeling bad for enjoying herself.

Lester Sterling stood from his chair and helped Regina do the same. They walked down the center of the tables toward the stage which, Lyla just noticed, had no podium anymore. She had been so distracted by the screen that seemed to emerge from out of nowhere that she didn't notice a microphone stand had replaced the wooden podium. The couple walked the three steps onto the stage and stood front and center.

"Testing," Lester said, and his deep voice came from the unseen speakers that had previously been playing classical music.

Sue and Lori jumped because they had still been talking and were completely oblivious to the Sterlings taking the stage.

"I guess it's working," he said, giving the ladies a chuckle.

Lyla's smile widened when she realized he had a sense of humor.

"Good evening, ladies. Nine of you know me, and one of you just met me, but I'll say it anyway, I am Lester Sterling, and this is my lovely wife of thirty years, Regina."

Regina, at his side, leaned into the microphone and said, "Hello, everyone."

There were muffled greetings and waves from the two tables.

"Hello," Lyla said, following suit.

Lester stepped forward again.

"As it is custom at Claymont for us to formally welcome new residents and for me to give my little talk, I believe it would be in poor taste if we didn't acknowledge the tragedy that occurred this morning."

The room was deathly silent.

"Antonio Dinardi, one of our beloved staff members…no, one of our family, died unexpectedly today. Many of you knew Antonio and interacted with him as he and his brother, Mariano, played many roles here at Claymont, not to mention their larger-than-life personalities. I am truly sorry for the loss that everyone in this room has suffered, and especially to Mariano, who is not with us tonight. He's understandably home with family. Dante and Julia will be pulling double duty until we hire additional help, so take it easy on them. Well, maybe not Dante, but give Julia a break."

There was a slight chuckle that eased the tension in the room. Julia looked at their table behind her and saw Dante with his hands up in a what-did-I-do? kind of gesture.

"I'm kidding. We all love Dante. Show him extra grace because we know how grumpy he can be under the best of circumstances."

"No argument there," Dante said from the back, which spurred more faint laughter.

"In all seriousness, this tragedy should never have occurred, and the windows in all rooms were inspected today by local contractors. Each one was checked and checked again. We could not get the window that malfunctioned to replicate what happened, but we replaced it anyway. Above all else, everyone's safety is priority number one. If you don't feel safe, everything else is irrelevant. And safety comes in various forms: physical and emotional. If any of you have concerns about anything or anyone in this building, feel free to address me or Regina, and we will handle it. You don't have to do it right now. We will be here for the week, and I hope, for the residents who have been with us since our last visit, that you feel comfortable enough to approach us with such concerns. Are we clear on that?"

Some girls nodded, some replied, "Yes," but everyone acknowledged the sentiment.

"And now for my regular speech that I do, not only to properly inform new residents, but to remind current residents of why you all are here and hopefully provide inspiration and motivation during times when you just don't feel like writing. I, myself, am not an author. My brain is numbers, not letters, I like to say. Regina is the same way."

She nodded.

"However, our daughter, Janie, was a writer. She did not take after us. From the day that girl could lift a crayon she was expressing herself creatively in one medium or the next. In early elementary school, she found her true calling: writing. She started by writing and illustrating her own books. She would draw her little stories on white paper and staple them together. I can't tell you how many of those she wrote.

"As she matured, so did her writing abilities and ambitions. Janie began writing short stories. She always excelled in English classes and even formed a creative writing club in middle school. I remember getting a call from a guidance counselor when Janie was in seventh grade," he said with a growing smile. "The counselor was concerned about Janie and wanted us to come in and meet with her and the principal about her stories. I remember laughing because I knew exactly what it was about, but at these private schools you have to play by their rules even though you're the ones keeping them in business.

"So we go to this meeting, and the principal pulls out one of Janie's stories and handed it to me—to us, Regina and I. 'No Escape' was the title. I'll never forget that. It was about a teenager who became possessed by the devil and shot up her school."

Lyla widened her eyes.

Well, no shit you'd get a phone call home.

"We explained to them that Janie writes about lots of things across many genres, but horror was primarily her favorite. She drew on the real-life horrors and combined them with genre fiction. The principal even said that although it was highly disturbing, it was one of the most well-written and effective stories she'd ever read…from anyone. They knew Janie well enough to know she was not a threat. They were just doing their due diligence by having the meeting, but she couldn't write about school shootings or anything that could be misconstrued if it fell into the wrong hands.

"Janie just sat there the whole time, listening, taking it all in and contemplating her response as she often did. When the principal asked her if she would comply with that, Janie said no, and she was quitting the creative writing club, effectively ending it since she ran it. I remember her saying, 'I'm not going to censor myself because some people can't tell the difference between fact and fiction.' That commitment—that borderline defiance—I know she got that from me. Without it, I never would've made anything of myself, but it has its pitfalls."

She likes horror, and she doesn't hold back. She sounds awesome.

"We never received any more concerned phone calls after that. Janie went on to graduate high school as the valedictorian. She went to New York University and studied writing. She could've gone to any school in the country on a full academic scholarship, and that's the one she chose. We lived in the Upper East Side of New York, so it took us by surprise that she wanted to stay close to home. We certainly didn't mind, though.

"She hit the ground running like we knew she would. But we noticed a change in her demeanor with each passing semester. She said she was working on a novel in her free time. She seemed so withdrawn. She would talk about her friends, but we never met any of them when she came to visit. By the time she graduated, she was living in her own apartment downtown. It was obvious that she was in poor mental health.

"When we found out she didn't apply for graduate school and had no plan, we confronted her. She said she was depressed but claimed it was because of her novel. We said she should apply to an MFA program the next semester, and she finally admitted she'd stopped working on her novel. She said she became too distracted and had picked up a new habit."

Lyla leaned forward, seeing the tears forming on Lester's face as Regina looked down and wiped her eyes.

"We knew something was wrong, but we had no idea our daughter had resorted to drugs. We arranged for her to go to treatment, and she was willing. Janie stayed with us that night. We found her dead the next morning. It was ruled as an accidental overdose. That was six years ago."

Lyla didn't realize she was crying. She didn't understand how Lester wasn't bawling and then remembered that he'd given this speech many times and has probably worked his way through it by now. Regina wiped her eyes again and looked up, standing strong as she faced the small crowd.

"You see…" Lester began, losing some of that bass from his voice as he struggled to keep it together. "Writing was everything to Janie. She had so much potential, such a promising future ahead of her, but she lost her voice. She never got to tell her story.

"We were obviously shocked and devastated by her passing, and losing a child is something no parent ever gets over. You just learn to live with it and try to honor your child's memory to the best of your ability.

"Ladies, this is the reason you're sitting here tonight. We knew that we couldn't just let our grief eat at us. Janie wouldn't want that. And so, we did what we thought she would want us to do. We created a space where young writers can come and be away from the distractions of the bustle of everyday life. Our mission was to provide a safe haven for residents to worry about nothing but their art. Maybe if Janie had had a fairy tale castle in the heart of Italy to go to and write, things would have turned out differently.

"Regina and I purchased this historic property and turned it into a livable residence. All of the luxury amenities are here for you because I believe one of my daughter's favorite novels says, 'All work and no play makes Jack a dull boy.' Am I correct on that, Lyla?"

Lyla froze when she heard him directly address her. She felt like the teacher had randomly called on her in class to solve an equation. But she quickly shook it off with a nervous laugh and said, "That's correct. Great book, too."

Lester turned to Regina and said, "Since Lyla is our resident horror writer, I had to quote Stephen King to try and impress her."

Regina shook her head and leaned toward the microphone.

"He does that to every new resident, Lyla."

Lyla breathed a sigh of relief as the ladies surrounding her nodded.

"Yes, and I will keep doing it," he said with a wink. "Where was I? Oh yes, so we bought the castle and quickly realized we knew nothing about writing or mentorships and programs. But we knew plenty of famous authors, some of the most respected and acclaimed authors working today. We made an arrangement with one of them, but they insisted on remaining anonymous, fearing that knowledge of their identity would alter the purity of the process.

"They didn't want anyone writing what they thought would appeal to them or fear writing something that wouldn't appeal to them. This author insisted on just being referred to as 'The Reader', and we understood and agreed. This is why The Reader lives in seclusion. The air of mystery and intrigue of an unknown editor living in a one-thousand-year-old castle only excited us more, and we knew Janie would love it.

"Our next task was finding someone to organize this crazy idea, someone creative and passionate enough to design a program that best suited the needs *and* the wants of our potential residents. And that's when we brought Julia onboard."

The girls clapped and turned to look back at Julia at her table with Dante. She smiled and blew a kiss.

"Yes, give her all the praise she deserves," Lester continued. "Our final piece of the puzzle was to hire a local to Umbria to be our Program Director. We truly lucked out when Dante came to us. If you haven't noticed already, Dante is one of the most handy, pragmatic, and effective people I've ever had the pleasure of employing, and I've ran several *Fortune* 500 companies. Let's hear it for our Jack-of-all-trades, Dante."

Everyone applauded and turned around again as Dante stood up and took an exaggerated bow and sat back down. He held up his wine glass in toast and then gulped the rest.

"Those two are the heart and brain of Claymont. The rest of our staff, from the kitchen, to security, to the grounds crew, they are the bones that keep everything together. You all, however, are the soul of this place. I thank you all for your service and dedication to a program that means so much to me and my wife and, hopefully, to you residents as well."

Everyone clapped until Lester gave a gesture for them stop.

"I'll wrap this up so you all can immediately go to bed and get your rest like I know you will…" he said with a smirk and a raised eyebrow.

Lyla watched her friends laugh in mock agreement as Lester just nodded his head.

"In summation, I want us to honor the memory of not just our daughter, Janie, but Antonio as well as past residents, by proceeding with business-as-usual tomorrow. They would want you to keep working, keep writing, keep enjoying life. I've already spoken to The Reader, and we are in agreement as well. However, if you feel like you need more time to process this loss, The Reader suggested to waive all writing goals for the week as an option. You're still welcome to submit your work, and The Reader will edit and return it like always. Sound fair enough?"

Everyone nodded.

"Okay then. Enough of me. Regina did you have anything to add?"

She forced a smile and leaned toward the mic.

"I just want to thank you all again for being here. You have no idea what your presence truly means to our family. Like Lester said, we'll be here all week. Feel free to talk to us about anything. I hope you all have a better day tomorrow. Oh, and Lyla," she said.

Lyla snapped to attention for the second time that evening.

"Welcome to Claymont. We expect nothing but greatness from you."

NINETEEN

At nine-thirty, Lyla went on the patio with Linh and Deja. She didn't want to drink too much. The Sterling's dinner speech had reinvigorated her sense of purpose. She planned to get a good night's rest, wake up early, and get to work on her novel. The only reason she was even still downstairs was because Lester and Regina were mingling about, taking the time to talk briefly with each resident like seasoned dinner party hosts. It was only a matter of time before they made their way to her, and she needed to talk about some things before they did.

"Guys, why didn't you tell me about the Sterling's daughter?" she asked her two friends who were sitting on either side of her at the patio table.

"Janie?" Deja asked.

"Well, who else would I be talking about?"

"Who wants to talk about that?" Linh said. "It's fucking depressing. And Julia told us not to mention her until the Sterlings gave their introduction speech thingy."

"Yep," Deja said. "She'll tell you the same thing. It's part of the program, as she likes to say."

"That's so fucking sad."

"It is what it is," Linh said.

"I related to what Lester said Janie went through though. There were so many similarities that it creeped me out."

Deja squinted at her.

"Which parts? Are you a secret billionaire heiress?"

"The sadness. The feeling that I need to write but have nothing to say."

Linh lit a cigarette while Deja leaned forward.

"Look, this might sound a little cold, but I didn't grow up with shit. I had to work twice as hard as everyone else all the way through school. I'm not naturally brilliant or a trust fund baby. I paid my way through college. I guess that's one thing I had in common with Janie Sterling: no student loan debt."

"So you're judging her for being a trust fund baby, but here you are living off the same money she did, doing something she literally died for?"

Just like at breakfast the previous day, Deja was shocked into silence.

"I'm sorry. That came out harsher than I meant for it to," Lyla said and took her last drink of wine for the night.

Deja sighed and leaned back.

"No, you're right. That's the booze and jealousy talking. It is sad they lost a daughter, and the fact they created this place as a way to honor her puts everything in perspective. Love is love, and loss is loss, no matter how much money you have."

"Ohh, you should totally use that line in your book," Linh said.

Lyla smiled and shook her head. She looked back and saw that the Sterlings were no longer there.

"Why do you keep looking back there?" Deja asked.

"I was seeing if the Sterlings were still down here."

"Why?"

"It looked like they were talking to everyone individually. I just wanted to thank them again and tell them that I appreciate what they're doing."

"That speech really moved you, didn't it?" Deja asked

"Yeah," Lyla said and stood up. "I think I'm going to go lie down. I need to really focus on why I'm here. I plan on getting started tomorrow morning."

"Boo. Party pooper." Linh said and finished her glass. "Wait, are you going to be good with, you know, everything that happened in your room?"

Lyla could see it in Linh's eyes that she wasn't just referring to Antonio's accident.

"No, but I'm not going to sit around and wait to feel good before I do something. I'm not going to let fear dictate my life."

"Now *that* should go in a book," Deja said and looked at Linh.

Lyla gave a slight smile and said, "Goodnight. I'll see you all in the morning."

"Get some rest, girl," Deja said.

"Will do."

Lyla opened the door and stepped inside the dining hall. She set her empty glass on the table with the others and headed upstairs.

As she stepped onto the third-floor landing, she saw light coming from the spiral staircase above. She heard people talking and, despite what her moral compass told her to do, she stayed and listened. It was definitely Lester and Regina. His voice echoed like he was in the stairwell. Regina said something, but she couldn't make out what they were talking about. The light turned off, and the tower was once again only lit by the occasional torch lamp.

Their footsteps got louder as they descended. Lyla almost hurried away, but they stopped directly above her and began moving forward like they were walking across the fourth-floor hall.

Well, that is where they stay.

But they were walking downstairs.

Her eyes widened when she realized that meant they had come from the fifth floor. It excited her to know that someone had an interaction with the mysterious person who she definitely knew was a female. She recalled the figure in the window. She wondered which famous author masqueraded as The Reader. If she was at the top of the writing food chain, and the Sterlings approached her with such an offer, would she do it? She wondered how much it would cost to get someone to completely uproot their life and move to a castle in Italy and basically live as a recluse. A list of female authors from every genre ran through her mind, and in that moment, she wanted nothing more than to please The Reader.

A door unlocked from way above her. She listened as it squeaked open but never shut. Her pulse quickened when she realized the last time she checked the time was at nine-thirty. It felt like thirty minutes had passed. Ten o'clock was The Reader's time to roam the grounds, to take walks. That's what Julia had said, right?

Lyla stood silently, waiting to hear a door close that never did. Was The Reader just standing there? She tilted her head so her ear pointed upstairs, and she held her breath and waited. Other girls laughed from the first floor, and it sounded like they were coming her way.

Shit.

She would have to move now. The last thing she needed was for her new roommates to think she was weirder than they probably already did.

But what would The Reader do? Continue to just stand there as the parade of drunk girls stumbled to their rooms?

Lyla sighed and almost stepped into the hall when she heard something move beside her.

"Lyyyyylaaaa."

Lyla turned just in time to see a woman walking backwards up the stairs. She disappeared around the curve and made no sound as she moved.

"Lyla!" Kay said from behind her.

She jumped and put her hand on her chest.

"Sorry! Didn't mean to scare you," Kay said. "What are you doing just standing here?"

"I, uh, I thought I saw something," Lyla admitted, too shocked to even try and think of a lie.

"You wouldn't be the first," Kay said as she walked to her room.

Lyla quickly followed behind her.

"Wait. What do you mean by that?"

"Oh, this place is haunted. Didn't you know that?"

"Are you being serious or just messing with me?"

Kay stopped at her door.

"Both, I guess."

"What the hell does that mean?"

"It means I don't believe in ghosts, but other residents have said they've seen some weird shit."

"Like who?" Lyla asked, stunned that no one had mentioned anything like that before to her.

They also didn't tell you about Janie. Maybe it's part of the program.

"Look, Lyla, I'm not trying to freak you out, okay? Just forget it. There's no such thing as ghosts. I'll see you tomorrow," Kay said, opening her door.

Lyla stepped in the room and put her hand on the door.

"Kay, who else said they saw something?"

Kay crossed her arms and looked down and back up.

"Ann did. The girl who used to live in your room."

Lyla just nodded and stepped back, balling her fists as she turned toward her room.

"Lyla, I'm sorry. I—"

"Nope. Don't worry about it. Just another fucking layer to the legend of Claymont. Can't wait to sleep tonight!" Lyla yelled before slamming her door and locking it, unable to shake the image of the woman on the staircase.

She walked straight to the bathtub and turned it on, adjusting the water until steam filled the room. She shut the bathroom door, undressed, and slid into the scalding liquid until the burn overrode her thoughts. The hot water filled around her body as she lay completely flat with her knees bent so her head rested on the bottom of the tub. As the water inched up her body and eventually covered it, she just stared at the ceiling and noticed something odd.

The colorful tiles were all shiny and rectangular and reminded her of stained-glass windows in a church. But on one of the black tiles directly above her, she spotted a crudely painted little white cross. The longer she stared at it, the more the tile itself seemed slightly different than the others. It didn't lay flush. The right end jutted out just a tiny bit, hardly noticeable at first glance.

Lyla washed quickly, abandoning the idea of soaking her troubles away. She dried off, threw on a robe and hurried into her room to get the chair from the writing desk, wheeling it into the bathroom and positioning it against the tub. As carefully as she could, she climbed the wobbly chair, trying not to slip from the still-dripping bathwater. She steadied herself and reached both hands, feeling the tile. The corner poked the tip of her finger, solidifying her suspicion that it was out of place for some reason. Careful not to cause too much damage, she gently tugged at the loose corner, but it didn't budge. She knew if she pulled any harder, she'd risk breaking the piece off.

"Shit."

The little white cross looked like it had been painted on with Wite-Out. She felt the texture of it, and it was smooth, not chalky.

"Is that fingernail polish?"

She pushed on the tile. It rose just enough to let her know something small and malleable was underneath. Someone had tucked something in there. That same someone was probably the one who painted the cross on the tile with fingernail polish. She'd been told Ann had fled in the middle of the night. The pieces were coming together in the narrative puzzle she was creating in her mind.

Lyla hopped off the chair and nearly fell on her ass when she landed on the wet floor, but she didn't care. Adrenaline pumped through her body as she hurried to her toiletry bag and withdrew a pair of tweezers. She climbed back on the chair as recklessly as she had when she jumped off it. The little metal prongs slid effortlessly into the slit. She eased them forward, careful not to push what could be in there back to the point where she couldn't retrieve it.

Her eyes lit up when she felt resistance. She had to twist her fingers to get enough leverage to pinch down with the tweezers. Something prevented them from fully closing.

Got it.

She felt like she was a kid at a claw machine whose loosely gripped prize could fall at any moment. Once the tweezers were almost all the way out, she pinched down as much as she could and jerked. The click of metal was not what she wanted to hear, and her fears were confirmed when she looked at the empty tool. She glanced back up at the tile and saw the progress she had made. The corner of what looked like paper poked out. She tossed the tweezers back on the sink and heard them clink as they cartwheeled to a stop.

Lyla reached up and pinched the exposed part and slid it out, analyzing the folded piece of paper. It was no bigger than a matchbook, but it was dense. She stepped off the chair, slowly this time, and sat down, holding it in the palm of her hand as it naturally unfolded. Somehow, she knew that that contents of whatever was written inside would change things. It would be something she couldn't unsee, a truth she wouldn't be able to deny. She sighed and began to open it, one careful fold at a time.

A door slammed behind her, startling her so badly that she almost dropped the note on the wet floor. She felt foolish when she realized it was just Linh entering her own room. She listened to her next-door neighbor rummaging around like she was opening drawers and settling in for the night. Lyla shut the bathroom door and made sure her bedroom door was locked.

With the speed and excitement of a child tearing through a Christmas present, she finally opened the letter and immediately recognized it as the same paper that was stacked on her desk. Every muscle in her body tensed as she read the handwritten note.

If you're reading this, you need to leave.

My name is Ann Finley. I've been a resident at Claymont for six months now, and I'm in fear for my life. I'm leaving this note in the event that something happens to me, and the Sterlings lure someone else into the program. If so, that's you. This is not a joke. I thought I was going crazy at first, but I know I'm not now. I don't fully understand what's going on here, but I've seen enough, and I'll write as objectively as I can until it's time for me to sneak out of this place in a few hours when everyone is in their rooms.

When I first arrived, I was just as overwhelmed as I'm sure you were. The carriage ride, the castle, the food, the library, and the luxury lifestyle seduced me, just as it was designed to. Lester Sterling gave a speech about the conception of the program and how it was in honor of his daughter, Janie. It moved me and made me feel privileged to be there.

Even though I thought the rules were weird, especially anything related to The Reader, I began my writer's journey. I hit my weekly goals and then some. Everything Julia said about the program being designed to increase productivity proved to be true. It was amazing to crank out so many words per week. I would proudly head down to the library and print my pages. I felt like a real writer every time I walked my weeks' worth of work up to The Reader's mailbox.

My fellow residents and I would all talk about the detailed feedback and notes we'd receive on our stories and how brilliant the suggestions were. The Reader was an amazing editor, always giving us constructive criticism and treated all ten of our works like they were all future bestsellers. I guess the first time I noticed something was off was about three months into my stay. The farther I got into my novel, the less feedback I received. When we'd compare our manuscripts, the other residents—even the ones who have been here longer than me—were still getting thorough notes. I would get feedback like, "Love it," "Great," "Yes," and then it turned into nothing but checkmarks like I was in elementary school.

The other girls took it as a sign that the reader obviously liked my work-in-progress more than anyone else's, and they started treating me like I was some sort of teacher's pet. I didn't get bullied or anything like that, but I just felt like an outsider. But even with that drama going on, I still felt proud of my work. The last batch of pages I submitted came back with nothing but crudely drawn smiley faces in the margins. It creeped me the hell out, but I didn't want to say anything to the girls. If they were getting constructive criticism or substantial edit revisions and all I was getting were smiley faces, who knows how they would've reacted.

Over the next week, I kept my distance. I didn't even write anything. And the longer I went without writing, the more I felt like I was being watched. I also began to see things. It started with shadows out of the corner of my eyes, nothing that I could seriously pin down as real. Then I noticed some of the other girls would—how do I say this without sounding like a lunatic—not behave like themselves. But that would only happen when I was alone with them. Fuck it, I'll say it. Sometimes, I felt like I was talking to someone who was possessed. They just had completely different demeanors and body postures, and I could just feel something else inside of them looking at me through their blank eyes. And that's not even the worst of it. The really creepy stuff happened at night in my bedroom, your bedroom if you're a resident and hopefully not a random custodian or anyone else on the Sterlings' payroll.

After that first week of not submitting anything to The Reader's box, Julia informed me that I "lost my privileges" until I resumed hitting the goals in my contract. Like I gave a shit at that point. I still didn't write. I think that's what triggered the bedroom visits. I pray that you haven't experienced those yet. They started with sounds, mostly from the closet, sometimes under the bed. I'd always turn the light on, but I never saw anything. She was toying with me. I know that now.

A second week passed, and I still didn't submit anything. I didn't get my privileges back, and I had completely withdrawn from the rest of the girls. One night, I heard someone whisper my name. I sat up in bed and saw her standing in my closet. I freaked out and turned on the light, but she was gone. No one went in or out of my room in that time. I knew then that I was dealing with a malevolent presence. I didn't dismiss it or try to rationalize it as I had before.

The next day, I told Julia I wanted to leave Claymont. My excuse was that I just wasn't inspired anymore and didn't want to take up a bed and prevent some other writer on the waiting list from getting accepted. She tried to talk me out of it. She said there were only a handful of other Claymont residents who left, but they didn't have the talent that I did. I told her that I had already made up my mind but thanked her anyway. She insisted that I talk to the Sterlings personally before leaving. She said they were arriving at the end of the week anyway, and if I still felt the same after meeting with them, they would arrange for immediate transportation back to the States. Reluctantly, I agreed. That was earlier this week.

The last few nights have been the worst. I kept the light on, but I couldn't fall asleep. Just when I started to doze off, the sound of my door shutting woke me up. It was Linh, my next-door neighbor. I guess I should say that it was Linh's body, but she wasn't the one controlling it. She was just standing there, eyes open, and with this look like she was disappointed in me and mad at the same time. I can't really explain it. The really fucked up part was that her eye color even looked different. They were lighter like they had a glow to them. She kept asking me why I wasn't working on my story. She just repeated it over and over without even giving me a chance to respond. The last time she asked me, it was in a different person's voice. I screamed, and then she snapped out of it. It was like whatever was possessing her had just left. She was scared and confused and had no memory of coming to my room. After we talked for a minute, I think she was more freaked out than I was.

It's only gotten worse since then, and my sleep deprivation surely isn't helping. I saw the woman in the closet again. Two nights ago, she was lying face down on the ceiling above my bed. I thought I was having some sort of night terror and tried to slap myself awake, but I couldn't move my arms. I was paralyzed and forced to watch as her head turned backwards. Last night she crawled in through my window and under my bed. She stayed there all night while I was paralyzed again. She just kept repeating my name and saying, "Don't go." At some point my body just called it quits, and I began to fall asleep. I heard her open the window, and that snapped me out of it. I watched her crawl up the castle wall. She made sure to look at me one more time when she closed the window while hanging upside down. I stayed still until the sun came up, and I was positive that she was back on the fifth floor.

Jesus, in just reading that back I realize how fucking nuts I sound, but if you're still reading this and you've experienced anything remotely similar to what I've described, then you know it's real. Don't doubt yourself. There is a darkness here, and it's tied directly to the Sterlings. They arrived here this morning. I went down for breakfast, and there they were, sitting right at their back table like they were waiting for me. As soon as I saw them, I went to the buffet and put eggs on my plate even though I didn't plan on eating anything. I haven't had an appetite all week. I feel like this place is draining me, and I feel like it was designed to do that from day one.

Even though I didn't want to speak to them, I had to. It was inevitable, and at the time, I really believed they would fly me home. As soon as I turned around, Lester invited me over to their table. I sat down, and they immediately started with the questions. They wanted to know why I wanted to leave. I lied and said that I suffered from depression. I knew their history with their daughter—well, the one they want you to know, at least—so I played on that to tug at their heart-strings. Oh, how blind I was. They told me The Reader had told them I was the best writer who had come through Clay-mont. I have to admit, even in my fragile state, that gave me a little ego boost. I told them how appreciative I was and there was nothing wrong with the program, and it was just my own bullshit. Once they saw that I was definitely leaving, Regina actually had tears in her eyes. Lester told me he had already looked into flights in the event they couldn't convince me to stay and the next flight out was tomorrow morning. The thought of spending another night in this room, on these grounds, terrified me, but then he said something that both intrigued and terrified me at the same time: he insisted that I say goodbye to The Reader. He said the other girls who left in the past had broken his heart, but The Reader had never asked to meet any of them. That was the whole point. You weren't supposed to know who The Reader was, but Lester actually convinced me I had made such a strong impression on The Reader that they wanted to personally wish me good luck. I would also have to sign a confidentiality agreement as well, which, looking back on it now, was a nice cherry on top of their mountain of deception. They said they would come to my room at ten p.m. and escort me to the fifth floor.

I agreed, and they told me to enjoy my last day at Clay-mont, and I was free to do what I wished, overriding all of Julia's consequence rules. I spent most of today hanging around outside, drinking coffee and just trying to act as normally as I could because I knew all the other residents would say goodbye to me at some point. I was half right about that, though. All of them came to me individually and at random times, but it wasn't really them. It was like the same thing that happened with Linh. They would approach me with those blue eyes and strange smile, and they all said the same thing. Word for word. "Ann, I heard you're leaving. Don't go." No matter how I responded, they would just give me a quick hug and hurry off like they had somewhere important to be.

I made myself eat a little bit of dinner, but I sat away from everyone. The only person who stopped by to give me a genuine farewell was Dante. He's a good man, as far as I can tell. I don't say this with one-hundred percent certainty, but if there's one person in this place that you can possibly trust, it's him. I don't think he fully knows what's going on here.

What's also bizarre is they didn't say goodbye to me as a group. They were getting along as they always did, drinking and eating and chatting like they didn't even know I was leaving. I couldn't take it anymore and went back to my room. The one you're currently standing in and will hopefully leave once you've read this. At 8:30, someone knocked on my door, and it surprised the hell out of me to see Regina standing there alone. She looked like she had been crying. I asked her if everything was okay, and she said it was and she was just checking on me before I met The Reader. I told her I needed to pack my things for the early flight tomorrow. She swallowed and turned her head away from me to wipe her tears. And then it dawned on me, a feeling of intense dread. She was acting as if this was the last time she would ever see me. Regina didn't come to my room to check on me before meeting The Reader. She came here like she knew something bad was going to happen to me, and this would be her last chance to say goodbye. She told me she would have someone bring me my belongings. But right before she left, she looked at me and said, "I'm so sorry," and walked down the hallway before I even thought to ask her what she was sorry about.

I watched her turn and walk up the stairs before I hurried down the hall. I listened to her walk across the fourth-floor hallway and go into their room. I snuck up the stairs and peered around the fourth-floor landing. The Sterlings were nowhere to be seen, but I heard Lester's deep voice and knew they were there. If they were planning on doing something to me on the fifth floor, I wanted to be prepared. So, for the first time since being at Claymont, I went to the top of The Keep.

I knew I was short on time but didn't know how much. I also had no idea what to expect once I got up there, so I crept as quietly as I could until I reached the top. This is going to sound crazy, but there's a certain step once you round the corner to get to the fifth floor where the atmosphere changes. I'm not talking about a cold spot or a draft. It feels like you're literally stepping into a crypt. The air is thick. It smells like dirt and decay. But the strangest thing about it is that I couldn't hear anything once I stepped into that realm, for lack of a better word. It shocked me so much that I took a step back, and the sounds of the castle resumed. The smell was gone. The moisture that hung in the air like it was a living thing was gone.

At that point, I forced myself up those remaining stairs and made it to the fifth-floor landing. The short hallway was completely barren. No decorations. No rug. No chandeliers, not that there was much room for one. And I didn't know why I never put it together because when you look at the castle from the outside, you can clearly see how the top floor of The Keep has no hallways connected to it. God, it smelled so awful. I wanted to go back, but my body wouldn't let me. I stared at the door to the left of the landing and gasped. The wooden door was rotten and moldy. Black and brown smudges covered it like it had suffered years of water damage. But the longer I looked, the more I noticed movement in the colors. It was no trick of the light, because there barely was any. The final stairwell torch light was at the last curve and provided just enough for me to see what was happening on the door.

I couldn't help but lean closer to analyze it and recoiled when I saw that it was filled with maggots, squiggling around like the structure was nothing but dirt. I'd jumped back too fast and stumbled into the wall. I stood there, too scared to move, praying that whatever was behind that hideous doorway to hell didn't hear me. I covered my nose and mouth to stifle my breathing. My heart was beating so hard that I thought its thumps would echo in the hallway. I had seen enough. The thing that resided behind that barrier was evil. I could feel it. I'd never experienced anything so alien in all my life. I thought I'd known terror, but this was beyond anything I could comprehend. And it was enough for me to get my ass out of there.

Just as I lifted my foot to take a step down, I saw two shadows at the crack of the door. Someone was standing on the other side, and I had no idea for how long. I froze. I knew I had to get out of there, but I felt trapped. I decided on what I thought was the lesser of two evils and quietly took a step back. One of the feet under the door did the same. I froze again, wondering if it was mimicking me. I moved my other foot, and it did the same. Not only did it know I was there, but it could see me or sense me somehow.

I didn't waste any more time. I turned and descended the stairs, moving as quickly and quietly as I could. As I approached the fourth-floor landing, I slowed down and poked

my head around the corner. The hallway was empty, so I sped
past it and kept going until I made it to my floor and took off
at a full sprint to my room. I shut the door and locked it and
have been in here ever since. The Sterlings are still in their
room and will be down to get me in an hour. If you're still
reading this, go to town, look up Ann Finley, and see if I'm
alive.

Let me make this clear. Lester and Regina Sterling are
not good people.

This place that you're in is a trap. LEAVE NOW. I
certainly am. Good luck to us both.

Lyla finished reading the hidden letter as her tears fell on the creased pages that Ann had risked her life to write. She sat there in a state of shocked melancholy, feeling like she'd just experienced Ann's final night alive. Even though she never met her, she now knew her from her writing; as a writer, Lyla knew that's how you truly get to know someone. She folded the paper back how it was, climbed on the bathroom chair, tucked it into the tile above the tub, and fixed it so no one else would notice it. She turned off the light and shut the door.

As she stumbled across the room feeling like she was torn between two realities, she crawled into bed and sat against the headboard with her arms wrapped around her folded legs. She sat that way and rocked, reflecting on the optimism she'd felt earlier that evening and how it had been replaced by sheer, utter hopelessness. She had to accept the fact that Claymont was not a writer's residency. If Ann's account was correct—and by her own admission, she was sleep deprived and starving herself—then something truly sinister was going on just two floors above her.

Lyla rocked herself with her eyes closed and the lights on until she came up with a plan. Tomorrow, she would go see a boy about a coffee, and once she was safely away from the curious ears and invasive cameras at Claymont, she would call her mom and dad, accepting the fact that the landlines at the residency were most likely being monitored like everything else. At that point, she just wanted to get home.

TWENTY

Lyla's eyes fluttered open as the sunshine caressed her face. She felt disoriented because of the angle at which she was looking at the window. Her body was still in a position like she was about to do a cannonball into a swimming pool. She lifted her head and realized that nothing had happened to her during the night. Despite the horrific tragedy depicted in Ann's letter, she saw no midnight figures or awoke to whispers of her name from the dark corner by her bedside. Still, the layout of the room was backwards, and it took her waking mind a second to realize that she had somehow rolled on her side with her head near the bottom of the bed and facing the window.

A gentle breeze fluttered the curtains and blew against her face. Birds chirped from outside, and a lawnmower hummed somewhere in the distance. Despite sleeping with no pillow and having a slight headache, this was the best morning she'd had since arriving at the residency.

Wait. Why the hell is the window open?

Lyla pushed herself up and let her equilibrium stabilize before she climbed out of bed. She walked around her room, looking for anything out of the ordinary, any clue that someone had been in her room, but she didn't find anything. Her bedroom door was still locked, there was nothing nefarious lurking in the closet, and everything on her desk was in order.

Another breeze WHOOSHED in, and that one was much stronger, blowing several of the pieces of paper off the stack by the typewriter. She hurried and shut the window, then turned around to pick up the papers. As she did, the tactile connection of her fingers touching the parchment, she was instantly transported back to the previous night, reading Ann's letter.

But then she noticed something that took her breath: the bathroom door was wide open. She distinctly remembered closing it before going to bed.

Maybe the breeze blew it open.

Don't be a fucking idiot.

Lyla gulped and placed the papers back on their stack on the desk as she cautiously approached the doorway. She looked inside, not sure what to expect, but everything looked fine at first glance. She stepped on the tile floor and picked up her toothbrush, put toothpaste on, and began brushing, staring at herself in the mirror. Her eyes gradually drifted up in the reflection until she looked at the ceiling. She let her toothbrush fall from her mouth as she stared at a tile with no white cross on it.

This isn't possible.

She spun around and saw what she prayed she wouldn't see. Not only had the cross been cleaned off, but the tile that had once harbored the bulky note now lay flush with the rest of the ceiling tiles. Her heart sank, and she almost collapsed.

"No," she muttered. "No, no, no, no."

Lyla pictured the ghastly woman in the decrepit dungeon crawling down the castle walls and slinking into her room while she slept. Somehow, the woman knew Lyla had found and read the note. It was too much of coincidence to think otherwise. For all she knew, the woman did all those things Ann mentioned. Maybe she stood by Lyla's bedside and watched her sleep. What if Lyla didn't roll around in her sleep but was positioned that way just to disorient her. Maybe the lady just stared at her from the ceiling with her head twisted backwards, grinning as Lyla breathed a dreamless sleep.

What startled her the most was that Ann's story had been stolen, erased, vanished from existence. The letter she had taken the time to write while she waited on the right moment to escape, specifically for the next resident in that room in the event that she died, was now taken, most likely by the very entity depicted in it. Lyla still had the story in her heart, though. She would keep it there and make sure Ann's tale would someday be told. People will eventually find out there was more to the former resident's death than just a freak taxi accident on a stormy night.

She looked at the clock and saw it was 7:10 a.m., still early. After taking a quick shower, she got dressed and made sure to put on shoes for a long walk. The thought to just use the landline at Claymont crossed her mind but only for a moment. There was nowhere private in the castle. She had to assume that to be safe. Someone could easily be listening in on every conversation made from that phone. There could be cameras tucked away in tiny crevices throughout the ancient structure.

As soon as she opened the door, she checked to see if anyone else was out there. The hall was empty, but she walked by Kay's room, and the door was open. Kay was putting her slippers on and still wore her pajamas and a robe.

"Good morning," she said when she noticed Lyla.

"Morning."

"Are you going down for breakfast?"

Trust no one.

"Yes. I'm starving, and I have a headache from hell…hoping some coffee will help."

"I'll come with you," Kay said and walked out and shut the door before Lyla had a chance to think of an excuse for her not to.

"Okay."

"So, are you going to get started on your novel today?" she asked.

"Yeah. I finally got some sleep and feel rested."

They approached the stairwell and began walking down the spiral, passing torchlights as they descended.

"That jetlag is a real bitch. It messed me up for a few days, too,"

Kay said. "I didn't have to deal with someone dying in my room though. That's so awful."

"I know. I don't think I'll ever unsee that."

They reached the first floor and walked down the red carpet with the pillars on both sides. Whirring and stomping sounds came from the rec area.

"Someone's up early," Lyla said.

"Lori. She's down here at seven almost every morning like she's training for a marathon."

Think of something. Get out of this situation.

She stopped, but Kay kept walking.

"Shoot," she said.

Kay stopped.

"What's wrong?"

"I was going to write on the patio with my coffee. I'm going to go grab my notebook. I'll meet you in there."

"Okay. But the patio gets busy in about an hour. Might not be the best place."

"Ehh, I'll hit up the library if I have to."

"Sounds good. See you in a few."

Lyla watched as Kay entered the dining hall doors. She turned around but not to go upstairs. She avoided that direction entirely. There would be no writing done; that priority set sail the night before and was long gone. Now, it was about safety and self-preservation. Without looking anywhere but straight ahead, she exited Claymont and hurried down the cement walkway to the main gates which were already open.

Once she stepped onto the stone road, she finally looked over her shoulder at The Keep, expecting to see some ghastly apparition in the fifth-floor window, but it was empty.

Or just too dark to see. Someone could still be watching you from the shadows.

Once she cleared the front facing fence and reached the corner where the tree line started, she began to jog. It had been a while since Lyla had run any sort of significant distance, but she was going downhill, the temperature was nice, and the thought of fleeing the castle kept her motivated. She increased her jog to a full-on sprint when she reached what she thought was the halfway point to the connecting road in Umbertide. Her safe haven awaited her, and that kicked in the adrenaline reserves.

Once she saw the road and the buildings as she rounded the bend, she slowed back down to a jog and then a walk, not wanting to cause a scene as she exited the entrance road to Claymont. She caught her breath and stepped onto the street and then the sidewalk across the road. For a moment, she felt a fleeting surge of panic when she couldn't remember which street led to the coffee shop, but she recognized the back of one of the brightly colored buildings and proceeded in that direction.

There weren't nearly as many people out that morning as there had been the day of the accident. She passed a few morning joggers, a couple on bicycles, and a group of people who looked like tourists on a horse-drawn carriage ride. There were hardly any vehicles on the road. She passed buildings that smelled like freshly baked breads, and her mouth watered. That was a good sign. She remembered seeing that place.

A wave of relief washed over her when she saw the coffee shop. She hurried across the road and walked toward the building, the smell of coffee already permeating the air.

"Lyla?" a familiar man's voice called from the alleyway.

She jumped, realizing how on edge she was and then breathed a sigh of relief to see Leo standing there with a cigarette in his hand.

"Hey, sorry. Are you a little jumpy this morning?" He smiled.

He must've been able to see the seriousness on her face beyond her initial fright because his smile dropped. She walked briskly through the alley.

"Leo, I need to talk to you."

He furrowed his brown and took a drag from his cigarette.

"What have you gotten yourself into? I don't want to be involved in any Claymont drama. Mama would make me work nonstop for a week."

"This is serious."

He looked her in the eyes and nodded.

"Okay, come on in," he said and opened the side door. "I'll make you something to drink, and you can tell me all about it."

She walked into the mostly empty café. Leo's brother was running the register, but she didn't see his mom.

"Mama is in the back baking pastries. Have a seat at the bar. You look like you need a triple-shot Leo espresso special."

She pulled out a barstool and sat, resting her elbows on the polished wooden bar.

"That sounds fantastic."

"So, what's up?" he asked while preparing her drink.

"There's something seriously messed up going on at Claymont."

"I told you I don't want to get involved in any drama with them. Julia helps me out, and you stay there. I can't lose that side gig."

"This is more important than your fucking side job."

He shot her a glare like he'd never been spoken to like that, especially from a young American girl.

"You're not being very nice," he finally said as the surface anger subsided.

"You're not taking me seriously. Aside from all the weird shit I've seen at that place, I found a note hidden in my room."

"Oh, a secret note? What did it say?" he said, still in a condescending tone that if he kept up with, she'd toss his special espresso straight in his face.

"You know the girl who got hit by the taxi? She stayed in the room I'm in now. She wrote a note and hid it in my bathroom ceiling."

He scrunched his face, but she could tell he was listening.

"I saw it poking out of one of the tiles. It was folded and shoved in there. She used fingernail polish to paint a tiny white cross on it. The only way anyone would notice it is if they were laying in the bathtub and looking straight up. The note was intended for the next resident in the event that something bad happened to her."

"That's...messed up."

"Yeah. And what's even more messed up is what she wrote."

He handed her the espresso and leaned on the bar.

"I'm listening."

"The Sterlings are keeping something seriously fucked up on the fifth floor of The Keep. Ann knew they were going to do something to her. Like she alluded to them taking her up there for…whatever is there. She talks about seeing the same kind of shit I've been seeing. I was kidding myself at first, and everyone had an excuse, especially me. I didn't want to believe that place was…"

"Was what?"

"Haunted."

"Lots of people think that place is haunted."

"No. I'm seeing the same person. A woman. I'm not sure how old she is. She has pale skin and dark hair. But that's just the visual stuff."

"What other stuff could there be? Sounds?"

Lyla took a much-needed sip of her hot drink and then another.

"You're trembling," Leo said.

She looked at her hands and noticed, forcing herself to not shake.

"What's the other stuff?" he asked.

"The other residents—the girls. Well, some of them. There are times when they're not themselves, and I know this is going to sound crazy because it sounds even more far-fetched the more I say it, but it's like they're possessed."

"That castle has so many legends and so many different ghost stories. There are people here who really buy into it. They tried to warn Julia and wrote letters to the Sterlings, pleading with them to not turn a place full of so much history of bloodshed into a luxury resort for Americans."

"It's not a resort. It's a residency for writers," Lyla said and then stopped, wondering why she was defending the integrity of the program. "Nevermind. I don't know what it is. The visions, the possessions, the letter—all of it has to mean something. What the fuck are they trying to do up there?"

"I don't know," Leo began. "But they knew what they were getting when they bought it. My mom actually thinks that's why they bought it. Umbria…umber…shadow. The darkness is in the ground the castle sits on and then you throw a thousand years of strife on top of that. Sounds like a perfect recipe for spirits to roam free."

Lyla's eyes widened like a light bulb just went off in her head.

"What?" Leo asked.

"I'm not seeing lots of spirits. I'm only seeing one."

"Okay…"

"The Sterlings, Lester's speech, the reason why they built a writers residency…"

"What about them?"

"It was all for their daughter, for Janie," Lyla said. "That came straight from their mouths."

"Yes, I know about that."

"Does it not strike you as odd that a couple who could buy property anywhere in the world would randomly choose this area? That castle? In Umbria with the shadows or whatever you said?"

"Yes, I guess so," Leo said, still not picking up what she was laying down.

"It doesn't matter how much money you have. You can't bribe life into bringing a loved one back from the dead."

"I still don't get it. I mean, I know what you're saying, but how does that relate to Umbria?"

"The Sterlings built their writers residency at that castle for Janie. You said it yourself; it's a fertile ground for spirits. What if they think there's a way to bring her back?"

Leo's eyes darted back and forth like he was scrolling through possible scenarios, trying to find the logic in what she was saying.

"Talk to me," she said. "What are you thinking?"

"You're only seeing one ghost?"

Lyla scoffed.

"One too many, but yeah, I'm just seeing one. Sounds like you're thinking what I'm thinking."

Leo put his hands on his hips. Lyla saw the outline of a phone in his pocket.

"I need to use that," she said.

"Huh?"

"Your phone."

He looked down at his shorts and saw the device, reaching for it and then stopping.

"Wait, aren't Claymont girls not supposed to use cell phones? Isn't that like a big no-no? I've heard Julia say that during every carriage ride."

"Do you think I give a fuck about Claymont or Julia's rules right now? I need to look at something and then call my parents and get away from this place," she said and tossed the rest of her espresso back like a shot of whiskey.

Leo took out his iPhone and held it, staring down at the screen as if in consideration.

"Are you sure you want to do this?"

Lyla didn't have time to waste. She snatched it out of his hands. He mumbled something in Italian that she was sure was a worried slew of cuss words, but she didn't care at that moment. She opened the internet browser. Everything was in Italian, but she didn't need anything but a search bar. She typed "Janie Sterling overdose, New York, NY." Results populated with links to news stories that she couldn't read, but she wasn't looking for articles anyway. A thumbnail image was attached to the first link. She clicked it and gasped.

"What?" Leo asked, leaning over the bar to look at the full-sized picture of Janie Sterling.

Lyla covered her mouth and just stared at those piercing blue eyes, eyes she'd seen before on residents at Claymont when the girls weren't "acting like themselves."

And it wasn't just that. The girl in the image had long black hair and skin the color of alabaster. Lyla scrolled down through paragraphs in Italian until she saw a full-body picture of Janie. In that one, she leaned against a tree on a college campus, holding her books and smiling in an obviously staged position. After looking at her tall, skinny frame, Lyla knew.

"She's the one," Lyla muttered, her heart skipping every few beats as her brain struggled to grasp this truth.

"The one?" Leo asked.

"She's the one ghost. I've been seeing Janie Sterling at the castle."

They looked at each other like they were both trying to make sense of the revelation. Lyla just shook her head and swiped out of the browser, bringing up the dial screen.

"I'm getting out of here," she said. "I don't care what the Sterlings are up to, and I'm not sticking around to find out. I won't end up like Ann."

Leo didn't say anything.

She typed her dad's phone number and hit the call button. It rang until it went to voicemail.

"Shit."

"No luck?"

"Did it look like I had any luck?" she barked in her highly caffeinated state.

"Well, it's still nighttime in the U.S." he said. "Early morning, technically."

"Oh yeah. He always silences his phone. Mom doesn't though," she said and began dialing.

The phone rang three times, and Lyla started to get nervous.

"Hello?" a tired and worried voice answered.

"Mom, it's Lyla."

"Lyla? What time is it?"

"It's morning over here. Listen, there's something I have to tell you. Are you awake yet?"

"Awake enough. Is everything okay?"

"No," she said, about to go on a tangent before Leo reached over the bar and grabbed the phone and ended the call. "What the fu—"

"She'll call right back. Calm down. Look, I don't know what you were about to tell her, but if it has anything to do with what we were just talking about, then you're going to sound crazy."

"I don't care how I sound."

The phone rang once. He silenced it but didn't ignore the call.

"Make up a real reason for having to come home. Say you're homesick. Say you're not getting along with the other residents. Say you got caught plagiarizing your story and got kicked out—anything but ghosts. Do you see what I'm getting at?"

She understood, and he was correct.

"Yeah."

He swiped his finger across the screen to answer and handed it back to her.

"Hey, Mom. Sorry, the phone service is horrible over here."

"That's okay. What's going on?"

"Look, I need to come home."

The other end of the line was silent. Lyla bit the side of her lip for what felt like forever. Her mom sighed.

"What's going on?" her dad said in the background. "Who are you talking to?"

"It's Lyla," her mom said to him. "Honey, what's wrong? I wasn't expecting to hear from you for a few more days. I didn't think you were allowed to use cell phones."

"I'm not. I'm not on property right now."

"Where are you?"

"At a coffee shop in Umbertide, just at the bottom of the hill from Claymont."

"Café," Leo whispered, correcting her.

Lyla didn't acknowledge him.

"What happened, Lyla?" her mom asked, sounding impatient.

"This program isn't for me. I need to come home."

"Why? Talk to me."

"It's not like I thought it would be," she continued. "The other residents have their own cliques. I just stay in my room all day. I'm not getting any writing done."

"Don't you have mentors there to help you?" her dad asked, causing Lyla to realize she was now on speaker phone.

"Hi, Dad. Yes, we have mentors, but that's another problem."

"What do you mean?" he asked. "What's the problem?"

"Fine, I'll be honest," Lyla began and let out a fake sigh, "I got drunk last night and kissed Dante. He's the program director."

"What?" her mom snapped.

"It was stupid. We were both wasted and ended up making out. One of the other staff members saw us and told the Sterlings; they're the people who fund Claymont."

"We know who the Sterlings are," her dad said. "Who is this Dante guy? Did he take advantage of you? If he's in some kind of position of power, then they need to shitcan his ass and give you another chance."

"You're not listening. I don't want another chance. It's turned into this whole toxic situation now. The other girls and staff members are mad at me because they all liked Dante, and he already got fired. The Sterlings did that last night."

"Oh, Lyla," her mom said. "I'm sorry you're going through this. Did they kick you out of the program?"

"No. I just needed to get out of there."

"Lyla," her dad started and paused like he was choosing his words carefully. "Now that that creep is out of the picture, can't you just get through this initial awkwardness and make it work? This is your dream. I'd hate to see you act on emotion and throw away a golden opportunity because some sleazeball took advantage of you."

"Dad, it's not like that. He didn't take advantage of me. It wasn't anything like that. It just sort of happened. That doesn't matter, though. I'm not running on emotion. This place didn't feel right after my first night. I can't focus here on a regular day, so who knows how hard it will be now that this happened. I just want to come home."

There was another long pause from their end of the call. She looked at Leo and shrugged her shoulders.

"That's really what you want?" her dad asked.

"Yes."

"Honey, you're sure you don't want to think on it for another day and see how things settle down?" her mom asked.

"Jesus, are you all not listening to me? I would want to come home even if the stuff from last night didn't happen. Will you help me or not?"

Her dad sighed and said, "Of course we'll help you. I take it the do-gooder Sterlings aren't going to foot the bill for you to fly first class back home if you decide to bail?"

"I highly doubt it, and I wouldn't even ask them. I don't want to see them."

"So, what do you need us to do, Lyla?"

"Will you book my flight and text this number back with the info?"

Leo gave her a what-the-fuck? look with his upturned palms. She just glared at him, and he seemed to understand he had no choice in the matter.

"Why can't we just text you?" her mom asked.

"They took my phone and put it in storage somewhere in the castle."

"Well, aren't they going to give it back to you when you tell them you're leaving?"

"Mom, I really don't even want to tell them I'm leaving. I just want to get a ride to the airport and get out of here."

"Lyla, you need to tell the Sterlings you're leaving, at least," she said.

The thought of going back to Claymont formed a sour pit in her stomach, but she knew she had to. She had no intention of telling the Sterlings or anyone else anything. They could keep her phone, but she needed to get her purse from her room. It had her ID, passport, and credit cards in it. She thought about bringing her MacBook with her, but if anyone saw her leaving with it they might think she was really leaving.

No, not if you play it right. You're a writer, remember? Go back there, get your stuff, and make sure they see you leave with your computer. Tell them you're going somewhere to write. Pretend to be happy. Act like you're still inspired by Lester's speech from last night and skip your ass right out the front doors.

"You're right," Lyla lied. "I'll do that. Just please book the flight right now and text this number as soon as you do."

After a moment of what she could only assume was her parents' mutual acceptance of their disappointment, her dad cleared his throat.

"We'll take care of it, Lyla."

"Thank you. I love you guys."

"Love you, too," they both said.

"Bye."

Lyla ended the call and handed the phone back to Leo.

"So, what do you want me to do when they text?"

"Just wait on me to come back. I won't be gone long. How late do you work?"

"We close after the lunch rush."

"When's that?"

"Fourteen-ish."

What the hell is he talking about?

She remembered they weren't in the U.S. There was no a.m. or p.m. It's what she'd always been taught to call military time, the twenty-four-hour clock.

Okay, so he'll be here until 2 p.m.

"If I'm not back before then, I want you to call the police and tell them a girl from Claymont stole money from your register or something."

He grinned, apparently holding back his laughter.

"What's funny?" she asked.

"Sorry, it's just that the police don't get involved with Claymont. Hell, they barely do anything in Umbertide."

"They were there yesterday morning…after the accident."

If that's even what it was.

"Well, yeah, probably just to write whatever narrative the Sterlings wanted them to put on the official record."

"Are you saying I can't even trust the police here?"

He shook his head like he was dealing with a child.

"If I were you, I wouldn't trust anyone."

TWENTY-ONE

Lyla hurried through town the same way she'd come. She wasn't running; she knew better than to make a scene. Plus, she needed to conserve her energy for the trudge up the hill. Her hurried walk was sufficient enough to serve its dual purpose of getting back to the castle as quickly as possible, abating the fear she had that the police Leo claimed were in the Sterlings pocket would leap out from a random alley and take her to the station to "ask her a few questions."

But nothing happened, of course. No one gave her a second glance as she passed by the locals and tourists and eventually ended back up at the start of the grand road to Claymont. She took a deep breath and stepped onto the stone, single-lane street and began her upward trek.

Even though she wanted to get away from Umbria as fast as she could, she was in no hurry to get back to the castle and get her things. It was the step she wished she could skip in the plan. As she walked, her mind kept returning to the picture of Janie Sterling she'd seen from the article on Leo's phone. Janie had been close to her age when she died. All of the current Claymont residents were around the same age, in fact. The voice in her that didn't want to accept the obvious wouldn't shut up.

Maybe they only accept young women who are the same age as their daughter to make themselves feel better, to make them feel like they're helping Janie directly. The program was created in her honor, after all.

But then the voice of reason, the voice she was too afraid to listen to, would speak.

Or maybe they're trying to bring their daughter back from the dead and will stop at nothing, spare no expense, to do so if they believe it could work. That's why all of you are the same age, and you're all writers. They want as close to a match as possible.

Lyla closed her eyes and rubbed her temples.

"This is fucking insane."

The sun beat down on the back of her neck, as perspiration began to form in all the usual places. Her legs were already tired from the run down the hill. Walking back up with such a short turnaround proved to be more difficult than she'd anticipated. She tried to distract her mind from her cramping calves by taking a mental step back and reassessing Claymont as a whole, starting with the rules that govern it. She understood the no cell phone policy, but why have a landline?

It's probably recorded. Just another illusion of choice in their manipulation.

Why the charade with The Reader and the weekly homework with feedback?

Because they're trying to find a match for Janie. They need someone who writes and sounds like their daughter.

Are Julia and Dante and all the other Claymont staff in cahoots with the Sterlings?

I don't see how they couldn't be.

What really happens at ten p.m. every night?

Whatever is in that room is allowed out.

But why would a ghost need a walk?

I don't know.

Why do some random residents seem like they're possessed? What happened in the library with the ladders? Why are you seeing her in your room?

I DON'T KNOW.

Lyla kicked some random pebbles off the road.

She neared the end of the tree line on the right and approached the corner of the fence. Her mission was to act normal, get her stuff, and get out without talking to anyone. No, she thought, she should talk to someone. She needed to tell at least one person that she was going somewhere to write alone. It would be an easy enough lie to sell with a person having died in her room. That would buy her some time. Whenever they would notice she broke curfew, Lyla would hopefully be flying back to West Virginia.

You can do this.

A confident grin teased her lips.

"Lyla," a voice whispered.

She jumped and looked around.

"Lyla!" the familiar voice whispered even louder.

It came from her right. Linh was crouched between two trees, hidden from the castle. She kept looking over her shoulders and had a worried look on her face.

"What are you doing?" Lyla asked.

Linh shook so badly trying to light a cigarette that her Ray-Bans nearly fell off her face. Lyla watched her put the lighter back in her purse.

"Why do you have your purse? And why are you hiding down there?"

"Come over here," Linh said. "Away from the road so no one can see you."

Lyla wasted no time shimmying out of sight. She crouched down beside her friend who looked like she'd seen a ghost.

"What's wrong?"

"I'm freaking the fuck out, that's what."

"What happened?"

Linh grimaced.

"God, this is going to sound weird."

"Try me."

"Okay, so I was on my way to breakfast, and as soon as I stepped in the stairwell, I forgot I needed to put my pages in The Reader's box. Well, I technically didn't have to, but I got them done and wanted feedback. I ran back and got them and went to the fourth floor to deposit. But, like right when I turned around, I heard people yelling and then something broke like a vase or something. It was coming from the Sterling's room.

"Don't ask me why I had the balls to do this, but I opened Dante's door and locked it behind me. I walked through his office and tapped on his bedroom door. I was going to make up some excuse about my plumbing if he was in, but it was empty, thank God. I walked to the wall that separates his room from the Sterlings, and I put my ear to it."

"And you weren't sleepwalking?"

"No! I was fully awake." Linh said and took another drag from her cigarette. "I heard them fighting in there."

"Who?"

"Lester and Regina. They were arguing. It was kind of hard to make out what they were saying, but they were yelling. Well, she was, at least."

"What were they fighting about, Linh?"

Linh looked down and shook her head and then back up at Lyla.

"Regina said, 'You're going to kill her like you killed Janie and the others.'"

Lyla felt herself shaking and nearly fell over. She gulped, trying to process what she'd just heard.

"What?"

Linh repeated herself.

"I heard Regina fucking Sterling say, 'You're going to kill her like you killed Janie and the others.'"

"And she was talking to Lester?"

"Yes. He shushed her as soon as she said it. He said, 'Be quiet or she'll hear you.'"

"Who was he talking about hearing them?"

"Fuck if I know!"

"I just heard her say, 'I can't do this anymore,' and then it sounded like they both started crying."

Lyla took a deep breath and closed her eyes.

"What does this mean? What does this mean?" she said in quick succession like she was trying to force a puzzle piece where it didn't fit.

"I don't know, but I hurried the hell out of there. I ran to my room and got my shit and was coming to find you in town."

"Then why are you hiding in the trees?"

"Because I heard someone coming up the hill and didn't know who it was until I saw it was you. I'm fucking freaked out, man! I'm not going back in that place."

"Okay, okay. Fuck. Here's what we do. You go to Umbertide and wait for me at the coffee shop."

"What? Why?"

"I already made plans to leave. My parents are going to book the first flight out of here and text Leo all the information. I just came here to get my passport and computer and was going to act like I needed some space to go write somewhere other than Claymont…uh, like the bookstore. I'm still going to do that, but I'll also say that I'm meeting you there."

"Don't tell them I left!"

"They're going to know that you left. If I act natural and say that we're going somewhere, it'll buy us time. Don't go to the fucking bookstore, though. Go to the coffee shop and tell Leo you talked to me on the way out. Mention that you know my parents are going to text him, so he'll know you're telling the truth."

"Okay, will do," she said and then, "be careful, Lyla."

"I've got this. Just be ready."

Linh nodded, peeked once more toward the castle fence shrouded by shrubbery and trees, and hurried down the road. Lyla backed up and turned toward Claymont. Her heart immediately started pounding. The confidence she'd try to inspire in Linh had faded from her as soon as she saw the top of the building from her shielded vantage point.

"Here we go," she said and walked parallel to the fence, now in full view of the front of the castle.

She looked around the front area and saw no one on the grass. A faint buzzing came from the distance, behind the castle somewhere in the courtyard, and Lyla assumed it was one of the groundskeepers on a lawnmower.

They'd have to work 24/7 to keep this place looking this pristine.

As she stepped toward the front gate, she read the sign mounted that read *CLAYMONT RESIDENCY FOR WRITERS* and couldn't help but be impressed by its elegance. Even if the entire program was a façade for something sinister, she had to give Julia props for her design skills.

"Speak of the devil," she muttered as she watched Julia walk out of the massive front doors to The Keep.

"Lyla?" she asked as the two women approached each other on the stone path.

"Yeah?"

"What are you doing?"

"I went on a walk. I needed to get some fresh air."

"Well, remember to sign out next time. Did you happen to stop by the coffee shop?" she asked with a coy smile.

"Yeah. How'd you know?"

"Well for one, you smell like you've been marinating in cigarettes and coffee, and two, I happen to know that a certain young man you seemed smitten with works there."

"Leo?"

"All the girls have a crush on Leo at one point. You'll grow out of it once you realize he's not necessarily the one-woman type. You're better off flirting with the horse."

It took Lyla a moment to realize what she meant, and then she faked a laugh.

"Oh, yeah. Aldo."

"What are your plans for the day?" she asked, putting her hands on her hips like she just transitioned from friend to mentor.

"I was actually going to try and get some writing done."

"Really?"

"Yeah. Does that surprise you?"

"A bit, yes, with everything that's been going on."

"Do you not think it's a good idea or something?"

"Oh, I think it's a great idea. In fact, I've got a bit of a challenge for you if you're up for it."

"What sort of challenge? I'm supposed to be meeting Linh at the bookstore soon to write with her."

"It's part of the program. Linh can wait. If it makes you feel better, I'll have someone phone the book shop and tell her you'll be just a little while longer."

Shit. She can't call the book shop because Linh's going to the coffee shop.

"I don't know, Julia. Can't this wait for another day?"

Julia's casual demeanor turned all business in an instant.

"No. I have other residents to attend to and assist. This is mandatory, and it would have been done already if it wasn't for the accident in your room."

"You mean the decapitation? It just seems a bit minimized when everyone keeps calling it 'the accident.'"

Julia cocked her head and smirked.

"Antonio was my friend. I've worked with him and Mariano since their first days here. If you're implying that I'm numb to the situation, you're confusing professionalism with apathy."

She seemed sincere.

"I'm sorry. I didn't mean to imply that you didn't care."

Julia lit a cigarette.

"Apology accepted. Now, let me get you back on track with your schedule as far as my duties are concerned. You said you were in the mood to write anyway."

"Okay."

"Let's take a walk to the courtyard."

Julia didn't wait for Lyla's agreement; she just strolled through the grass. Lyla reluctantly followed her as they walked past the front of the castle. Just as they were about to round The Keep and venture down the side, Lyla felt compelled to look back at the fifth-floor window. Only darkness stared back.

Lyla sighed.

"Something wrong, dear?" Julia asked.

"No. Just tired of all this walking, I guess."

"Ha! You have to move around. It keeps the blood pumping and the creative juices flowing."

Lyla didn't say anything.

"Morning, ladies," Julia said to the four residents on the back patio.

They all greeted her in their own ways. Lyla looked at Rachel, Rae,

Sue, and Becky with their empty plates and coffee cups piled on the table at which they sat. Lori was sprawled out on the lounge with her laptop open, typing away like she was in the zone. Lyla spotted Brittany sitting with Deja in the dining hall through the glass doors. The only resident she didn't see was Kay.

"Are you taking Lyla to the guest house?" Becky asked with a knowing grin that raised a red flag.

"Spoiler alert," Julia said.

"Oh, my bad," Becky said, and the girls laughed, obviously all in the know with what was going on.

"Good luck, Lyla," Rachel said.

Lyla glared at them and then hurried to keep pace with Julia.

"What are they talking about?" she asked, trying to mask the worry in her tone.

Julia smirked.

"I don't want to ruin the surprise. That's half the challenge."

"Why are we going to the guest house?"

"You'll see."

"I hate surprises."

"Everything you ever wanted lies on the other side of fear. Someone said that somewhere, and it's always stuck with me."

Lyla didn't respond. It was too early in the fucking morning for philosophy, and she had more pressing matters to attend to. She just needed to get through whatever awaited her in the guest house and get back to the coffee shop. The fact that all the other girls knew where the two of them were going and why, provided her with some comfort. It had to have something to do with writing and not a trap where Dante leaped out with an axe because she knew too much.

They were about halfway to the guest house—which was really just a separate building within the castle walls. As far as she knew, Claymont didn't have guests come over. And now that she thought about it, she'd never heard any of the other residents even talk about it.

"This sun is rather unforgiving, isn't it?" Julia began. "At least you got your exercise in early."

"Oh, I'm still sweating. So, why do they call this the guest house?"

"Because that's exactly what it was when this castle was in its heyday. People who were important to the owners during the different regime changes would stay there."

"And what is it now?"

Julia flicked her cigarette toward the castle wall to her left.

"You'll see."

Lyla shook her head in frustration, accepting the fact that she would get no further information. They walked in silence the rest of the way across the courtyard until they reached the one-story structure whose roof ran parallel with the rear castle wall, kept in the back like a dirty secret. Julia stepped onto the cement porch and stopped at the door. She withdrew her keyring and unlocked it.

"Why was it locked?" Lyla asked.

"Oh, for crying out loud, just come on, and you'll see. I promise it's not nearly as interesting as whatever plot your little horror machine making mind has concocted."

Lyla squinted at her. Julia pushed the door open and walked in.

Get it over with so you can get to the coffee shop.

"Okay. I'm coming," she said and stepped past Julia who held the door open for her.

The smells of cut grass and gasoline stopped her in her tracks as she entered the cool building. Julia shut the door, and just before the room went completely dark, she flicked the light switch, bringing life to two fluorescent tube lights hanging from the ceiling.

Lyla scanned her surroundings. Lawn and gardening equipment hung from one wall corkboard: leaf blowers, weed whackers, hedge trimmers, chainsaws, rakes, and shovels. Riding lawn mowers and push mowers were in a neat row beneath it. Across from that wall hung every tool imaginable with three massive toolboxes the size of her dresser sitting side-by-side. Tanks of gasoline with red plastic containers and funnels beside them were shoved against the far wall. A shelf full of engine and motor oils hung above them. She was in a glorified tool shed. All of the equipment looked like the most expensive version of everything that was in there, but the shed smell was the same as her dad's back home.

"I don't get it," Lyla said. "What are we doing?"

Julia smiled and took a step to the left to reveal the school desk behind her. She grabbed it by the front and slid it to the center of the room. As soon as she did that, another odor assaulted her senses: fertilizer. The wall behind Julia contained all the gardening equipment, and bags of soil, potting mix, and fertilizer were stacked against it.

"Eww," Lyla said. "It smells like shit and manual labor in here."

Julia laughed and gestured to the desk.

"That's precisely the point. Have a seat."

The desk had cobwebs on it, and Lyla was pretty sure she saw something scurry across it.

"I don't want to sit in that thing. It's disgusting."

"Again, part of the plan. Now have a seat."

Get. It. Over. With.

"I didn't see this room on the website," she said as she approached the desk. "What kind of test is this?"

"Endurance."

Lyla furrowed her brow. There was something in the way Julia looked at her that made her want to ace whatever test this was. She silenced her natural repulsion and sat, keeping eye contact with her instructor the entire time. She'd be damned if she was going to let this bitch get the better of her.

"Under your desk, you will find a pen and a notebook. Retrieve them now, please."

Lyla reached down and felt the notebook and the metal pen that probably cost a hundred dollars and placed them both on the desk.

"Okay, Lyla, here's your assignment. You will be given a writing prompt—"

Julia stopped speaking when the door opened. She turned to see one of the yard workers—a local who looked at Julia and Lyla and then went about his business like they weren't even there. Lyla watched him until Julia snapped her fingers like a stern teacher.

"You will be given a writing prompt, and you will have precisely thirty minutes to write whatever you can."

The man reeked of body odor in that way only being outdoors can produce as he unscrewed a red gas can and began filling it from one of the large drums. He coughed and sniffed, clearing his throat before he spat in the corner.

"Eww," Lyla said, watching him and then looking back at Julia. "How am I supposed to concentrate with all this?"

"All what?" Julia asked with mock offense, almost like she knew the question was coming.

"The disgusting smell, the fucking bugs on my desk, and workers walking in and out of here."

"That's the test, Lyla. A real writer can silence the senses. You have to ignore the distractions and disappear into your story."

"I haven't written a story longhand since elementary school," Lyla said, instantly realizing that's precisely why she was being forced to do it.

"Here's your prompt, and keep in mind you were supposed to have written about this before Lester's speech: You wake up, and you've lost the ability to speak."

Lyla understood why she had the upper hand in writing about this topic after listening to the Sterlings' presentation mentioning their daughter. It was the specific words he chose: "She never got to tell her story."

Okay, so the Sterlings want to hear how Lyla would relate to their daughter's struggle. It's fucking morbid, but just do it like a good little resident and get the hell out of here.

Julia looked at her watch and then back to Lyla.

"You have thirty minutes starting now," she said and left the building.

Lyla stared at the blank paper and the pen in her hand. She began her process the same way she always did; she closed her eyes and watched the movie in her mind. She embraced the darkness, the emptiness, until shapes and sensations began to form. Her feet walked on cold stone. The air reeked of rot and mildew. The only light came from an arched window across the room. And in that moment, Lyla knew exactly where her imagination had taken her. She was wandering around the fifth floor of The Keep.

Before she'd even opened her eyes, she'd written a paragraph.

TWENTY-TWO

Lyla finished the last few words of her short story as soon as the guest house door behind her opened. Groundskeepers had been going in and out ever since she'd started writing, and that was probably intentional. No, it was definitely intentional. Julia had probably been standing outside of the building the entire time, smoking and telling her little errand boys to keep up with steady interruptions to derail Lyla's train of thought.

Or test it?

Just the way the slower, more elegant way the door opened let her know it was Julia, and that her thirty minutes were up.

"Pen down," Julia said in a mock-teacher voice.

Lyla placed her pen on the desk and stared at the four handwritten pages, completely unaware of what was on them. She was lucid the whole time she'd been writing whatever she wrote, but it was as if she was on autopilot. The one aspect of the weird little experiment that sent a chill down her spine was the handwriting. She expected to look down and see her messy, out-of-practice scribbling, but that's not what she saw.

The first page was written in elegant cursive handwriting, the penmanship of a bygone era. She flipped the page, and the same writing continued on the back. Again, she turned the page, staring at her creation, realizing it wasn't her creation at all.

Julia snatched the papers before Lyla could analyze them any further.

"I'll take those," she said and slid them in a black leather designer bag that she didn't have before they came to the guest house. "You sure are a speedwriter. I think you're the first resident at Claymont I've ever seen write in cursive during this part of the program. It seems like a lost art."

Lyla was still trying to make sense of what just happened.

Act normal for now; analyze later. You need to get out of here. If she senses anything out of the ordinary, this whole plan could go to shit.

"Yeah, my mom insisted on it. I never broke the habit, I guess."

"Good for you."

Lyla squeezed out of the desk and pushed it back against the wall. Julia still stood between her and the door.

"So, how do you feel about it?"

"About what?" Lyla asked, suddenly feeling guilty of something even though she knew she did nothing wrong.

"What you wrote…and this little exercise, I guess."

Lyla had no idea what was on those pages, but the concept of what Julia was trying to do by forcing writers to generate ideas despite distracting surroundings did fascinate her on a craftsman level.

"My story is what it is, I guess. I do respect the method to your madness, though. It definitely makes me feel like I can endure an annoying housefly buzzing around while I'm trying to write on my couch with my MacBook," Lyla said, her sincerity surprising even herself.

That brought what appeared to be a genuine look of satisfaction to Julia's face.

"Good."

Lyla followed her outside. They crossed the courtyard. From her vantage point that far away from the castle, she could see the pool area on the left and the patio to the right. A couple of the girls were in the pool, but she couldn't see which ones. Two other residents were on the patio. Lori was still in the lounge with her laptop like she hadn't moved since they'd last seen her.

"Hey, Julia. What time is it?"

"Almost noon."

"Really? Shit."

Julia looked over her shoulder as she continued to walk.

"Don't worry. I'm sure Linh is still waiting on you. With any luck, she started writing without you. The Reader has given her very positive feedback."

Lyla thought of Linh standing in her bedroom staring at her with those blue eyes that weren't hers. The image made her stomach churn. Including that incident, Linh has lost control or—she still hated saying it—been possessed by something three times that she knew of.

"I'm curious what you wrote about in there," Julia said as they neared the patio.

"Are you going to read it?"

"Oh no. That's strictly forbidden. Even though the 'writing crucible' idea was all mine, the writing prompt was provided by Lester and Regina. They're the only ones who read it."

"Not even The Reader?"

"I wouldn't know."

So there are things that Julia doesn't know. The Sterlings keep her at some level of distance. Maybe she doesn't have every piece of the puzzle either.

"Oh. So, do you need me for anything else?" Lyla asked.

"Nope. You're free to go to town and work with Linh or leer at Leo until your heart's content."

Lyla forced a laugh.

"Okay."

Julia crossed the patio and nodded at Lori who didn't look up from her screen. She held the door open, and Lyla followed her in. The French woman walked like she was on a mission, immediately turning right and heading straight for the table in the dining hall where the Sterlings sat. Lyla's heart skipped a beat at the sight of them.

Both of them smiled and waved.

They are professional bullshitters. How can they sit there, looking like a happily married couple you'd see in a fucking Hallmark movie, and pretend like they didn't just have a heated argument this morning?

"That means they want you to come with me," Julie whispered while barely moving her mouth.

Both of them approached the couple who stood and greeted them.

"Julia, Lyla, good to see you both on this beautiful day," Lester said.

"You, too. Both of you," Lyla said.

Regina smiled and couldn't help but look at Julia and the bag she held.

"Regina and I were just discussing your submission piece," he said, catching Lyla off guard.

"You were?"

"Oh yes," he said. "I know you haven't had a chance to begin your work here yet, and I'd like to personally apologize for the rough start you've had. Ideally, you would've written your 'pressure piece,' as Julia so aptly dubbed the method, before my speech. I know that hearing of our daughter's passing, and her life story undoubtedly influenced your response either directly or on a subconscious level at the very least. But we have to play the hands we are dealt. This is a bit unorthodox for us, but if you don't object, Regina and I would like to read your submission now."

He looked at Julia, and she quickly pulled the pages from her bag.

Jesus, I don't even know what I wrote.

"Oh, okay," she began, feeling flustered but realizing that was okay because it would help sell the lie she was about to tell. "I get super self-conscious when people read my work in front of me. I hope you don't mind if I excuse myself."

"Not at all, dear," Regina said. "Feel free to go about your day. Don't let us keep you."

Has she been crying?

"Okay, thank you."

"No, thank you," Lester said with a steely cold gaze.

Lyla smiled awkwardly and took a step back from the table.

"Sit with us, Julia," Lester said in a tone she hadn't heard from him before.

He sounded like a boss talking with an employee, which he technically was. Lyla just found it hard to believe that a woman as strong and cool as Julia would obey his stern command.

God only knows how much he's paying her.

Or what he could do to her...

As soon as she opened the doors to the main hall, she took a deep breath and composed herself. She looked around and didn't see anyone, but that didn't mean she wasn't being watched, whether by someone unseen, cameras, or the presence that likes to visit her at night.

Lyla hurried down the red carpet and didn't stop until she reached the stairs. Someone was coming down, and it wasn't one of the girls. This person was wearing boots, and his heavy steps echoed in the stairwell. For a brief moment, she thought about just running out the castle doors and not stopping until she reached town.

Who cares about your passport and money right now? You just need to get out of here. Certainly, American citizens have lost their passports before. There must be a protocol for that scenario. Just get to the coffee shop and —

"Lyla?" Dante said, nearly stumbling as he took his last step out of the stairwell.

Shit.

His breath smelled like whiskey, and he looked like he hadn't showered or shaved since the last time she saw him. Dark circles hung like toothless grins under his eyes. Still, even with his disheveled appearance—and maybe even in spite of it—she couldn't help but find him attractive.

"Hey, Dante," she said, doing her best not to sound nervous. "How are you holding up?"

"How am I holding up?" he chuckled. "Peachy. Living the dream. Isn't that what they say in America?"

"Yeah, I guess."

He sniffed and forced a grin. There was something knowing in his gaze. Something that made her blood run cold because it was almost apologetic like he was going along with a program that didn't sit right with his morals.

"Is there anything I can help you with today?" he asked and suppressed a belch.

Lyla grimaced at the smell of booze that oozed from his pours.

"No, thank you. I'm just on my way to my room."

"Got some writing to do?" he asked and put his hand on the wall, blocking the entrance to the stairs, intentionally or not.

"Yes, as a matter of fact, I do."

"You were up pretty early this morning. Did you already knock some words out, as you writers like to say?"

"How do you know I was up early?"

"Because I was, too. I saw you leave from my office."

"Oh, I went into town. I needed a good walk to jar some ideas loose. It's what I do when all else fails."

Dante took his hand off the stone wall and crossed his arms, looking at her like he was sizing her up.

"Can I ask you something, just between us?"

"Sure," she said like she had any choice in the matter.

"After you left, I went down for breakfast and came back and noticed that someone had been in my room while I was gone. Do you have any idea why Linh went in my room this morning?"

She felt the blood drain from her face, and her throat went dry.

"I mean," he began, "I know I have an open-door policy. Residents pop in all the time when I'm not there and leave me notes, normally something to add to my to-do list. But this wasn't that. She went in my private quarters."

"How do you know?"

"Well, I saw her go in my office from the hallway camera. She was in there for longer than it would take to write a note or leave something for me—which she didn't do—and she left my residence door open. I always have it shut. As far as I can tell, she didn't take anything."

Lyla used every muscle in her face to act like she was hearing about it for the first time.

"That is weird. I'm sure it's just a misunderstanding. If nothing was missing, maybe she was just looking for you. You know how Linh can be," Lyla said and mimed like she was smoking a joint.

Dante half-smiled.

"Right, right. No, you're probably right. Probably nothing."

He stepped out of her way.

"Sorry, didn't mean to hold you up," he said.

"No worries," she said and was about to walk up the stairs but stopped and looked over her shoulder. "I hope I'm not out of line in saying this—"

"Uh oh, this ought to be good."

"The Sterlings are in there, meeting with Julia," she said, nodding toward the dining hall. "If I were you, I'd maybe shave and take a shower. You look like a walking hangover."

He gave that same confident half-grin like he was flattered that she was concerned for his job.

Like he has you right where he wants you?

No.

"Thanks, I appreciate the honesty. Seriously thanks for looking out for me."

"You're welcome."

"This place will definitely do it to you," he muttered and put his hands on his hips. "Eh, fuck it. I'm not too worried about it. When you have the stature that I do, you can get away with anything," he said with a wink.

"Right," Lyla said and awkwardly turned back to the stairs.

"Oh, Lyla, one more thing."

Good God, when will this conversation end?

"I don't know if you noticed that you had a loose tile in your bathroom ceiling just above the tub…"

She looked over her shoulder and shook her head.

"Oh, well I went ahead and fixed that for you."

What the fuck? That was fixed when you woke up this morning. Don't let him know that you know.

"Really? I didn't even see it. I appreciate it, though."

As she ascended the spiral staircase, he said, "Anytime."

TWENTY-THREE

Lyla entered her room and immediately shut and locked the door. She breathed a sigh of relief at just being by herself. It was only early afternoon, and she already had enough surprises and strange social interactions to last her the rest of the year.

"Back to the plan. Back to the plan," she mumbled to herself, scanning the room for her essentials.

She hurried to her desk and unplugged her MacBook and put it in her computer bag. Her purse sat on the floor beside the desk, but she didn't want to make it too obvious that she was skipping town. The only item she really needed out of there was her wallet and passport. She picked it up and placed it on the desk, rummaging through it until she found what she was looking for. She tucked them both in the zippered part of her bag right beside her laptop.

This is it.

She scanned the room one more time.

You're leaving with just the clothes on your back.

But I'm leaving. *That's something Ann didn't have the luxury of doing.*

Just to give it a final once over like she did any time she left for a trip, she stepped in the bathroom to see if there was something she wasn't thinking of on the counter but didn't see anything. As she turned around to walk back out, something on the ceiling above the tub caught her eye.

What the hell?

The same piece of tile hung down, maybe even further this time like it still had something under it. Dante had said he'd fixed it. That meant he read the note, and she assumed he would've taken it. Lyla remembered the only mention of him in the letter, and she recalled the rumors that he had a "thing" with Ann. She had said that she didn't know for sure, but she thought he was the one person she could trust at Claymont. After that interaction Lyla just had with the man, it certainly didn't feel that way.

Still, he had said he'd fixed it, and he clearly hadn't.

"Shit."

She grabbed the chair from her desk and pulled it back into the bathroom like she had once before. After climbing atop, she carefully fingered the corner of the tile, and a folded piece of paper fell out and landed on the floor. She hopped off and picked it up. The first thing she noticed was the brightness of the note. Whatever this was, it had been written on new paper. She eyeballed the stack of white paper on her desk and the pen beside it. It didn't have its lid on.

Lyla racked her brain but couldn't remember if she'd ever used it. The pangs of panic felt like two hands climbing up her back and reaching inside to squeeze her lungs. She took a deep breath, something she had grown accustomed to doing even more than usual since she'd arrived at Claymont, and then she unfolded the note.

Her eyes widened and her jaw dropped. This was not the same note that Ann had left as a warning for the next resident. This was a brand-new note, a new warning. In what looked like the same black ink from that pen on her desk, someone had scribbled, *Leave now! Don't end up like Ann.*

Lyla's hands trembled.

What is going on?

Dante had said he'd repaired the tile. He made sure to tell her that just before she came up here. She hadn't noticed the white cross and the bulging tile the first couple of nights she was there, so why did it stand out so prominently the night she found it? Did Dante put it there? Had he had Ann's note all along? Did he paint the cross?

Yes! He did! It was a warning. He had a thing for Ann. He's probably held a resentment against the Sterlings and anyone else in their employ for what happened. Maybe he'd seen one too many "accidents" and Ann was the last straw. He was a local, after all. Sure, some of the townspeople looked at him like he was worse than the Americans because he was one of their own. And now they viewed him as Lester and Regina Sterling's henchman. No wonder he drank so much and stayed at the castle more than he let on. He's looking for a way out...a way to make amends for Ann!

In that moment, Lyla felt pity for Dante, the lonely program director of Claymont and the reviled outcast from Umbertide.

KNOCK. KNOCK. KNOCK.

Lyla jumped at the sound of someone pounding on her bedroom door. She quickly balled up the paper and flushed it.

"One second!" she said and washed her hands to really sell that she had been using the restroom.

She carried the chair back to her desk and made sure there wasn't anything too obviously incriminating left out. Everything appeared to be in order, so she crossed the room and stopped at the door.

KNOCK. KNOCK. KNOCK.

Lyla jumped again, pissed at herself for getting startled.

"Lyla, it's Julia."

She hesitated even opening the door, but what choice did she have?

You're just gathering your things and heading into town to meet up with Linh and write at the bookstore. You've got this.

She unlocked the door and opened it.

Lyla looked at her suspiciously.

"Why'd you have the door locked?" she asked.

"What kind of question is that?" Lyla responded, genuinely perplexed as to why it would seem that odd for a resident to have her bedroom door locked.

"There's no need for locked doors here is all I was saying. But it's neither here nor there," she said, walking in and shutting the door behind her.

"Is there something else you have planned for me? I don't have time for any other surprises. No offense, I'm just supposed to be in town right now working on my book, and I'm already late from the pressure cooker in the guest house."

Julia crossed the room and sat on her bed. She patted the spot on the mattress beside her. She was smiling. That was odd. Julia was always laid back when she wasn't carrying out official Claymont business, but Lyla had never seen her so joyous. She was acting like she had a secret she couldn't wait to share with her, and the giddiness radiated from her expression and body language.

Lyla didn't know what was more off-putting: Julia's dominating teacher persona she'd met in the guest house while she scribbled out the story she still didn't remember writing or seeing the French businesswoman so excited. Regardless, Lyla did as she was told and took a seat beside her.

"What's going on, Julia? You're kind of freaking me out right now."

Julia laughed and took out her pack of cigarettes, not bothering to ask if Lyla minded if she smoked in her bedroom. Hell, Lyla wasn't even sure anyone was allowed to smoke inside the castle.

I guess rules don't apply to the woman who makes them. Julia is a do as I say and not as I do type of person.

"Oh, you don't need to be freaked out. But you're probably going to freak out when I tell you the news."

"What is it?" Lyla asked with equal parts trepidation and genuine excitement—again, allowing her writer's ego to poke its head out of the soil of her brain like a curious gopher.

"Lester and Regina read your piece."

Lyla suddenly felt nauseous, not really sure where this was headed, unable to see any positive possible outcomes.

"They *fucking* love it!" she said, eyes beaming. She gripped Lyla's hands like she was trying to transmit her enthusiasm through touch. "They're taking it to The Reader right now!"

The Reader.

The nickname left a sour taste in her mouth, but she had to act happy about it.

"Seriously?" she asked, with genuine disbelief, considering the fact that she had no idea what was written on those four pages.

"Yes! Do you know what this means?"

"No. What does it mean?"

"The Sterlings have *never* had a reaction to anything that's been produced in the guest house. I've seen them impressed by submission pieces, like they were with yours, but they've never gone straight to The Reader with a glorified writing exercise."

"Wow. I, uh, I don't know how to feel right now," Lyla said, even more baffled than before.

"Fucking elated! That's how you should feel! If The Reader likes what you wrote as much as they do, then you could get the fast track to publication. You know they can get you in with any publishing house in the world, right?"

"So I've heard."

"Why are you not freaking out right now?"

"I am…I think I'm just in a state of shock," Lyla said, which wasn't a total lie. "I still need to go to the bookstore. Linh is waiting for me."

Julia shook her head.

"Linh can wait. She'll get impatient soon enough and come back. Trust me. I know Linh. She'll probably start wondering where you are, buy a few books or find another reason not to write, and then hold a resentment against you for making her wait. Sorry about that. Well, not really. The reason you stood her up was because I forced you to produce the best piece of writing the Sterlings have read since we started this place!"

Linh and Leo have to come through for her. Surely, with her being gone this long and probably a lot longer by the way things are going, they'll…

They'll what? Leo said the cops were crooked and in the Sterling's pockets. He's not going to call any authorities.

But he could call Mom and Dad, especially if Linh showed up and told him the crazy shit she overheard. They'd definitely do something to save her and all the other residents if they knew people's lives were at stake. Hopefully Leo would at least tell his mom. That woman didn't seem like she'd back down from a fight, and if there were so many locals who were as sick of the Sterlings as Leo had said, she didn't see why they wouldn't band together to put an end to Claymont once and for all.

"Oh, I don't feel comfortable with that. I need to at least run down to town and tell her. It was my idea to meet down there. She didn't even want to leave the castle. I had to practically beg her to come with me so I could bounce some story ideas off her."

"Nope. Not today."

"What do you mean?"

"If The Reader responds to the story the way The Sterlings anticipated, then you'll be taking a trip to the fifth floor."

The details of Ann's warning note flashed through her mind. She'd said it was a tomb with an otherworldly atmosphere. She described seeing The Reader's feet at the crack under the door back up as she did. Lyla recalled her own eerie encounter of seeing the woman mimic her actions from the window at the front of The Keep. Her stomach was a bowling ball of dread.

"What's the matter?" Julia asked, seemingly genuinely surprised.

Lyla could read people. She'd done it in college in order to find the group of friends who were as genuine about their crafts as she was. Her skill sometimes came out so bluntly that it ruined relationships before they even began like at the interrogation breakfast where she had to go around the table and say something about each resident.

But as she sat on the bed beside Julia, a terrible epiphany came over her. The skill that she relied on more than she realized was obscured when it came to anyone complimenting her writing. That's why she didn't immediately pick up on Lester and Regina's motives, because whatever they were, they weren't good. It's the same reason why she had such a difficult time seeing if Julia was bullshitting her or not, even in that very moment.

Linh heard Regina accuse Lester of killing their daughter and warning him that he's about to potentially kill someone else. Were they talking about you?

Two light taps came from the bedroom door.

"Come in," Julia said like it was her room.

The doorknob turned, and Dante slowly peeked inside.

"Dante, what are you doing here? Don't you have a shower and a shave to attend to?" Julia said, as she puffed her cigarette.

"Lester and Regina want to see you in their quarters," he said to her.

Julia got up and hurried to the bathroom. Lyla heard a brief hiss and the toilet flush. She walked out sans cigarette.

"Since when are we allowed to smoke in the building?" Dante asked.

"Oh, chill out," Julia said to him and then directed her attention toward Lyla. "Moment of truth. Keep your fingers crossed."

Dante held the door open for her as she walked out and turned right.

"Use some mouthwash, for Christ's sake," Julia said from the hall.

Dante didn't say anything or move from the open door.

"Aren't you coming?" Julia asked from farther down.

"They told me to stay with Lyla until they talked to you."

"Okay…"

Dante looked to his left like he was waiting for her to disappear in the stairwell. She must've been far enough away because he shut the door and whipped his head toward Lyla with raised eyebrows and fear in his eyes.

"You have to get out of here, now."

"Dante, what's going on?"

"Did you not see my note? I know you saw Ann's note."

"I did. What is going on here?"

"There's no time, Lyla. You have to get out of here right now. I don't want you to become Claymont's latest 'accident'," he said, leaning against the door for support.

Good Lord, he can barely stand. How drunk is he?

It didn't matter. His booze was his problem. She didn't need to hear anything else. Lyla grabbed her bag. She looked around, fearing she was forgetting something.

"Come on," he said.

"Okay, shit."

Dante opened the door for her, and a fresh exhale of bourbon stained her face. She held her breath as she ran down the stone steps that were dangerous at a normal pace, but moving as quickly as she was caused her to nearly stumble. She regained her balance at the second-floor landing and kept moving.

As soon as she headed to the first floor, she realized Dante wasn't following her.

What the hell is he doing?

He's probably going to the meeting with the Sterlings and Julia right now.

Fuck! There probably is no meeting with the Sterlings and Julia. Dante just made that up to get Julia out of the room. It's only a matter of time before they realize something is wrong.

Dante grunted. Something thudded upstairs. Lyla froze. A *thwack* echoed in the stairwell. Lyla listened to a massive weight tumbling, breaking, and grunting down the stairs until it came to an abrupt stop.

Run.

Dante is shitfaced. He fell and could be seriously hurt…or worse.

Or he was pushed. Either way, he did it for you to get the hell out of here, so move!

Lyla finally made it to the first floor and ran straight into Lester. He'd come out of nowhere and stopped her like a brick wall. The man was more than double her age but was cut like the stone that composed the castle.

"Oof!" he said.

Lyla looked at him like she'd just bumped into Michael Myers on the streets of Haddonfield.

"My dear, are you alright?"

"Yes, I'm fine," she said. "Are you?"

"Aside from the wind getting knocked out of me, I'll survive," he said with a smile. "I took some serious hits when I played lacrosse for Stanford, but this one rivaled any of those."

"Sorry. I was just on my way out. I have to hurry and meet Linh at the bookstore in town."

In the sudden shock of literally running into Lester, she'd forgotten about Dante. But the shrill shriek from the second floor filled the stairwell like a train whistle. Another scream, but that one was from a different resident. Lester shot Lyla a glare.

"What's happened?" he asked.

Lyla opened her mouth but could only shake her head.

"Someone help!" a resident shouted.

Lyla thought it sounded like Rae.

"Dante fell down the stairs, and he's hurt!" Deja screamed.

Lester's eyes darted to Lyla.

"Why were you really running, Lyla?" he said with that deep voice in an accusatory tone. "I think it's best you come with me so we can sort this out."

Lyla didn't have a chance to resist. Lester started walking up the steps. His imposing frame blocked the staircase, and Lyla could only back up.

There were more footsteps above them. It sounded like two sets quickly descending.

"Holy shit," Julia said from just around the curve.

"Lester!" Regina yelled.

"I'm coming," he said.

Lyla finally turned around when she reached the second-floor landing. Dante's broken body lay in a growing pool of blood. He was on his side with an arm wrapped around his back. A bone protruded from the back of his broken neck. A few of his front teeth were missing, and one eyeball had popped forward.

Lyla turned and vomited all over the steps behind her. It splashed against the stone and coated Lester's legs. He didn't even acknowledge it though. He was staring at Dante's corpse, the residents who'd initially discovered him, and Regina and Julia standing beyond the body on the stairs leading to the third floor.

"Julia," he said, immediately getting her attention. "Get the residents out of here. Call the drivers and take them out for the day."

Her eyes were wide, and her body was shaking, but she did as she was told and stepped around Dante and into the second-floor hallway.

"Let's go," Julia said to Rae and Deja. "Go get your stuff while I round up the others."

The two girls didn't move, and that's all it took for Julia to snap back into professional mode.

"Ladies! We have to clear out. Go!"

They listened.

"Regina," Lester began. "Go to our room and call for an ambulance."

She didn't waste any time hurrying back to the fourth floor.

"You," he said to Lyla with a hint of disgust buried in his tone. "Run to the third floor and see if any residents are in their rooms. If they are, tell them to get ready to leave and to wait for Julia to escort them downstairs."

"Okay," Lyla said, gagging as she stepped over Dante's mangled body that smelled like a broken bottle of Jack Daniels and copper.

She hurried to the next floor and ran down the hallway banging on doors, one after another, not waiting for anyone to answer. She would address them if they came out. Once she reached the final door, she turned around and saw an empty hallway. Linh was hopefully still in town, trying to figure something out with Leo. She prayed Mom and Dad were coming through with a flight for her and she could get out of this godforsaken place.

"Okay, let's go, ladies. Just don't look as you pass by the accident," Julia said.

She must've gotten more than just Rae and Deja because Lyla heard a mix of gasps and shocked exclamations as she pictured them entering the staircase and finding it impossible to not look at the crooked man shattered on the stone. Lyla saw Regina pass by her floor on her way down.

"The police are on the way," she said.

"Okay," Lester said.

"Good God. I can't imagine what his blood-alcohol levels are right now. He must've just fallen."

Lyla just stood against the wall opposite the first doorway in the hall, trying to process what had just happened.

Dante was piss drunk. He could've easily fallen down the steps. Hell, you almost did, and you're sober.

He also tried to warn you and sent Julia away so you could escape. Now he's dead, and they know he lied to them.

Lyla listened as Lester's loud footsteps grew louder as he ascended the spiral staircase.

TWENTY-FOUR

Lyla stood in place and watched the tall man stop at the third-floor landing and glare at her down the hallway. His steps were so loud that she didn't even hear Regina following him. But while Lester stayed put, Regina said something to him, patted him on the arm, and walked toward Lyla. Lester turned away and continued up the staircase.

The commotion from the first two floors had all but died out once Julia had ushered the rest of the residents out of the castle. She wondered if Dante still lay on the stone, twisted like a pretzel and leaking like a half-eaten jelly doughnut. Sometimes she hated having a writer's mind, a pictorial imagination—not that she needed to create a horrifying image after seeing the real thing; that one was permanently seared in her brain, no doubt.

"Lyla, are you okay?" Regina asked as she closed the gap between them.

The two ladies stood in the hallway lit by chandeliers and light from the archers' windows. Lester's stomping continued to echo down. He was going to the fifth floor. They would've heard him if he'd gone to their private living quarters on the floor above them.

Lyla wanted to scream out that she was not fucking okay, and all she wanted to do was get back to West Virginia and forget Claymont ever existed. But that wasn't the way out of the climax of her current predicament, and she knew it.

"I'm terrified," she said, knowing the best lies are embedded with truths. "I just want to leave, Regina. I can't deal with all this…this…"

"Death?" Regina said, finishing her sentence for her.

"Yes."

"May we step into your room and talk for a moment?"

The way she asked it, with tears in her eyes, gave Lyla some hope that there could be room to negotiate her way out of there.

"Yeah, okay," she said and led the way.

Regina didn't shut the door behind her. She walked straight to Lyla's bed and sat down like Julia had.

"Have a seat, Lyla. You're in shock over this terrible situation, but we need to talk about something important, and I don't want you collapsing on me. I can't deal with any more medical emergencies."

Lyla did as she was told. She knew she had to gain the woman's trust. She had to give a little to get some in return.

"I want to ask you something, and I want you to tell me the truth. Can you promise to do that for me?"

Regina looked like she had tears in her eyes, like a woman who'd been through a lifetime of misery and carried with her the burden of having lost a child and being forced to endure the rest of her days with a hole in her heart.

"Yes, of course."

"Julia came to my room shortly before all this pandemonium ensued."

Lyla waited for her to continue her story, but she just stared at her. Regina was trying to read her reaction. Lyla knew how to read people by catching them off guard and that's exactly what Mrs. Sterling was attempting to do now.

Don't budge.

Lyla continued to pretend like she had no idea where she was going with the conversation. Regina, seemingly satisfied, continued speaking.

"She told me Dante had sent her to our room. She said Lester and I wanted to speak with her privately."

Half-truths. Give her half-truths.

"He did. I was talking with Julia when he knocked on my door and said that, actually."

"What were you all talking about?"

"I don't want to get her in trouble if I'm speaking out of school here…"

"Oh, you don't have to worry about that. Julia is family to us."

"Okay, she told me that you all loved my submission piece that got me accepted into the residency, but you were blown away by what I wrote in the guest house."

Regina nodded and said, "Is that all?"

"No," Lyla said and swallowed, her dry tongue grating against the roof of her mouth. "She tried to talk me out of leaving Claymont."

"How did she go about doing that?"

"She said that you and Lester had never gotten so excited over a resident's work before and that you all were taking the new piece directly to The Reader," Lyla said and broke eye contact, looking at the floor with forced shame. "She also said that if The Reader liked what I wrote then I was pretty much guaranteed an agent and a big publishing deal."

Even though she wasn't looking directly at Regina, she saw her smile from her periphery.

"She's right about, well, all of that."

For a few seconds, Lyla succumbed to the temptation and pictured her life as an international bestselling author, commanding multi-million-dollar advances, having publishers begging for her latest horror tale, and each one of her books turned into modern classic horror cinema.

Focus.

"I do need to tell you something, though," Regina said, and Lyla met her gaze.

"What is it?"

"Lester and I never asked Dante to send Julia to our floor."

"You didn't?" Lyla reacted like she was baffled. "Then why would he say that?"

"Why, indeed."

The ensuing silence kicked Lyla's anxiety into hyperdrive with each passing second.

"I know Dante entered this room after Julia left."

Regina left it at that, placing the ball firmly on Lyla's side of the court.

Don't hesitate. If you hesitate, she'll see it.

"He did."

"Well, what did he say?"

"He was drunk," Lyla said and hated herself for the excuse she knew would buy her some time. "He came in and tried to kiss me." She forced her eyes to water, but she didn't have to try too hard. "I… I'd be lying if I said I didn't want him to. Honestly, if he didn't reek of alcohol, I probably would've done it. God, I'm so stupid."

Regina patted Lyla's back.

"That's why I ran out of my room. I don't know if he tried to chase me because he thought I was going to tell on him or something, but I feel like this is all my fault."

"It is not your fault. It's mine…and Lester's."

Lyla looked at her with ruffled eyebrows.

"This isn't the first time Dante has broken boundaries with a resident," Regina said. "Ann, the girl who stayed in this room before you, also had a thing for Dante. From what the other residents said, she was a bit obsessed with him and didn't exactly keep it a secret. Dante, according to his testimony, did have relations with her, but he broke it off rather quickly. That was the night Ann left. We all believe she was heartbroken and fled in the middle of the night to avoid any embarrassing confrontation. And, well, that's when tragedy struck. It was rainy, the driver didn't see her, and you know the rest of the story."

Lyla just nodded.

"I'm sorry this happened. We should have terminated him on the spot. It's just so difficult to find good help locally. I don't mean for that to sound like an excuse, but I'm sure you've witnessed firsthand how some of the people in the area view our little program."

Again, Lyla only nodded.

"Do you accept my apology?"

"Yes. I just want to move forward and forget about it."

Lyla knew that's exactly what Regina wanted to hear. The woman perked up a bit.

"Good. That's what we want, too. And I have just the news that I think will help us do that."

Lyla waited.

"The Reader wants to meet you and offer you a deal."

"Really?"

"Yes!" Regina said and stood up. "Lester is with her right now. They're waiting on us."

Her.

"Oh, wow. I, um, don't know how to feel right now. So much has happened. Is it wrong to feel excited about your dreams when you just witnessed a nightmare?"

Regina smiled, still with a sadness lingering behind them that someone not as keen on reading people wouldn't detect.

"Absolutely not. And while we're up there, Julia will be working with the medics and police to get everything cleaned up. Our maintenance crew will do the rest. When you walk back down those stairs after meeting with The Reader, you won't have to worry about the mess."

"Okay," Lyla said, as solemnly as she could and stood up. "I guess I don't need this right now," she said, still holding her wallet with her passport.

"Not now."

Lyla placed the wallet on the computer desk and slid a pen in her pocket. She turned around to face Regina.

"I'm ready."

Regina smiled and approached the door. Lyla stepped forward, knowing this was her only way out. But she had hope. She'd set the pieces in motion for her escape. Linh and Leo had to come through for her. She'd been gone for so long and knew she wouldn't be going back. They would get someone to help her. They must.

Don't forget about Janie Sterling. "All of Claymont was for her." These *apparitions you've been seeing, the residents acting like they were possessed—all of them with blue eyes—and the obituary picture of Janie that looked so much like the figure who kept sneaking into her room, could very well be the spirit of their dead daughter. And even though you don't believe in that shit, you've seen enough to be stupid to rule it out as a possibility. Plus, if Janie is waiting for her, don't you think she'd be very interested to find out that her own father killed her?*

"Well then, after you," Regina said as she opened the door to the hallway.

Lyla took a deep breath and walked out with Regina right behind her.

"I have to admit, I'm a bit nervous," Lyla said.

"There's nothing to be nervous about. Your skills got you here."

As they approached the stairwell, Lyla listened for any sounds of emergency service personnel, but all was quiet. Dante's corpse was most likely still sprawled across the second-floor landing, cold and bled out.

A door opened and shut from above, and Lyla knew it wasn't the floor above them. Someone had just opened the door at the top of The Keep, and judging by the heavy *thuds* of the descending footfalls, Lester Sterling was on his way down. Lyla paused.

"Lester will meet us on the fourth floor," Regina said, allowing Lyla to go up first.

Great. Now you're trapped between them.

"Come on up, Lyla," Lester said in his deep but warm tone.

Lyla began to walk up, slowly, step by step like a prisoner on death row taking her final stroll. As soon as she rounded the curve, she saw Lester standing at the fourth-floor landing with a welcoming smile, the same one he'd sported the first time she'd seen him at the bottom of the staircase on the night of his presentation and grand dinner.

Once she was a few steps away from him, she could see the same troubled look in his eyes that his wife had. To say they were hiding something would be the understatement of the decade; Lyla knew that. But what confused her the most was the sadness. She saw no malicious intent or sadistic glee. The two of them looked like parents who had just lost their daughter, or, at the very least, were continuing to relive it.

Lester gestured for Lyla to walk past him. She looked at the stone stairs and remembered what Ann had said about the change in the atmosphere. If there was tangible validity to the supernatural experiences described in the former resident's warning letter, Lyla was about to find out.

TWENTY-FIVE

"Go on," Regina encouraged. "She's waiting for you."

Lyla looked over her shoulder at the couple.

"Yes, it's best not to keep her waiting," Lester said.

Lyla turned back around and stared at the spiraling staircase of stone that led only to darkness. She took a step.

And then another.

And then another.

As she rounded the curve, it was like she walked into a cave, one that was both chilly and full of sticky humidity, a sensation she'd never felt before. She stopped immediately.

"What's wrong with the air?"

"Ahh, that's centuries of life and death, my dear," Lester said. "The earth the castle is built upon exhales its memories and minerals throughout the structure, and it all collects up here—the fifth floor of The Keep."

Umber.

"Forgive the smell of this hallway," Regina cut in. "There was nothing we could do about that without damaging the castle itself, and the locals wouldn't take too kindly to it anyway. I assure you that The Reader's quarters are as pleasant as money can buy."

Come on, Linh. Come through for me, please.

Lyla felt a hand on her shoulder, and she jumped.

"It's quite alright," Lester said as he walked behind her.

She took another step because she feared he would pick her up and carry her to the room if she refused.

"That's it," he said, releasing his hand.

Lyla made it around the turn and saw the final few stairs that led to a landing with no light. She tasted the air and nearly gagged. A thick invisible fog filled the tiny space, smelling of rot. If she were writing a story about the place, she'd compare it to the inside of a tomb or the waft of death that would surely rush from a lifted sarcophagus of some Egyptian pharaoh.

A small sliver of light shined through the crack under the door. It was an amber glow, flickering like flames burning inside the room. She tried to recall what Ann's letter had said.

Did she mention anything about fire? Or was it a pale light?

The one distinct image she recalled from the cautionary tale was the feet that stood on the other side of the door. Lyla didn't see anything. If there was a person inside, he or she wasn't standing by the door, ready to mimic her movements.

"Just step onto the landing and make way. I'll get the door," Lester said.

Lyla gladly backed away from the glowing room that looked like it contained the fires of Hell itself. The door seemed to move. No, it was covered in moving things. Ann had said maggots. She pretended not to notice and watched Lester withdraw a set of keys from his pocket and unlock The Reader's door.

"Why would you need to lock her in the room?" Lyla wondered out loud.

Lester looked back at her.

"Oh, it's not to keep her in," he chuckled. "She can come and go as she pleases. It's to keep curious residents from trying to sneak a peek."

"Yes," Regina said from behind her. "Two of our ladies from the first year were intoxicated one night and decided that it would be a good idea to catch a glimpse of The Reader."

"Did they get in?"

"Oh yes."

"What happened to them?"

Lester unlocked the door and said, "They were immediately discharged and signed a non-disclosure agreement. Hence, the lock."

He pulled the key out and put the ring back in his pocket.

"After you," he said.

You have the upper hand. Show no fear. Keep them thinking you're a naïve young lady who will do anything to be the queen of horror literature.

Lyla nodded and approached the door. She could feel the warmth at her feet, but the doorknob was cool to the touch.

Bizarre.

After a deep breath of the dank air, she opened it and stepped inside. Lester and Regina rushed in and shut the door. Lyla acknowledged their hurried entry but was too focused on making sense of the surroundings to analyze their strange behavior.

There was no furniture or luxury living accommodations. The room was barren save for the candelabras resting atop two wooden tables pushed against the walls on her left and right. The stone floor matched the ceiling, and shadows danced no matter where she looked. The infamous arch-shaped window she'd seen the figure in was straight ahead and open, yet she felt no draft; it was as if the air from the outside world dared not enter this dwelling.

Regina brushed by Lyla and walked past the table in the center of the square-shaped room and stood next to the window, staring out at the darkening sky. From the walkway leading up to the castle's front doors, Lyla imagined she would look quite like a shadowy silhouette.

Was it her? Was Regina Sterling the mysterious figure? If she wore her dark hair down, she very well could be. Holy shit.

Wait, what's with the table?

Lyla studied the sturdy table made of thick, dark wood. The longer she peered at it, the stranger it appeared. It looked more dusty and darker in some spots than others as if someone had smeared a brown pigment all over it.

Umber.

The table-length box that sat on top was covered in it, too—so much so, that it was difficult to tell where one started and the other one ended. She noticed that the box was also secured by a thin, taut rope to the table. Lyla's brain slowly came back to reality, overcoming its shocked state that she didn't know she was in until she snapped out of it. But by then, it was too late.

Don't freak out.

"Here she comes," Regina said from the window.

Who?

"Good. She's right on time," Lester said, standing beside Lyla.

Lyla looked at the room's centerpiece and prayed it was anything other than what she thought it was.

"What's going on?" she finally asked, careful to make her tone sound more inquisitive than afraid.

"You walked onto these grounds by choice, yes?" he asked.

"Yes."

"And you entered the castle and accepted a room on your own accord, yes?"

"Yes."

"You ascended the steps and crossed the threshold into this dwelling of your own free will, yes?"

"Yes."

"Good. It's essential that we acknowledge that you've passed every measure of our program by your own volition."

"Why?" Lyla asked, unable to stifle the tremble in her voice that time.

"That's just how the ritual has to happen," Regina said, still staring outside.

The ritual.

"A ritual? What kind of a ritual, Mr. and Mrs. Sterling?" she asked, still trying to give off the impression that what was happening was a normal part of the residency.

A door opened and shut below them. Lyla turned to Lester and saw that he looked more distraught than ever before, or maybe it was the shadows of the flames playing tricks on her. She honestly couldn't tell anymore. Faint footsteps gradually got louder as someone ascended the staircase. Neither one of them had addressed her question. It was then that something shined in Lester's hand as the flicker of light hit the knife just right.

"Lester, what's with the knife?" she asked as she took a step back toward the door.

"It's for the rope," he said with no discernible emotion.

She looked back at the box she knew was a casket and the stretches of rope that bound it.

After a moment of silence as she worked up the nerve to speak, she finally asked, "What's in the box?"

"Lester?" a woman said from behind the door, startling Lyla.

"Come in," he said.

The door opened, and Julia cautiously stepped in, looking at the scene before her much like Lyla had done.

"Are the residents in the hotel?" he asked.

"Yes. Everything is taken care of."

"And you've arranged for their flights and know precisely what to tell them?"

"Yes. I'll follow every instruction, Lester. You don't have to worry."

"Good."

Julia appeared out of her element, being the one receiving the orders and seeming somewhat out of the loop. She gave Lyla one quick glance and immediately looked away when she met her gaze.

She's ashamed of something.

"Thank you, Julia," Regina said, finally turning to face them.

She walked around the table and stood beside Julia.

"Is she…the one?" Julia asked.

Regina nodded and smiled as tears fell down her cheeks.

They're talking about you. Get ready for anything.

Lyla couldn't tell if Regina's tears came from a source of joy or despair…or both.

"So, I'm finished?" Julia asked.

"Yes," Lester began. "Regina, give her the address."

Regina withdrew a small piece of paper and handed it to Julia.

"This is where she is?" Julia asked, looking back and forth between the Sterlings. "Sasha is at this address?"

"Yes. That's one of our properties in Paris. She's with Sophie, as you know. You are now free to get her. We'll let Sophie know her nanny services are no longer required. And for your pain and suffering, and especially your silence regarding this matter, you'll see that one billion dollars has been wired to your account."

Now, Julia was crying.

"Go home Julia," Regina said. "Thank you for everything you've done for us. I know it hasn't been easy. From one mother to another, I can't tell you how sorry I am for what we've done."

Julia just nodded, looked at both of them and began to back out of the room like she was half-expecting Lester to literally stab her in the back as soon as she let down her guard. She locked eyes with Lyla and mouthed the words, "I'm sorry." And just as quickly as she'd come, Julia left, descending the stairs and fleeing into the night where an idling car awaited her on the stone road.

Julia was working for the Sterlings against her will from the very beginning. They kidnapped her fucking daughter to make her do it. No one lured her away from her glamorous job in Paris to come and live in Umbertide and run a writer's residency. They needed her, and she delivered.

But what did they need her for? Yes, she claimed to have created the logistics, the rules, the experience, and even the décor. But what was the end game? The entire history of The Claymont Residency for Writers transpired just to lead to this very moment? Julia had called you "the one." What—who—were they searching for. What are you "the one" for?

Oh my God. Has it really been in front of you the whole time? Lester had said this was all to honor Janie's memory because she never got to tell her story. Did they need someone to do that? And what do these fucking lunatics plan to do with that box?

"Look," Lyla began. "I don't know what's going on here, and I don't want to know. I just want to leave."

"I think you know exactly what's going on here, Lyla," Lester said, taking a step closer to her.

He lifted the knife and turned it in his hand, so the flames illuminated the blade like he's making sure she gets a good view of the weapon. She took a step back and bumped into the table, but it didn't budge.

"Careful now," he said. "I wasn't lying when I said this blade is for that rope, but I will use it on you if I must. Rest assured. I do not want that to happen."

"Me either," Lyla said. "What do you need me to do?"

Lester and Regina looked at each other like they were surprised by her compliance and then turned their gazes back on her.

"I need you to climb on the top of that box and lie on your back."

Her stomach iced over. He continued to stare at her, expression unchanging.

"I don't think I can."

"Oh, don't doubt yourself, Lyla. I never took you for the timid type."

"No, I mean, I don't think I can physically get up there. It's too high off the ground."

"Give her a boost, Lester," Regina said.

He briefly regarded his wife and then turned back to face her. Lyla faced the box, carefully pulling the fountain pen from her pocket and shielding it with her arm. She watched Lester take a knee behind her and place the knife on the ground so he could cup his hands together.

"Okay, give me your foot," he said.

She lifted her right foot and placed it in his hands. Just as he strained to give her the extra step she needed, Lyla gripped the pen and swung her arm around. The metal tip made a wet popping sound as the pen stabbed through his left cheek.

Shit.

She'd been aiming for his neck, but that blow would have to do. It would serve as much of a distraction as she needed, at least. Lester's eyes bulged with shocked terror. Lyla took off toward the door but felt his firm grip snatch her ankle just before she could clear his reach. His squeezing hand was a python that jerked with the strength of a desperate man who'd worked too hard to let her ruin his master scheme.

Lyla fell face first onto the door, losing consciousness before having a chance to feel any pain.

TWENTY-SIX

"Lyla."

Her mind was swirling in the tar of oblivion, but a voice kept calling her back.

"Lyla, wake up."

It was a woman's voice, a familiar one. She felt herself being pulled back into the world with each word. A sudden smack jolted her eyes open. The pain on the right side of her cheek let her know that she had been slapped. Her vision was blurry, and her head throbbed. Something was wrong with her equilibrium. She wasn't on her feet.

Of course you're not on your feet. You just woke up.

So where am I?

Lyla blinked and saw a stone wall. No, it was a ceiling. There was no light hanging from it, though. Orange flames cast a flickering glow across it like she was looking at a river of lava.

Candles... Stone ceiling... You're on your back on the fifth floor of The Keep.

But she wasn't on the ground. She tried to move. Something held her down on the slab of wood.

"Lyla, look at me," Regina said.

It was her voice that you heard. It was her hand that you felt.

Anger boiled inside. Lyla tried to strike the woman, but the ropes binding her down wouldn't allow it. She attempted to look to the side and felt the taut rope rub into her forehead.

Ropes… You're tied to the top of the box on the table. This must be part of their ritual.

"Lyla, are you lucid?" Regina asked.

Before she could answer, Lester stepped into her field of vision, looking down on her as he held a blood-soaked garment against his face. Lyla couldn't help but smile.

If only it had been his throat…

"She's with us," he said. "I don't blame you for what you did. I would've done the same thing if I was in your position."

Lyla swallowed before trying to speak and winced. Her parched tongue was a razor going down the back of her throat.

"What are you going to do to me?" she forced herself to say.

"Is it not obvious to you by now, Lyla?" he said. "You are the horror writer, after all."

Why does he sound so remorseful? He doesn't want to be doing this. So, what is it that he doesn't want to do? What is this ritual?

It doesn't matter. You have to stall whatever it is. You still have Linh out there. You still have Leo. They know the truth. They could still be trying to save you. Don't give up.

"This is about Janie," she said.

"Of course it is," Regina replied from behind her in the direction of the window where she had retreated out of view. "And we don't want to do this, but we have to."

"No, you don't!"

Lester pounded his fist against the box—the casket—on which she was tethered.

"You don't understand," he bellowed, angry but remorseful. "Janie never got to finish her story. She overdosed on what was supposed to be her final fix before going to treatment. Her spirit…her spirit cannot rest until she is able to do so."

"And that's why I'm here? To be some sort of conduit for Janie to finish her story?"

"You're the only one who can now," Lester said. "We thought Ann could, but she chose her fate the moment she ran out of here that night. She could've put an end to all this."

Something in the box moved. Lyla froze. She didn't have to guess to figure out who it was. She understood what was boxed up and sealed shut as soon as she stepped foot into the damned crypt. Janie Sterling's corpse or whatever remained of it, lay mere inches below her back, and it had just moved. The thought sent chill bumps down her arms.

But you planned for this. You knew it all along. And if Janie's spirit was not at rest and somehow strengthened by this plot of land, then she would probably want to know what really happened to her.

"You're so full of shit," Lyla said.

The movement beneath her stopped.

"What did you say?" Lester asked.

"You," Lyla began. "And her. You're both so full of shit that you sound like you actually believe it. God, you're good liars."

"What are you talking about?" Regina asked from out of her line of sight.

"You killed your own daughter," she said, looking directly at Lester.

The box under Lyla began to shake.

Lester heard it that time and peered, wide-eyed at the phenomenon.

"And you," Lyla said, angling her head as much as she could toward Regina. "You knew about it. You cosigned it. You kept his secret."

The couple looked at each other, mouths agape.

"How'd you do it, Lester? The newspapers said she overdosed. What'd you do? Spike her heroin with a little something extra?"

"You don't understand—"

The box rocked, picking up intensity like a john boat in choppy water.

It's working...

"Bullshit! I understand perfectly. 'The Sterlings' couldn't have a junkie for a daughter. It would be a blemish on their lily-white reputation. Why chance having her go to rehab and potentially fuck up?"

Both of them were speechless.

"I bet you never even supported her passion. The daughter of one of the wealthiest families in America only aspires to get high and write commercial fiction. You all wouldn't dare have an heir like that."

"How could you possibly know that?" Regina asked, finally stepping into Lyla's view.

"Someone heard you all yesterday, fighting in your room. She heard you tell him that he killed Janie and would kill someone else," Lyla said and then glared at Lester. "Who's the 'someone else,' Lester? Me?"

The box stopped so suddenly that Lyla almost forgot it was rocking in the first place.

"I've done many, many regrettable things in my time, young lady. You don't get to this position in life without cutting a few throats and turning a blind eye to house fires you helped start. And once you make it to the top of the mountain, you have to be willing to kick the next climber in the face if you want to stay there. That's how you maintain power."

"So, you kicked Janie in the face? Is that it, you cowardly, small man?" Lyla spit in Lester's face.

Lester raised his hand to smack Lyla, but Regina stepped in front of him.

"You *can't* hurt her," she said like it was a reminder. "Put the bandage back on your face. You're still bleeding."

"Oh, Mother," a raspy voice whispered from above them.

Lyla kept her gaze fixed on the Sterlings as they stared at the ceiling, all the color having drained from their skin.

"Why stop hurting me now?" the voice said.

Her heart stopped, and she couldn't move.

Look. Turn your head. Face her.

I can't.

Yes, you can. You've been creating demons and monsters your whole life.

I write about them. They're fake. I just want to scare people.

You do more than that. You face your fears and free the ghosts. Now look!

The box against her back vibrated like an earthquake, forcing her to turn her head. She gasped at the uncanny sight.

Janie Sterling hovered above her, a pale face surrounded by flowing black hair like she was underwater. Her eyes were bright blue against a shade of white flesh that only death can produce. Her limbs moved like a squid's tentacles, and a black gelatinous substance swirled around her naked body like it was concealing autopsy scars.

"Janie…" Lester said, sobbing as he stepped closer. "Please—"

One of her hands shot toward him, and he shut up.

Janie seemed to have no interest in her parents. Her glowing eyes never left Lyla's.

"Is it true?" she asked, through clenched teeth, seething with rage.

"Yes," Lyla said.

The box vibrated, threatening to come apart from the fury of the remains inside.

"But I think you suspected it already," Lyla continued. "That's why you're still here. That's the story you need to tell, isn't it?"

Janie remained emotionless and expressionless, giving Lyla the courage to continue.

"You manipulated your parents to get to this point. Their ritual has nothing to do with you inhabiting my body so your parents can have you back like some shitty horror movie. You tricked them into this. You had them orchestrate their own demise by bringing you a vessel, but not just any vessel. Every resident at Claymont has been auditioning for your possession and not even realizing it," Lyla said, laughing hysterically.

The Sterlings continued to watch in shock.

"Ann almost made it, didn't she? She was selected, but she figured out something was wrong. The choice to leave killed her."

Lyla glared at Lester and Regina.

"Which one of you killed her? Who threw her into that taxi? Or was that just a cover-up on top of a cover-up?" She turned back to Janie. "But Ann lacked the final piece of the puzzle. Lester asked me three times if I was doing this on my own free will, and that's what you need for the possession to be permanent."

Lyla stared into Janie's eyes, and Janie stared back. They shared an understanding.

"Janie Sterling," Lyla began with rage already coursing through her, "You've already used my hand once before in the guest house to test it out. Do it again. I give you permission to tell your story."

The apparition above her nodded and then dropped, hitting Lyla like an ocean wave, covering her in the tar-like substance that instantly seeped into her pores. The casket burst with the collision, sending splinters and a knife-wielding Lester across the room. Lyla heard the crunch of brittle bones beneath her and felt them pierce the flesh on her back.

Lyla spasmed on the table. She shut her eyes and dug her fingernails into the wood, gritting her teeth like she was being electrocuted.

Relax. Breathe in.

She did, and everything stopped as she sank into a black morass deep within herself.

By the time her eyelids finally opened, she wasn't the one who did it.

TWENTY-SEVEN

Lyla floated in the dark. She saw a light appear and willed herself toward it. The next thing she knew, she was staring at the stone ceiling again. The ropes holding her down split as she sat up faster than she'd ever moved in her life. And she understood why. It wasn't her moving. She wasn't calling the shots anymore.

Lyla Robbins had rented out her body to a girl who'd been neglected and disowned by her parents and then murdered by her father. She did it so that they—Janie and Lyla—could tell that story. It would be the end of the Sterling family dynasty, and she was sure that Janie would be perfectly okay with that. It would be the most shocking true crime story since *In Cold Blood* but contain the supernatural allure of *The Amityville Horror*. Lyla always thought she just wanted to entertain and scare readers, but she now knew telling this story was far more important.

Lyla's head whipped to her right, but she didn't make it do that. She could see what was happening but couldn't control anything. It was as if she had no body, only a soul forced to watch the show through her own eyes.

Lester was still finding his bearings as he leaned against the wall. Regina just stared at her in shock.

The door is right there. Run! Get out while you can!

But something was off. Lyla could sense it. A cold, invasive presence. She couldn't understand what it was thinking, but she felt its emotions, and it had no intention of fleeing the room.

"Lester," Regina called, snapping him out of his delirium. "Do it! Do it now!"

Do what? She'd said that like this was part of their plan all along.

Lyla realized that she didn't know everything about the situation, and it was too late to do anything about it.

Lester looked at the knife in his hand and back at Lyla.

"Janie?" he asked.

"Dad."

His pointy Adam's apple dipped down and back up, and then he slowly approached her as she sat on the table, legs hanging off the side like a patient sitting on a doctor's exam table.

"I'm sorry for what I've done, and I'm sorry for what I have to do now."

He swung the knife at her throat.

Janie kicked him in the stomach, knocking the air out of him as the blade missed by an inch. She snatched the knife from his grip and stabbed him in the side of his abdomen. He wailed and fell back against the wall.

"No!" Regina screamed and ran to her husband.

Janie grabbed a pointed piece of broken wood from the table and hopped off.

No, what is going on.

Regina turned to see Lyla standing beside her. She glanced at the wooden stake, and her eyes went wide. Janie gripped her mom's hair, jerked her head back to expose her neck, and gouged her throat. Regina gurgled and coughed blood as she fell to her side, still trying to crawl to her husband.

Oh, my God. No. No. No. This isn't what I wanted.

Janie picked up one of the candelabras and poured the pools of wax on her mom's face. She tried to scream but only spat more red globs. Janie turned it upside down and admired the heavy metal base. She looked down at Regina who was reaching for the knife still buried in her husband's side.

"Even in a new body, you still can't look at me," Janie said.

Regina looked up just in time to see the metal base split her skull on the stone floor.

"No!" Lester cried.

Stop! Janie, stop! This isn't why I let you in!

Janie dropped the candelabra with a *clank* that echoed in the chamber and knelt beside her father.

"Your turn," she said.

"Wait!"

Janie slowly pulled the knife from his body, savoring every wince and cry that came from his mouth.

"Lyla!" Lester screamed. "Lyla, I know you're in there. I need you to listen to me."

I am.

"She is," Janie said.

"Lyla, I know you thought what you were doing was right, but you need to know that we were never trying to bring Janie back. That's not what this is about. We were trying to put her spirit to rest."

Janie laughed.

What is he talking about?

"We thought that if we did what she wanted and provided her with a host she could inhabit, we could do just that. Lyla, you were going to be a sacrifice, but your death would have ended this charade for good. I am so sorry. If only you knew the whole story…"

No sooner than he spoke those words, Lyla disappeared into a montage of memories, hopping from one scene to the next.

She sees Janie filling a syringe on the floor of her room at her parents' house, poking her arm until she finds a vein that still works. She pulls the plunger back, and blood mixes with the heroin. She pushes the shot, falls back as the wave of euphoria washes over her, and then she tips over and stops breathing.

————

She sees Lester and Regina, looking a few years younger, enter their New York home after the funeral. Regina falls on the couch, and Lester pours a cup of bourbon and downs it.

"We did everything we could," he said. "One more day. Why couldn't she have made it one more day?" he cries and throws the glass, shattering it against the wall.

Regina just closes her eyes, unfazed.

"We didn't do everything, Lester, and you know it."

"What's that supposed to mean?"

"We didn't support her. I knew something was off, but I chose to ignore it because it was more convenient. I guess I was just hoping she'd snap out of it."

"We gave her what she needed but not everything she wanted. We taught her the value of working for something. We didn't spoil her, Regina."

"I'm not talking about that, and you know it. You never wanted an artist for a daughter. I remember the scowl on your face as soon as she told you what she wanted to major in, and when her grades began to go down and she called us less, we did nothing to intervene."

"We made mistakes, but when she came to us for help, we arranged for it. We were there, goddamn it! How were we supposed to know she'd overdose the night before going to treatment?"

————

She sees Janie sitting in a bathroom stall with a phone to her ear. Loud music blares from the club she's in.

"Dad? It's me."

...

"I know you told me not to call you unless—"

...

"Dad, I feel like I'm dying. I will pay you back. I promise."

"Dad?"

"Daddy?"

———

She sees Lester with a phone to his ear, tears in his eyes as he hears Janie keep asking for him.

"You're already dead to me," he says and ends the call.

———

She sees Lester and Regina in their bed. Lester is sleeping on his back while Regina is curled on her side, holding a framed picture of Janie's high school senior portrait.

The portrait cracks, causing her to gasp. She pulls it up and looks at it, and the glass explodes on her face. She drops it on the floor where it lands beside Janie's body. The corpse is positioned in the same way it was when they discovered her. Regina screams, and Lester wakes up.

"What's going on?" he asks.

He looks at his wife screaming at something on her side of the bed and sits up. Once he sees what it is, he grabs Regina's arm and watches in horror as Janie's corpse starts to move. Her lifeless eyes find her parents, and she pushes herself up.

"Janie?" Lester says.

Janie looks as dead as the day they buried her only a week prior. The Sterlings watch in stunned silence as their dead daughter walks around their bed, opens the bedroom door, and shuts it behind her.

———

She sees Regina taking a shower as Janie strokes the curtain until Regina screams.

———

She sees Lester getting up in the middle of the night and walk to the bathroom, but he keeps stopping because he hears something behind him. He takes a few steps and turns around only to find himself alone. He walks faster and hears the same noise but this time he realizes it's coming from above him. He looks up and sees Janie on all-fours looking down at him with her head twisted completely around.

———

She sees Lester and Regina sitting in their pajamas at the kitchen table, drinking coffee in the middle of the night. They've aged. They know their daughter's body is on the tile floor beside them, laughing without moving. This is something they're used to now.

"Fine," Lester says. "I'll meet with the medium."

———

She sees the Sterlings sitting on their living room couch as a gray-haired man paces the room.

"And you've been living like this since she passed?" the medium asks.

"Yes," Lester says.

"For almost a year now," Regina says.

"Why do you think her spirit is manifesting in this malicious manner?"

"Isn't that why you're here?" Lester retorts.

"Don't be rude, Lester," Regina says.

Lester sighs and says, "We didn't exactly have the best relationship. If I'm being frank, I had certain expectations for her life that she failed to meet."

"Like what?"

"In short, she always wanted to be an artist, and I did my best to prevent that from happening."

"How so?"

Lester clenches his fists.

"I never showed interest in her writing when she was a child. She liked to write horror stories and even got in trouble at school for writing them. I never held my tongue on what an embarrassment she was to the family. I told her I wouldn't pay for her college if she was going to major in a useless degree, and I didn't. She worked her way through college and barely graduated because of the toll it took on her. I think that's why she got into drugs in the first place. But that's not the worst thing I did to her."

Regina sits up like she's about to hear something for the first time.

"She called me one night and begged me to help her get into an MFA program. Because of her grades and financial situation, she needed all the help she could get. Not only did I refuse to contribute a dime, but I also found every program she applied to and made sure she didn't get into them. All it took was a generous donation."

Regina shakes her head and stomps the ground. Lester glances at her over his shoulder.

"I'm sorry I never told you."

"You killed our daughter, you arrogant prick."

Lester clasps his hands and stares at the floor between his feet like a child in trouble.

The medium takes a deep breath and continues pacing the room.

"Your daughter wants you to make amends."

"How?" Regina asks.

"That, I don't know. But for your all's sake, I hope you find out."

―――――

She sees Lester and Regina sleeping in their bed. Regina sits straight up so fast that it wakes Lester. Her eyes open and are a glowing blue. Lester looks at her and recoils.

"Happy anniversary, Dad," Regina says, but Lester knows he's not talking to his wife. "I died exactly one year ago today. Check the clock and note the time of death if you don't believe me."

"I believe you, Janie. What do you want me to do? How can I end this?"

She smiled.

"You're going to give me a second chance, but this time you're going to support me."

"How?"

"I need you to find someone. A writer. One like me."

"What am I going to do with her and how would I even find her?"

"You're going to establish a residency for young female writers in Umbria, Italy. There's a castle just outside Umbertide. Buy it. The veil between life and death is especially thin there. Take my body there and get someone to design a program to find the new me."

Lester sat there in shock, but he was listening.

"And what if I don't?"

"I'll stop Mom's heart right now and torment you for the rest of your lonely life until the day comes when jumping out of your penthouse window seems like a dream compared to the hell I've put you through."

———

She sees the Sterlings hire a man to kidnap Julia's daughter.

———

She sees Julia sitting with the Sterlings at a villa in France, sobbing as she agrees to the plan to create a program designed to kill, at the very least, one young girl.

———

She sees Julia personally mount the final sign to the gates outside of the newly refurbished castle, now called The Claymont Residency for Writers.

———

She sees Janie's casket inside the fifth floor of The Keep and watches the lid come off every night at ten PM. Janie's strengthened corpse crawls across the floor and down the side of the castle roaming the grounds, absorbing the umber so her spirit can stay tethered to this world.

———

She sees a resident strapped to the casket die as soon as Janie's spirit entered her body.

———

She watches Lester dispose of body after body as each attempt failed. Every time the Sterlings ask Janie why it didn't work, she tells them they weren't a perfect fit.

———

She watches Regina and Julia create cover stories for each death.

———

She watches Lester and Regina meet with the medium in their home in New York.

"If she possesses a body successfully—if she finds the right match and the host dies—would that free her spirit?" Regina asks.

"In theory, her spirit would be intertwined with the host's. So, yes, killing the host would vanquish both spirits to the other side. Janie wouldn't be strong enough to stay tethered to her remains. You would put both of their souls to rest, but you would also be committing murder."

———

She watches Janie practice controlling a host by possessing residents for minutes at a time, mostly while they're asleep.

———

She sees everything that she read in Ann's note happen. Ann flees to the gate and waits for the taxi. Janie crawls out of the tower and into the woods to make sure Ann doesn't leave. When she sees the terror in Ann's eyes, she knows she will never willingly let her in. She gives the okay to Lester from across the road and watches as he throws her under the taxi.

———

She sees herself and Julia being watched by Janie through Kay's eyes as she peers around the library as the two of them walk through the courtyard after just signing the contract.

———

She sees herself sleeping in her bed at Claymont through Janie's eyes.

———

She sees Janie release the window that decapitated Antonio.

———

She sees Dante levitate and get smashed against the wall and thrown down the stairs.

———

She sees Janie take control of Linh and forces her to hide in the bushes outside of the castle until she returned from Umbertide. Janie makes sure Linh is wearing sunglasses that conceal the only tell she couldn't control: her blue eyes.

———

Lyla realized that everything 'Linh' had told her was a lie. She had been talking to Janie outside of Claymont. Everything 'Linh' had said was just to get Lyla that much closer to surrendering her body to Janie. No one's coming to rescue her.

TWENTY-EIGHT

Lyla was powerless to do anything about what happened next. She was a viewer through eyes that were no longer hers. She could still smell, hear, taste, and feel, but Janie was in total control. All that remained of her was awareness, fear, and regret.

"You want her to know the whole story, Dad?" Janie asked, still kneeling in front of her bleeding father.

Lester nodded his head.

"There is no 'whole story.' Stories never end. They live on long after we die," she said as she stood up. "That's what you and Mom never understood about the one thing in life that I loved. All your money and your stature and material shit that you covet dies when you die. But stories…they're eternal."

"I'm sorry, Janie." Lester mumbled. "I failed you."

"Too late for that, Dad," she said and kicked him in his stab wound. "Now get up."

He whimpered and winced as he used the wall to help get to his feet. He held his injured side and looked at her.

"What do you want from me?" he asked, slowly backing away. "If I could go back and undo everything, I would. I should've listened to you. I should've encouraged you—"

Janie stabbed his other side and withdrew the blade.

Lester screamed and tripped on his dead wife's legs, falling on his tailbone.

"I bet that hurt. Did you feel that zing up your spine?" Janie asked, as she cocked her head. "No, probably not. You don't have a backbone."

He crawled backward until he reached the wall opposite the door. The top of his head touched the bottom of the arched-shaped window.

Lyla was forced to watch. She screamed from the inside for Janie to stop. She begged for her to leave her body. But the more she fought, the further back from the light she receded. She thought of her own mom and dad and how she'd give up anything just for a chance to see them again. Hugging them goodbye in Charleston, West Virginia felt like a lifetime ago.

"Get up."

Lester pulled his hand from his new wound and looked at his dripping palm.

"Stand up unless you want me to play connect the dots with those two holes."

He glared at her and strained until he finally stood shakily on both legs.

Lyla remembered one of the visions that flashed through her mind. It was a threat Janie had made. She told Lester that if he didn't do exactly what she demanded, she would kill Regina and terrorize Lester until he jumped from his penthouse window in New York.

"I'm sorry," Lester said.

"I told you it's too late for that."

"I wasn't talking to you, Janie."

Lester looked deep into her eyes, and for the briefest second, Lyla thought he could see her trapped deep down inside her own body. For the first time since the ritual started, Janie was speechless as she watched her dad sit on the windowsill.

"I'm sorry for bringing you here, and I beg your forgiveness for what's to come."

He leaned back through the open window like a scuba diver departing a ship.

Janie took a step forward even though Lyla was begging for her not to. She looked at the splattered remains and smiled. Janie dropped the knife on the floor and turned around. Now that everything was quiet, she took a moment to admire her new body. She took slow steps toward the door, absorbing everything about Lyla—her history, thoughts, beliefs, dreams, and desires. Because she knew that once she crossed that threshold and departed the fifth floor, the screaming girl inside her would be gone forever.

Tomorrow, she would gather the girl's belongings and hail a cab to Umbertide. She would stop at the coffee shop and get that flight information from Leo, letting him know about the 'accident' with Dante and how that caused the Sterlings to get into a heated fight and remove all the residents from the grounds. She was so paranoid about doing anything the Sterlings commanded, stayed behind and hid in her room. It was only after hearing Lester and Regina's shouting match coming from upstairs that she had the will to run. She would tell him that she stayed at a different hotel and checked out first thing in the morning. She would tell him that she'd forever be grateful to him and seal the deal with a kiss.

After that, she would have the taxi take her to the airport where she would call her new parents and tell them where she was and that she'd be home just as fast as the planes would get her there. She would let them know she loved them and not to worry because even though Claymont didn't work out for her, it did help her find her voice, and she had quite the story to tell.

And maybe one day she would work up the nerve to take another trip abroad and leave the nest for good. They would naturally wonder why she would choose Paris, and she would tell them she wanted to catch up with her old mentor from Claymont but leave out all the gory details because as a writer, she knows that sometimes, less is more.

Janie finally reached the door and grabbed the knob. A smile crept across her face as the voice inside pleaded for the last time. She opened it and stepped through, her mind and body her own, fully becoming Lyla, in the flesh.

———

Thank you for reading. Sign up for the Wicked House Newsletter to never miss out on a new release!

ACKNOWLEDGMENTS

Each book I write or story I tell is a new venture, but they're always made possible by the loving support of my family. I'm blessed to have a mom who nurtured my creativity from the first monster I drew to the stories I tell as an adult. My wife and children light up my dark mind, often brightening my day against my will. I can always count on the warmth and levity that fills my home to welcome me back after a long writing session of mining the bleak or abhorrent.

The list of my author friends and contemporaries continues to expand the longer I hang around. I remain eternally grateful for the core four who compose my Authors Anonymous homegroup: John Durgin, Gage Greenwood, Felix Blackwell, and Sammy Scott. We hold each other accountable and share our highs and lows. Also, Duncan Ralston, Leigh Kenny, Dan Franklin, and M.L. Rayner never fail to make me laugh at least once a day. That's something I'll never take for granted.

And to the writers higher up the food chain who have taken the time to help me in one way or another, you have no idea how much that motivates and inspires me to be better. Or maybe you do, and that's why you continue to give back. My thanks to Brian Keene, Joe Lansdale, Josh Malerman, Clay McLeod Chapman, Wrath James White, Jeff Strand, and Joe Hill for your graciousness, kindness, and wisdom. I need to give a special acknowledgment to Stephen Graham Jones. Man, I don't know that I can ever repay you for your generosity and just leading by example. What I will do is promise to pay it forward and hopefully do for the next newbie what you've done for me.

Lastly, to my readers who've been with me from day one to the person who just discovered me with this book, thank you. I have to give a shoutout to the Books of Horror group on Facebook and The Haunted Minds Book Club—both of which are filled with lovely people who tolerate me on a daily basis. And to all my Patreon subscribers, please know that your extra support enables me to continue to live my dream. Much love to this growing legion of loyalty, laughter, and learning:

Julia Terry, Daunya Gentolizo, Nicole Scardina, Robin Moore, Ashley Chmielewski, Bree White, Crystal Evans, Joseph Miller, Meredith Foster, Monique Beasley, Stefanie Silvestri, Alyssa Cook, Amanda Ruzsa, April Haas, Brittany Powers, Carrie Hibbard, George Benson, Heather Rogers, Jennifer Whitney, Ju Collins, Kelly Jobes, Lara Watkins, Lisa Breanne, Liz Wallace, Mary Sepko, Mike Hughes, Miranda Isenberg, Montez Oudenaarden, Morgan Huggins, Paige French, Rebecca Cavanaugh, Ryan Gairdner, Sara Dougherty, Shana Caldwell, Shanda Langley, Sonya Brooks, Trudy Meiser, Ugur Kutay, Angel Nellson, Blazingangel74, Carisa Kyle, Cormac Kincaid, Desiree Macias, Jennifer Rose, Jesseca Spyra, Jim Donohue, JoAnna Martin, Jonathan Edward Durham, Joseph Towner, Karen Larsen, Kathleen Benton, Khaleesi, Lisa Meehan, Lori Foley, Monika Hoppe, Raven Stone, Rikki Goodwin, Tia Barker, Aaron Masters, Andrew Nicolle, April Butler, Ashley Cox, Ashley Beattie, Cade, Debbie Thornton, Jane Kessell, Jasmin Carter, Kaela Kalicky, Kate Curry, Kathy McKnight, Kelsey Chambers, Meredith Jensen, Michelle Marie, Molly Mix, Nicole Sonnenburg, Rose Evans Craft, Sarah Bell, and Эми Кларк.

THANK YOU FOR READING
LYLA, IN THE FLESH

We hope you enjoyed it as much as we enjoyed bringing it to you. We just wanted to take a moment to encourage you to review the book. Follow this link: Lyla, In The Flesh to be directed to the book's Amazon product page to leave your review.

Every review helps further the author's reach and, ultimately, helps them continue writing fantastic books for us all to enjoy.

Thank you for reading. Sign up for The Wicked House Newsletter to never miss out on a new release!

Don't forget to follow us on socials!

Facebook | Instagram | Twitter | Website | Amazon

———

Looking for more great Horror and Dark Fantasy?

———

For a full listing of all our books, visit www.WICKEDHOUSE.com.